THE SILVER DRAGON

THE SILVER DRAGON

CALEB MCLEAN

CJM Publishing

Published by CJM Publishing

ISBN: 978-0-6480195-0-3

Typesetting services by BOOKOW.COM

*To My God, My Family, and My Friends, for
helping me pull this off*

PROLOGUE

A strangled roar echoed through the concrete room, followed by a screech of metal and a clash of chains. Men in white lab coats rushed frantically around, yelling out panicked commands and warnings. Blocky machines fitted with leavers, buttons and spiralling wires were being pushed hurriedly out of the way, opening a large space in the middle of the darkened room. The roarings grew louder and shook the lights dangling from the ceiling.

Amid the panic one thing stood out: a single man. He wore a simple black tux with a white undersuit and tie. A briefcase hung loosely by his side, lightly swaying under force of the cries. His nearly black hair was combed neatly to the back of his head. His hard face stared, remorseless, into the space that had been cleared. A large, barely healed scar stretched from the tip of his chin down across his neck and under his shirt, pulsing angrily against his skin. A black glove covered his left hand, making no movement, while his right tapped relentlessly against his leg.

'Sir, we are ready,' said one of the men in white coats.

The scarred man nodded, grunting in response.

The scientist hesitated before calling out to his fellow colleague, 'Bring it in!'

The roars reached a head-pounding volume and the very building shook with fear. With a deafening crack, the creature was finally restrained. A large green dragon was being pulled into the room, the men in white coats trying their best to drag her forwards. Metal chains were wound around her wings and maw. With choked roars she lashed out with claws and mace-like tail, cracking and cratering the cement walls.

The scarred man began to walk slowly forwards, studying the dragon with an intense interest. He didn't panic. No fear was in his eyes as he approached the monster, his black shoes clicking against the floor with every step. The green dragon saw him and stopped her thrashing, staring as a newfound fear crept into her. With a slight whimper, she took a small step backwards.

The scarred man smirked. He knelt down against the floor and placed his suitcase with the utmost care against the ground. It opened with an audible click, making the dragon flinch. Slowly and deliberately, the man pulled out a silvery device with glowing red light flashing on top of it. It was the shape of a handgun, but with a drill piece for a barrel. The man clicked the trigger and the drill spun as he smirked. The dragon began to struggle against the chains once more, growling and thrashing.

The scarred man pulled another device from the suitcase. A small red dome beeped intermittently, connected by wires to a flat, disc-shaped base. The man attached it to his gun-like drill and turned to the dragon that towered above him.

The green dragon snorted, threw back her head and, with a cry, shattered the chains around her maw. She lashed out the instant she was free: a small green boulder shot from her maw, colliding with the floor and creating a large explosion of rock. The scarred man calmly stepped to the side, dodging one that was directed at him. With a single movement, he brought the drill up, aimed it at the dragon, and pressed the trigger.

The dome device shot forwards like a discus, heading straight for the now-free dragon. The wires reached out with a seeming life of their own, wrapping themselves around her head. She screeched as a clawed hand scratched at the device, which had already drilled itself into the dragon's head, between her horns. The dragon screeched in pain, rearing back and roaring in agony. She fell to the floor with a deep thump and a groan.

The scarred man smiled and walked calmly towards the dragon. He lightly tapped her on the jaw, and her eyes flickered open. She tried instinctively to lash out at the man, but something stopped her. Something took control of her body, racking it with pain. She tried again to strike the human, but was again unable. Her eyes widened with fear as she realised what had happened, and she reluctantly bowed her head in defeat.

The man gurgled a laugh that couldn't have been made by a human. He stroked the creature's nose and grinned, making the dragon flinch again. He walked away and placed his drill back in the suitcase. His experiment had worked, and now it was time to start the real battle.

CHAPTER 1:
THE FAMILY

A silver flash swept through the undergrowth, running on all fours at the speed of a jaguar. It passed through the trees easily, slipping through like a snake. Iron wings were open slightly, guiding its form as it ran. To anyone overhead it would look as if a shooting star pierced the forest. To anyone on the ground it was gone too fast to even register.

It found its way up a mountainside, leaping from rock to rock as easily as a mountain goat. It had slowed down now, and its form was exposed—a dragon. It had the same shape and structure: four legs, a tail, pairs of wings and horns, and dull yellow scales winding from its sharp talons to cover its underbelly and sides. But what could only be described as iron covered its back and stretched along its wings, creating an almost mirror-like sheen. The metal covered its tail and wound up its neck, covering only the top of its body, like a shell.

It flared its wings in the last jump to the top of the mountain, screeching to a stop on glinting talons. It was about the size of a large horse, suggesting a young dragon of maybe five or six, a teenager in dragon years. Its slim figure suggested it was female, with thin wings and a narrow tail.

With a small sigh, the dragon turned and looked over the valley she had just run through. A long lush forest stretched into the distance, full of many animals that made excellent prey. Towards the middle was a large lake that made a lovely bathing place. Mountains surrounded either side, protecting the inhabitants from the outside influence of humans, forming a dragon haven.

A rustle of movement caught her attention and she turned to see two red dragons burst forth from the forest. They ran side by side, each eager to beat the other to the top of a mountain, where the metallic dragoness was waiting. She could only grin at the two males' competitiveness. One suddenly lashed out with his tail, catching the other's legs and tripping him up. A laugh followed as the red dragon bounded up beside the female.

'You boys are impossible,' she said with a small chuckle.

'Says you,' snorted the male with a flick of his tail, 'You're, like, the fastest on four legs, though in the air I reckon I could catch up.'

He flared his wings just to make his point. The dragoness rolled her eyes, knowing only too well how superior she was in the air. Her speed on the ground was nothing compared to her speed in the sky.

'Silver, could you bite him for me!' yelled the other male with a growl as he pulled himself from where he'd been stuck between two rocks.

He was the biggest of the three and, in Silver's opinion, the dumbest. While he was nearly impossible to defeat in an all-out when sparring, brawn and fire were the only things he used to attack, never speed or cunning, traits that she prided herself on.

The other red dragon had heard the mock threat and jumped backwards before Silver had a chance to grab at him. She only smiled sweetly at her brother and turned towards the other one, who slowly crawled up the side of the mountain.

'Stop being a hatchling, Blaze,' Silver called. 'Get up here before Dad gets here.'

Blaze snorted with annoyance and pulled himself up to the small plateau where Silver and his brother were. He shook himself, and checked his wings and scales for any scuff marks. To his annoyance, some dirt had smudged his usually ruby-red scales. He glared at his brother.

'You're going to pay for that, Raize,' he said.

Raize only grinned cheekily. He was the troublemaker of the lot, always tricking their parents and other dragons. Occasionally he got into huge trouble with other inhabitants of the valley, and only his status as the leader's son prevented his exile. He was now under watch and was forbidden to leave the cave without permission, which he had today.

A chuckle sounded from behind them, spinning the young dragons to around in surprise.

'You three are amusing to watch sometimes,' said a larger dragon, revealing himself from a dark cave struck into the mountain.

'Dad, Raize tripped me up,' said Blaze with a snort. 'Punish him!'

The large dragon laughed. He wasn't red like the two males, but had his daughter's appearance, with yellow scales up his underbelly and a metallic shell across his back and wings. He was stockier than Silver, however, and was obviously more strength than speed.

'There was never a rule that said I couldn't,' said Raize, though he shuffled slightly away from his far larger father.

'He's right,' said the father. 'It was never a rule.'

Blaze's wings dropped with disbelief.

'However, I would prefer if you didn't pull a stunt like that again, Raize,' the father said. 'It is unsportsmanlike.'

Blaze grinned, and Raize looked away with a snort. Silver watched without making a sound. Males were so confusing sometimes. With a small amused snort of her own, she turned to her father.

'Where's mother?' she asked.

'Hunting. She should be back any time now,' was the reply.

Silver sighed; she had wanted to join her mother. Hunting was something she excelled at—from the air, at least. Her shining shell always gave her away from the ground, but she was slowly learning how to hide it. One of the skills her father was teaching her was the ability to darken her metal shell, turning it almost peat black. This didn't make the shell camouflaged, but it stopped from shining whenever light found it.

Metallic dragons had a number of abilities, most of which Silver was still struggling to gain a hold of. Her father continued to encourage her, saying that she would get it right eventually, but she was finding it extremely frustrating. Her brothers were fire dragons, and only had to worry about one thing: fire. Their abilities were simple and easy, but hers were so much more complicated, even if more powerful.

'There she is!' said the father with a grin, looking at a red dragoness flying towards them in the sky. 'Welcome back, Scarlet, love. What have you got for us today?'

The red dragoness landed with a small thud on the plateau. She wasn't quite as big as her mate, but was still double the size of her largest hatchling. She was a fire dragon with a great temper when annoyed, but a loving heart that would do anything to keep her mate and hatchlings safe. Silver and Scarlet were as close as mother and daughter could be, being the only females in an otherwise male family.

Scarlet dropped a large pig in front of her hatchlings. Raize immediately dug in while Blaze nodded his thanks before following his brother. Silver let them eat first. She wasn't very hungry and she wanted to catch her own food a bit later, when she went to see Liam, the only human who lived in Dragon Valley. Occasional tourists came to see the dragon society for themselves, but human interaction was nearly non-existent.

'Silver, are you not hungry?' asked Scarlet with a hint of worry for her daughter.

She shook her head. 'No, I'll go hunting later. Let the boys eat first.'

Scarlet sighed and padded over to Silver. She sat by her and looked into the distance.

'May I ask what you're thinking about?' she said.

Silver hesitated. While the valley was a paradise that was comfortable, familiar and above all else safe, she longed to see the human world. Here they were so protected by the mountains and their abilities that she hadn't had the opportunity to see for herself what humans were really like. From the stories she had been told, they seemed horrible, but Liam didn't seem all too bad, and nor did the valley's few tourists.

'Hey, Mum, do you mind if I go flying? Just for a bit?' she asked.

'Not at all. Just don't cross the mountains or bother Liam. He's busy at the moment,' Scarlet replied.

Silver smiled before turning her back to her family and taking to the air with a few flaps of her silver wings. Once the wind caught her, she soared higher and smiled. Flying was amazing—the greatest thing about being a dragon. She could go without anything else as long as she could fly. She turned in the air, tilting her wings and moving her tail a little to guide herself. It was also silent up there, the only sound being the wind. And then there was the view; standing on top of mountains was fine, but flying above them was even greater. She felt as if she could see everything, and when she got high enough she could even see a slight slant as the earth circled around.

'Silver, fancy meeting you up here,' said an all-too-familiar voice.

Her peace broken, Silver growled slightly and looked at the culprit, a yellow dragon. He flew upside down under her. His name came to Silver's head—Zepos. He was an increasingly annoying lightning dragon, about a year older then her, who was constantly butting in at times when she wanted to be alone. She was pretty sure Zepos had fallen head over heels with her. Not that she was surprised; she wasn't vain, but being the only eligible female metal dragon, she had quite a number of males vying for her attention. Zepos was especially annoying because he tried so much harder to gain her attention. Most of the time she had to resist the temptation to coat his face in metal.

'What do you want?' she half-growled at him.

Zepos grinned and flipped into the air, levelling out to fly alongside Silver. 'Nothing much, just wondering what you were doing up here all alone.'

'Trying to get away from everyone,' she said, giving him a sideways glance.

'That's sweet of you. Trying to fly off by yourself … just to be with me,' Zepos hummed contently.

She growled slightly, annoyed at his behaviour. He seemed to never give up. She pulled herself into a steep dive, angling down towards the trees below. Zepos grunted in surprise, before diving down to follow her. She levelled out just above the trees, sighing when Zepos again joined her.

'So … I was wondering if you wanted to join us in a couple of days. Some friends and I are planning a day at the lake. It would be great to have you join us, just for some fun.' He angled himself so he was flying upside down again, showing off.

'No,' she said.

'Oh, why not?' asked Zepos.

'Because I don't want to,' was her simple reply.

'Yes, you do,' he said cheekily.

He jabbed Silver's hind leg with his tail, prompting an angry snarl.

'Leave me alone, Zepos. I'm not in the mood for your antics today.'

The electric dragon snorted. 'Fine. See you around.'

Zepos flew off as Silver sighed in reply. She rounded off as she came to a mountain, landing on a large stone pillar that protruded from the ground. She sat down on her haunches and sighed, looking at the wall of mountains that barred her way. It was so tempting just to take off into the air and fly over them, towards the human lands. But she couldn't do that, not without suffering the wrath and disappointment of her parents. The metal at the end of her tail rippled and formed a small blade that she used to slice off a piece of rock from the pillar. She watched it tumble down the mountainside. One day, when she was old enough, she would go, but until then, she was trapped in the valley.

CHAPTER 2:
A PROBLEM

SILVER watched as the sun began to descend to the horizon, casting luminous colours across the sky. Fiery orange and yellow danced off her shell, casting her in an almost celestial light but annoying her to no end—she would be visible from all sides of the valley. With a slight growl, she took off from her perch and flew into the sky, trying to darken her shell, but to no avail.

Her stomach growled hungrily. Not having eaten was going to be a problem now. Her family had probably already finished their meal, so she'd have to hunt by herself. Not that she minded, but at sunset she was most exposed. If she was going to hunt, she'd have to wait until she less resembled a beacon in the sky.

An idea came to Silver and she tilted her wings, descending towards a small wooden hut on the edge of the lake. It was a simple building, with walls of rough-hewn logs stacked neatly side by side and wooden slabs angling downwards for a roof. A simple door was built into the wall, and glassless windows were pocketed around the house. A thin ribbon of smoke reached up from a small iron chimney on the roof. A patio, also made from oak and large enough to accommodate a dragon, stretched out from the house.

Silver came to a landing outside the patio and carefully padded underneath its roof. As soon as she was out of the sun, her back stopped glowing and she sighed with relief. The sun's glare was more than she could handle, and it attracted a lot of heat. Under the shade, she could cool down easily.

As she walked up to the door of the house, she heard a number of voices from inside. Interested, she poked her head through one of the windows to see two humans chatting in front of a fireplace. Her sudden presence startled one of them, who leapt up in shock. She chuckled slightly as the other one turned to scold her.

"Silver? What are you doing here?" he said.

The fireplace cast an orange glow through the small and cosy room. The two humans were sitting on a long soft chair they called a sofa, made from soft purple velvet. On the far wall sat and a row of drawers and a small wooden benchtop that housed a metallic sink made by Silver's father. The only other piece of furniture was a round table near the makeshift kitchen.

Silver smiled and rested her head on the windowsill. "Nothing. I was bored and mum told me not to come and bother you, so I decided to come and bother you."

"They can talk?!" exclaimed the other human in the room, staring at Silver in fascination.

"Of course we can. Liam said that in his ... um, blog? So you should know." She turned her head to the other human. "You never told me we had a guest."

Liam shrugged. "He only came in this morning. You were out, so I didn't tell you."

Liam was a strange human, or at least that's what Silver's father had told her. He came to her neck in height and had long brown hair that flowed down his shoulders. He wore a plain grey T-shirt with a cartoon of a curled-up fire dragon on the front and long black cargo pants—he seemed oddly relaxed.

"Hmm," she said, and turned towards the new tourist. "What's your name?"

"Zach," said the human, still staring in wonder at the dragoness's iron skin.

To Silver the two humans looked similar, though Zach had starched blond hair while Liam's was a dark brown. Zach looked ready for adventure, with a single-strapped duffel bag sat beside his chair and a utility belt around his waist. If Silver didn't know better, she'd think he was going caving. In these parts, a human in a cave was a dead human.

She scoffed at this idea before turning to Liam again. "Do you have anything spare to eat? I'm hungry and it's sundown. Prey can see me from a mile away."

"Why didn't you grab anything sooner?" asked Liam.

"Wasn't hungry," she smiled sheepishly.

Liam sighed and got up from where he had been sitting. "Just wait there, I'll be back in a moment."

Silver beamed, backed away from the window and sat on her haunches outside, waiting for Liam. The two of them were very good friends. Older dragons mostly shunned Liam, but Silver, like many of the younger dragons, liked him. She understood the older dragons; they had long lived as the humans' captives, and only six years ago they had broken free under her father's leadership, but in her mind it was time to move on.

It wasn't long before Liam opened the door. He had a bag thrown over his shoulder that looked quite heavy, for him anyway. With a grunt, he hauled it in front of Silver's feet. The young dragon was instantly into it, tearing apart the bag to see what it contained. Venison —one of her favourite meals. She smiled and took a large bite.

"You owe me a deer," said Liam. "Skinned and gutted."

Silver gave him a smile and a nod, her maw covered in blood. She licked it clean before digging in once more, her hunger getting the better of her. As she ate, Zach joined Liam on the patio, watching her with a look of slight disgust on his face. Silver ignored him. Humans had a far stranger way of eating than dragons do.

Once she finished, she got up and shook some of the blood off her muzzle. "Thanks, Liam."

"Any time, Silver. But remember you owe me a deer," he said.

She nodded and turned to fly off. She would need to clean herself before she got home, so she made her way to the lake and dived in, washing off all the blood on her metal shell and scales. She made sure to keep a close lookout for Zepos, in case he wanted to join her. Luckily, no other dragons were at the river besides a large fire dragon lounging nearby.

After a small nod of greeting, she again took to the air and flew back to her cave, carved into the peak of one of the valley's central mountains, where her mother and father were waiting. They were probably wondering where she was; she and her siblings weren't supposed to be out after dark. Not that this stopped her, but she enjoyed her after-dark adventures more when her parents didn't know about them. She had plans for that night anyway, and didn't want to raise suspicions.

She landed outside the cave on a rocky outcrop large enough to hold a small family of dragons, and walked inside, out of the glare of the sun. As soon as she entered, something tackled her from the side and she squeaked in fright. Laughter soon followed. She rolled to her feet and glared at Raize.

"Hey!" she said.

Raize was laughing so hard puffs of fire were shooting from his maw and his tail lashed around, showing his amusement. With a growl, she shot a glob of liquefied metal at the fire dragon's tail. It landed and froze solid instantly, trapping the tail still. Now it was Silver's turn to laugh.

"Let me go!" said Raize, trying desperately to pull his tail out from underneath its shiny casing.

Silver stood and watched him, ignoring his pleas of help. A smile had spread across her face; it wasn't often she got her brother into such a predicament. Eventually, though, her soft heart forced her to cut the metal loose with her tail and free her brother. Raize shook his tail out, making sure nothing was injured, and glared at her.

She only grinned. "Serves you right for sneaking up on me," she said.

Raize didn't have an answer for that and only rolled his eyes and turned back to face into the cave. It was a small cave for five dragons, with a branch that led to where her mother and father slept and another to where the three siblings slept. There were no stalagmites or stalactites in the cave, for her father had broken them all down to create room for the family. It was still a bit cramped, however. Sleeping in the same rooms as two male fire dragons was a little annoying, and she longed for her own space.

When she walked in, she noticed that the rest of her family were waiting in the central cavern of the cave, a dome-shaped area with stone smoothed by its dragon occupants. Blaze was sitting by her mother, watching as the two of them walked in. He grinned at Silver and Raize, and Silver rolled her eyes in a gesture she had learned from Liam. Blaze snorted softly and turned back to where her father was sitting. Silver trotted up next to her mother with a small smile. Scarlet nodded a silent greeting to her daughter before turning her attention back to her mate, Elron, Silver's father.

"Ah, Silver," said Elron. "You're here. Good. There is something I need to tell you."

Silver sat down, curious as to what her father wanted to say. Usually when he got them all together it was to discuss a new advantage for the dragons, or to warn his family of an increasing number of humans passing close to the valley.

"For over the past month, dragons have been disappearing," said Elron, looking over them.

The siblings glanced at each other in surprise. Dragons disappearing was a serious matter. There were so few of them as it was that whenever one left or died it was a great source of grief for the dragons. Silver had only ever seen one dragon die, from a sickness that had plagued her body, and she'd been a few hundred years old. Some dragons were older, though no-one knew the age of the oldest. And now they were disappearing.

"How many have gone?" Scarlet asked anxiously.

"Three," replied Elron, "Maybe more. The first two I didn't pay much attention to because the occasional dragon does leave the mountains to find a home elsewhere … but three in one month I find very suspicious. They are elders, too, who don't really have the taste for adventure that the younger ones have."

"Do you have any idea what has happened to them?" said Scarlet.

Elron shook his head. "No, though I'm going to assume they have been taken or killed. I want you all to be on high alert. No going out after nightfall, and be aware of any suspicious humans in the valley. Don't go anywhere by yourself, especially you, Silver. Not until we get on top of this problem. Do you hear me?"

The two boys nodded their heads. They seemed worried, but Silver was simply annoyed. In her mind, her father was being overly paranoid. So what if a few old dragons suddenly disappeared? Maybe they just fell asleep in their caves and haven't woken up for a while. It wouldn't surprise her. Most older dragons were a bit boring, and annoying. She didn't want silly suspicions to stop her from going out on her own. Besides, she could look after herself, and she had plans for that very night.

"Dad, don't you think you're being a bit paranoid?" she asked.

"Maybe, but I'm not taking any chances," Elron said. "Not when it could mean the life of one of you three."

Silver snorted. "Come on, a few elder dragons disappeared. They probably went off together to look at the world. It's not the first time it's happened. Besides, I could defeat a group of humans easily."

"I know," growled Elron, "but elder dragons aren't usually ones to disappear, especially in groups, and if they *are* being taken then I have no doubt a younger dragon would easily fall as well. Now, enough of this conversation. We'll talk more in the morning. I want you three off to the nests. You hear me?"

The three of them nodded and turned towards their part of the cave. The two boys raced into their area. It was smaller than the central cavern, but with a similar shape and the same smoothed stone. A damp, earthen smell wafted from the walls, accompanied by a musky warmth that came from housing fire dragons.

Silver followed her brothers quietly. She was sure her father was just being over-protective. Even if elder dragons were being taken, they had probably been taken by surprise, and she wasn't one to let this happen, most of the time anyway. Besides, she had plans for that night and she wasn't going to let her father's stupid concerns stop her.

With a snort, she lay down in her iron nest, which she'd made herself and was very proud of. She settled her head against the cool surface of the nest and closed her eyes. She wanted to get some rest before she went out, even just for a small time.

CHAPTER 3:
SUSPICIOUS ACTIVITY

Silver's eyes snapped open, greeted by a wall of darkness shrouding the cave. She blinked a few times, trying to shrug off the sleepiness that covered her. A tongue of fire from a nearby dragon's lips licked the air and lit the room, and Silver winced at the sudden flair. It was probably Raize. He often snored in his sleep, and every snort would create a small tongue of fire. Classic fire dragon.

Sighing, she carefully got out of her metal nest. Because of the lack of light, it looked strangely black in the cave, besides Raize's sudden flares. She stepped out of the nest, keeping her metal tail from touching it, to prevent a metallic screech that would wake her brothers. Once free, she padded to the exit of the cave, rolling her wing joints to ready them for the short flight ahead.

She wouldn't be travelling far, so if she did run into any trouble, she'd just need to roar and wake the whole valley into a frenzy. Outside, she stretched her body like a cat and swished her tail from side to side, knowing that her metal shell would be cool after staying still overnight. Her father often had this problem as well; when metal dragons wake up, they're often stiff in the joints, and they need to move around a little before taking flight, lest it end badly. Luckily for Silver, she hadn't been asleep that long, and could easily warm up.

Satisfied, she took to the air with two beats of her metallic wings. It was a full moon, and the forest shone with a silver light that glinted from her wings and tail, but wasn't bright enough for her to bother darkening her sheen. It wasn't a glare, though any wakeful dragons—or dragon hunters—would see her easily. The thought worried her a little, but she quickly shook it off as she glided over her destination.

Pulling in her wings, Silver plunged into a steep dive, aiming for a small stream at the foot of a mountain. It didn't seem significant, except that it was well hidden among the trees, and auburn leaves piled up against the rocks that dotted its course. Silver landed beside the stream with a thud and padded under a small overhang. The hollow underneath was just big enough to accommodate her body, and she knew that soon she'd have to dig it out to fit inside.

Smiling, she pawed around in the leaves for a second, before gripping a twig in her talons and pulling. It took a couple of seconds, but the ground began to move. It opened much like a trapdoor, and Silver slipped inside, closing the door behind her with her tail.

Anyone but Silver would be shocked by what they saw underneath the curtain of growth. Smooth metal plating hugged the walls of the small tunnel underneath, reflecting the light of numerous fire torches.

Silver took a moment to look around, before padding down the tunnel. Each torch cast an orange-yellow glow that reflected down the tunnel and off Silver's shell. Every step she took echoed sullenly, summoning an eeriness that made Silver smile.

Eventually the tunnel ended, spreading out into a large cavern that probably encompassed most of the mountain. The cavern's walls weren't entirely covered with metal like the tunnel was, nor were they entirely lit by torches. Instead torches dotted the ground and steel platforms jutted across the room. On each platform stood a number of metallic statues, depicting dragons and humans, among a few shapeless sculptures. There were around twenty such structures in the cave, creating a small gleaming garden of statues.

Silver felt herself smile at her creations, and swished her tail in pride. This was the one place where she was able to just sit and let her passion take control. She loved using her metal breath to sculpt her lumps of metal into perfect shapes. Seeing the finished structures standing before her in their full glory made her shiver with excitement. For a while, she hadn't been able to get to this place because of her father's constant training, and the fact that dragons seemed to follow her everywhere. She didn't want any more attention, so she'd gone to great pains to keep this skill a secret.

Silver padded among the statues to one that was half-finished. It was a dragon, standing on hind legs with its wings outstretched—or at least that's what she imagined it would be once it was finished. At that moment it was merely a set of legs and half a torso—not much to look at. Sitting down in front of it, she sighed, wondering what to do with it next. She summoned a glob of metal from her throat and shot it in a stream at the edge of the statue, creating a mass of formless metal around the edge. She thinned her tail into a razor-sharp blade and began to work on the metal, coarsely cutting off chunks and then smoothing the surface. If she accidentally shaved off more than she meant to, she'd add a little more and tried again. It was strenuous work that most dragons would find boring, but it allowed Silver to stop thinking and just work, if only for a little while.

Eventually, time got away from her and she was forced to stop, knowing she'd been there for too long. Another metre had been added to the statue's torso, and she'd begun work on its tail. She was looking forward to beholding the finished product. Sighing, she rose from where she'd been sitting and made her way back through the tunnel to the door. She pushed it open slowly, waiting to see if anyone was outside. No-one was, so she pushed the door further open and pulled herself out.

She closed it and made sure all the leaves and sticks were still stuck on top, creating a seemingly natural forest floor. Satisfied, she walked out from under the small overhang and was about to take off into the air when something stopped her. A musky smell, like that of sweat and damp cloth, wafted past Silver's sensitive nose. It was human, but different from Liam's. Frowning, Silver began to stalk through the forest, willing the metal shell on her back to darken. This time it obeyed, and its usual gleam disappeared as it turned from silver to a deep grey—not perfect, but it would have to do.

It was still dark, but the horizon was lighting up as the sun rose slowly. Silver had stayed in her hideout longer than she'd thought. Shrugging, she followed the scent until it dissipated near the base of a mountain. Finding a cranny she could wedge herself into, she scanned the area for the source of the smell.

Her gaze lit on a human standing not far from her hiding spot, with a strange implement pressed against its ear, which it used to talk with other humans from far away. A cell phone, she thought it was called. The human looked familiar, and it only took a moment for Silver to realise it was Zach, the new tourist who had arrived the previous day. What was he doing out here?

Frowning, Silver strained her ears to pick up the human's speech.

"Are you ready for the attack?" Zach hissed into the phone.

There was a pause before he said, "Good. That was all I wanted to know. I think Liam is starting to suspect me. Do you think you can set it up for this morning, while all the dragons are asleep? It'll be easier then."

A pause as the human waited for an answer, then continued speaking. "Yes, but make sure Elron and his hatchling whelp are captured alive." Another pause. "You may kill the others if you wish, but I advise against it. These dragons are very close to their families, and if you kill one, others will start to rage. Dragons are really just humans with stronger bodies but less brains," he chuckled.

It took Silver a moment to realise what the human was talking about. Fear shot through her and she glanced at the sky. The sun was nearly up. Would she be able to get out of there without alerting Zach and whoever was on the other end of the phone? She'd have to risk it—the attack was going to happen soon. As stealthily as she could, she snuck out of the crevice and made her way to the forest.

Her dark grey shell was beginning to regain its sheen as her emotions clouded her focus on it. As the sun finally shone from the sky, it hit the now-silver shell on her back, casting a brilliant light over the forest. She cursed, using one of the words Liam had taught her, and quickly took off into the air. She had no doubt that Zach had seen her now, and her certainty was confirmed as two gunshots pierced the air. Silver shrieked in alarm and dove towards the forest, flapping her wings as hard as she could. Her silver form shot through the air with a speed she'd never flown at before. She flew so fast she nearly passed by her destination: home.

Pulling herself to a stop with a couple of wing beats, she quickly entered the cave.

"Dad! Mum! Wake up, quick!" she roared as loud as she could, running into her parents' side of the cave.

They were tangled up in each other's wings, lying side by side and sleeping peacefully. As Silver ran into the room they began to rouse. Elron raised his head and looked blearily at his daughter.

"Why are you up so early, Silver?" he asked.

"The humans are coming!" she yelled. "I heard Zach, the new tourist, talking to them. They're going to attack this morning! Get up!"

Elron was instantly on his feet. He nudged awake his mate, who at first murmured in annoyance, but woke up as quickly as her husband once she understood the situation.

"Silver, go and wake your brothers. Get them to the outside of the cave," he said.

Silver nodded quickly and broke into another run, quickly reaching the cavern she shared with her brothers. Raize and Blaze were still fast asleep, and fire still shot from Raize's nostrils with every breath. They woke, though, as Silver let out a clanging roar that sounded like steel gouging iron. Blaze snarled at his sister as he got to his feet, while Raize only groaned, screening his head with his wings.

"What was that for, Silver? It's not time to wake up yet, is it?" asked Blaze.

Silver shook her head. "Humans are coming."

Both Raize and Blaze were instantly on their feet. They followed Silver out into the rocky outcrop that jutted from the cliff outside their cave, looking out over the valley below. The sun was half above the horizon now, illuminating the valley. Oranges, purples and reds shone from Silver's back and over the valley. Elron and Scarlet were already there, waiting for their hatchlings.

"Cover your ears," said Elron. "This will be loud."

They all placed their wings over their heads. Elron opened his maw and let loose a clanging roar that burst from the mountainside and echoed down into the valley in a cacophony of sound. Even with her wings shielding her, Silver felt it reverberate through her whole body, rippling the metal on her back. Elron closed his mouth with a snap, and the thunder stopped. The family uncovered their heads and looked around.

A minute passed and dragons started appearing from their caves. A few of them took flight towards Elron's cave. Simultaneously, Silver spotted something in the distant sky. It was steadily coming closer, and the sound of an engine thrumming began to reverberate among the mountains.

"Look!" cried Silver, pointing her talon at the steadily approaching planes.

Elron growled as he spotted them, and turned towards his family. "Get ready. Hatchlings, remember what I taught you—guard each other and, if it comes to it, run."

The three of them nodded, and Elron took to the air. The rest of his family followed, and they were soon joined by other dragons, at first a few, and then seemingly the whole valley. Their numbers were greater than Silver had imagined, boosting her confidence. There was no way humans could fight this many dragons ... could they?

Chapter 4:
A Broken Peace

THE first wave of planes hit hard. Silver's heart hammered in her chest as she twisted and dove, leaving her back facing the hailstorm of bullets that rained on the dragons. Roars of rage and cries of pain reverberated through the air. Explosions lit up the sky and the elements commanded by the dragons—fire, air, water, earth—lanced across open space, catching planes in midair. A crackle of lightning boomed its thunder. Spears of razor ice pierced the heavens. Guns blasted and missiles flew. Elemental reds, blues and yellows riddled the normally peaceful sky. A few bullets caught Silver's shell, bouncing harmlessly off, but she felt the impact and winced slightly.

Levelling off, she grew metallic spikes on her tail. She looked up to the sky to see a jet flying towards her at a frightening speed. She flicked her tail once, sending a storm of spikes towards it. They hit their target, but hardly dented it. Growling in annoyance, she flapped her wings forcefully and soared again into the air, turning to fly upside down. The pilot couldn't follow such a tight turn and sped away, trying to get out of her range. She sent another volley of spikes after it, but missed.

Silver turned quickly to see what was becoming of the rest of the battle. The first wave of planes had passed, and it seemed the numbers of dragons had dwindled slightly. Her father stood out in the chaos because he was in what Silver liked to call the "full-metal" state, his shell having grown to cover his whole body. Metallic dragons were nearly invincible in this state, but it slowed them down considerably and exhaustion came much quicker.

Silver decided to follow her father's lead, however, and let her own metal shell expand around her until it encased her whole body. She instantly felt the extra weight and was forced to flap her wings much harder to keep up in the air. No sooner had she done this than the next wave hit. Bullets rained upwards from the forest below, fired by human ground forces that had somehow snuck into the valley while the planes had attacked. The bullets rang harmlessly off the shell on Silver's stomach, but other dragons weren't so lucky. They cried out in pain as the bullets penetrated scales and disabled wings. Many plunged from the air.

The metallic dragoness felt anger course through her. Who were these people to attack their valley? What had the dragons ever done to them? Tucking in her wings, Silver dived towards the humans below, crashing through the trees without a second thought. She landed on two soldiers who were stalking towards a downed earth dragon. She whipped out her tail at the other assailants around her, merely knocking them down because she hadn't bladed it. She opened her maw and shot a stream of liquefied metal at the soldiers, who cried out as the metal encased them.

Shivering, she trotted through the forest to where she had seen the downed earth dragon. She exhaled in relief when she saw him slowly getting up, recovering from the fall. He saw her and nodded, obviously in pain, before hauling himself to his feet and looking to the air. A sudden growl of surprise shot from him as something sped from the forest and towards the green earth dragon. It was red in colour, and before either dragon could react, it landed between the earth dragon's horns. He screeched in pain as wires that led from the bottom of the device sunk into his head. Silver roared out her surprise and raced to help him, but it was too late, and the dragon fell to the ground, unconscious.

Silver turned to see if she could find the hidden attacker, and growled. A man revealed himself from the undergrowth. He was different from the other humans she had seen. There was no scent of fear about him, and he held himself in a posture of calm confidence, like he wasn't afraid of the far bigger creature in front of him. He also held a device in his right hand, which looked like a handgun. An angry scar—likely carved by a dragon's talon—stretched down his neck, the remnant of a wound that would kill most men. As the two made eye contact, a dangerous smile lit across his face.

Unease wound its way through Silver as she gazed at the man, and for a moment neither dragon nor human moved, each surveying the other. With a snort, Silver shook her fear away. He was a human, and no human could match a dragon in combat. With a flick of her tail, she sent several spikes his sway, all directly on target until the man simply stepped to the right. The spikes missed him by inches and embedded themselves in trees behind him. Before Silver could attack again, he raised the device, holding it sideways and hitting a button that wasn't the trigger.

A small yellow circular object shot out from the side of the gun and flew towards her. It seemed to magnetise itself to Silver's shell, landing on her right foreleg with a dull clunk. The dragoness growled in surprise. The device beeped twice, the only warning she had before it exploded. The metal dragon was thrown to the side and into a tree with such force it snapped, falling over her.

Silver groaned and tried to get up, but her body hurt all over and her head was ringing. The broken tree didn't help either. She saw her vision go black for a moment before it cleared. The dragoness whimpered and tried to get up again, but the tree held her down. The sound of footsteps came to her attention, and she moved her head to gaze at the human, who was steadily walking towards her with an easy gait. She summoned some liquefied metal into her throat and shot some at him, which he easily sidestepped once again. With a yowl, she hauled herself up again, managing to lift the tree. She threw it to the side and formed a blade with her tail, launching herself at the man. He moved far faster than any other human she'd seen before, dodging her talons and ducking under her bladed tail.

Another yellow bomb shot from his gun, attaching itself to Silver's chest. The explosion threw her backwards and she landed belly up to the sky, moaning. Her vision flickered black again as she struggled to regain consciousness.

No! I will not lose! Not like this, she mentally roared at herself, before rolling to her feet and standing up shakily.

She glared at the man, charging again, but her strength failed and she collapsed midstride into the floor, sending up a shower of dust. A gurgling laugh bubbled from the man's throat, and he turned his gun towards her again. This time he pulled the trigger. A device like the one that had hit the green dragon shot from it. Wires sprung from the bottom and it landed in between her horns. The wires scratched across her metallic armour, desperately trying to pierce it. With a snarl she lashed out with her tail, spearing the device through the centre and throwing it to the side. It landed a few metres away and didn't move. With a defiant grimace, Silver again hauled herself to her feet.

"You're not going to defeat me that easily," she growled.

The man raised his eyebrow, not at all perturbed by the failure of his strange device. He again shot a yellow bomb at her. She tried to hit it from midair, and missed. The bomb went off on her shoulder, throwing her to the side once again. This time her body refused to get up, and she whimpered, trying to recover from the shock. Never had she been hit so hard. She knew it was only her metallic armour that was saving her now. Before she had a chance to recover, another bomb hit her and she was lifted into the air before crashing back down again. Unconsciousness called to Silver, and her head rung like a bell. Another bomb hit her and again she was thrown several metres. This time she landed on her back and fell into unconsciousness for nearly five seconds before waking up, panting heavily as she tried to recover her breath.

A chuckle sounded, and she turned her head to look at the approaching man. How had she been defeated so easily? The thought continued to rush through her head as the man walked slowly towards her, but he seemed to be a blur, as did the rest of the world. And instead of getting clearer, all the colours began to merge into a mass.

She couldn't hear anything but the ringing, and couldn't feel anything but a dull throb that pulsated through her entire body. She barely noticed the clanging roar that echoed among the trees, or the great crash as several trunks were torn from the ground and thrown towards the man, nor did she notice the great silver mass that landed in front of her, the very embodiment of rage. But she did hear her name roared above the din.

"Silver! Get up! Run, damn it! Run!" Her father's voice broke through her consciousness.

Her vision cleared up and she saw Elron standing in front of her, wings outstretched and staring at the man, who had fallen back. His smirk had widened, but his eyes had narrowed. He was probably aiming to get Silver before trying to defeat her father.

"Silver! Go! Get out of here. Fly as fast as you can! Go! The valley is lost," he roared.

His words shot her into action. She got to her feet and opened her wings, about to take to the air when something stopped her. She couldn't leave her father here to face this man alone. She shook herself, regaining sensation in her body and snarling back the confusion.

"Silver, go!" cried Elron.

"No, I'm not letting you face him alone," she yelled back, taking a few defiant steps towards the man, who seemed content to watch the dragons argue.

"Damn it, Silver," Elron yelled, taking a few steps back to shield her from the man, "stop being stubborn. Get out of here while you have a chance, before they get you too."

"But you can't defeat them all alone!" Silver said.

Elron glanced back at his daughter, sorrow framing his gaze. Her heart leapt in her chest. He already knew he wasn't going to win or escape. The valley had fallen. The few dragons still alive had fled, and Silver and he were the only two left to defend the valley. Even the most powerful dragon in the world wouldn't be able to fend them all off.

"Please, I can't lose you too." Elron was desperate.

With a silent nod, Silver took to the air with a single beat of her wings. A strangled cry from the man who had defeated her brought Elron's gaze back to him. He pointed his gun at the fleeing form of Silver, and fired, but Elron leapt in the way, catching the yellow explosive. Unlike with Silver, it only stunned him momentarily before he turned back towards the man with a growl.

Silver turned and beat her wings harder, letting her armour retract from her lower body, which restored the speed and agility she needed to escape. Her speed increased and her view widened as she gazed over the now-destroyed valley. Trees were torn up. Wildfires were spreading and mountains had fallen. Liam's hut had been burned down, and she could only hope he had survived.

The planes in the air instantly targeted her, as she was the only dragon still in the sky. Summoning the last of her strength, Silver increased her speed to the maximum, until only a silver blur could be seen as she shot through the air and over the mountains that had always been her boundary.

As she crossed over the mountain range, she couldn't help but think that she had finally got her wish to leave the dragon paradise. But she had never wanted it like this. Not like this. With a heavy heart she flew onward, trying to outpace the planes that would undoubtedly follow her.

Chapter 5: Silver's Flight

The ocean stretched vastly to the horizon. There was no land in sight, no mountains, no trees; not even a cloud. It was almost as if the world's maker had decided to stop creating and filled the seas with water just to occupy space. The only difference was the constant moving of the blue ocean as waves were created and destroyed over and over in a never-ending cycle that would continue until the end of days.

Silver watched as the world seemed to end before her, and hesitated. There was still land below her and the sight of the ocean before her made her hesitate. Never in her life had she seen such an empty expanse of water, and it scared her. Metallic dragons were not the best swimmers because their metal shells weighed them down. To fly over an ocean without a destination was nearly a death sentence, yet as she glanced behind her she knew that she didn't have much choice.

Two dark spots on the horizon were steadily closing in on her fleeing form, and it didn't help that the sun outlined her shell so brilliantly. She was like a beacon to anyone hunting dragons, and the two planes that had been following her for the past few hours wouldn't likely stop, so she continued over the vast blue ocean.

It was the perfect day for flying. A slight breeze blew a salty scent that Silver could only think was the sea, and the sun was shining brilliantly. It wasn't too hot, nor too cold, so Silver didn't have to worry about her metal shell heating up or freezing. She almost smiled as an updraft caught her and pulled her even higher into the sky. To any animal or human on the ground she would undoubtedly look like a shooting star.

She continued to fly, and the land behind her disappeared into the horizon. Now she was well and truly out in the open. There was nothing else out there but water, and she wondered if she had been the first dragon to find the end of the world. Her dad had said it was round, but the huge expanse before her led her to believe otherwise. There was no way there could be anything else out there. If there was, she would undoubtedly see it.

She glanced behind her to find out if she had finally lost the two planes, but the two dark spots in the distance were still following her. She growled. Her wings were beginning to tire, and began to hurt with every flap. She was lucky her dad had forced her into training for long-distance flights. At the time, she hadn't considered its significance, but now she was glad for them. At her best she could fly for nearly two days straight without rest, and with her life on the line she knew she could fly even longer, but that didn't stop her wing joints from hurting.

For hours they flew until the sun was at its pinnacle in the sky. Silver felt the metal on her back slowly heating up. She sighed and forced herself onwards, looking out for any sign of land. If she could find something that would help her, like a cave of some sort, then she may be able to hold off until nightfall where the heat wouldn't bother her so. But the hours passed and land didn't show itself.

With every minute, Silver grew more paranoid that she had found the end of the world. But when a long line on the horizon came into view she couldn't help but be overjoyed. Land, at last! Pushing herself for more speed, she began to get excited. On land she'd be able to hide and wait for them to stop looking for her. After that, she didn't know what she would do, but she would think of something.

As she came to the land, the heat had risen greatly, and the metal on her back was becoming uncomfortable. She half-growled at it, wishing the feeling away, but it persisted. Distracted by her hot shell, she almost missed the movement of human soldiers down on the shoreline. Only when the first wave of bullets passed her did she notice.

Silver roared in surprise and looked down to see nearly a hundred humans, all pointing weapons of different kinds at her. She whimpered, not wanting to fight anymore, but the humans were scarcely giving her a choice. A rocket from an RPG fired at her and she dodged to the side, flying with greater-than-normal agility as she began to speed up to escape the humans. She only hoped they destroyed the two planes following her as well.

The land below her was dry, like someone had sucked all moisture from it and dumped it in the ocean. The emptiness was beginning to make her sick. What kind of world was she in? Her father had spoken of amazing things like mountains that touched the sky and bushland that spread for as far as the eye could see, yet all she could see now was desert and the occasionally desolated human town. The heat was blistering. Silver's shell felt like it was melting into her back. She knew it wasn't—it had withstood the heat of fire before—but it was still painful.

Worse, the two black dots behind her still hadn't disappeared. She knew they had passed the army of humans, and wondered if the two groups had been working together. Liam had told her of the long-range communication devices that humans had created, so it was entirely possible. She growled at the thought. Did that mean the whole world was looking for her now?

She decided not to stop in this land. She didn't know how safe she would be while the planes were following her. Now she knew they were using long-range communication, she'd just have to fly far enough for the planes to stop following her long enough to find a hiding place. It was the only option.

The plus side of flying over the landscape was that it changed. It never stopped being hot, but it pleased her to see that the world wasn't all desert and ocean. After the desert, she first crossed a great expanse of yellow, almost-dead grassland. A savannah, or at least what she imagined a savannah to look like. The long grass then turned into rolling hills and then into mountains, not quite as big as those at home, but big enough for a dragon to live in. She was tempted to fly down in between them and find a cave to hide in, but the smell of humans stopped her. They seemed to be everywhere.

So she flew on until the ocean again revealed itself. By then the sun was dipping into the horizon, painting an enormity of purples, oranges and yellows. It was the most beautiful sunset she had ever seen, and if she had the chance she would have landed on a small outcrop to watch it. But alas, it wouldn't happen. The black dots behind her had become a constant presence and no matter what she did, she wouldn't be able to escape them, so she once again flew over the ocean.

Her hatred of the blue mass quickly intensified as she was reminded how far it stretched outwards. She wasn't scared by it anymore, but she was tired. Her wings were tiring, and she hoped she'd be able to fly for the rest of the night. She should have paced herself more.

Once again, the land behind her disappeared and she was left with the setting sun and the black dots. Once the sun had set, the planes behind her wouldn't be visible … but neither would she. Silver considered turning back now and making a break for the land, hoping that the planes wouldn't capture her, but she knew that would be foolish, and continued to fly.

A darkness on the horizon perked her up. At first, she thought it was land but soon realised that it was far too high up to be land. Her second guess was it was the darkness of night, but she dismissed that idea when she realised that even night wasn't as dark as what she saw ahead. It took her a few more minutes to realise what the dark mass was, and when she did, her heart fell. It was a storm. She recognised the formation now. She had seen quite a few in her time but had only flown through one. It ended with her smashing into a mountain and breaking one of her metallic wings, made of the hardest substance on earth. She began to turn to fly around the storm, when an idea popped into her head. She glanced behind and, sure enough, the two black dots were still present. She turned back to the storm and made a decision.

With a flap of her wings she powered towards the storm. If she could survive it then she would lose the two planes behind her. If she didn't, well … she couldn't think about that. Right now, the most important thing was getting through the wall of lightning, wind and rain.

* * *

In the cockpit of one of the planes, a pilot watched the storm steadily approach. He frowned as he watched the glinting piece of silver on the horizon continue to fly straight towards the great wall of cloud. He knew only too well how impossible it was to fly a plane through a force of nature as strong as that, no matter how well-equipped his plane.

"Sir?" he spoke into his radio, "A storm is rolling in fast and the dragon looks as if it's going to fly into it. Do I have your permission to turn around?"

"No!" came the stoic answer, "You are to come back with that dragoness or not at all."

"But, sir …" the pilot tried desperately.

"Did you just argue with a direct order, sergeant?" said the voice.

"No, sir," was the mumbled answer.

"Good. Now get the dragon."

The pilot switched his intercom off and took a deep breath, readjusting his grip on the steering wheel.

Well, it's been a good life, he thought.

* * *

Silver pierced the storm with as much speed as she could muster, hoping to break through it in a single push, but a ferocious updraft sent her spinning into the air with enough force to knock the wind from her. She half-groaned and beat her wings frantically to regain control of her body. It was futile.

The storm tossed the silver dragon around like a rag doll, throwing her up, down and side to side. Snake-like lightning zigzagged through the air, followed nearly instantly by a cataclysmic bang. Mountains of water reached high into the air before crashing with enough force to crack a ship's metal hull. The wind felt like giant hammers to the adolescent dragoness, and she could do little but struggle to stay aloft.

The more she fought the wind and rain, the quicker she exhausted herself, and she soon found that it was far easier just to ride the swirling currents, only fighting when she came to close to the ocean. If she went into the water, she doubted she'd be able to get out. The upside was she couldn't see the planes anymore, and she was sure they couldn't see her. Now the only problem was getting herself out of the storm.

An idea came to her and she transformed into her metal state, allowing her shell to cover her body. The difference was immediate. She wasn't thrown around so much in the storm anymore and she was able to fly in a more or less straight line. She didn't move as fast, however, and she knew it would take a while to get out of the storm, but she pushed herself on. A horse-sized dragon flying through a storm the size of a small country.

Thunder boomed constantly around her, and every lightning strike seemed to get closer. Little did she know that metal attracts lightning, especially so high in the air. A blue bolt stung Silver. She roared in surprise as a million volts of electricity surged through her, lighting her up like a beacon in the sky, but she felt no pain. She felt its power, but if anything, she wanted it to strike again. Silver didn't know how to unleash its power, however, so she did what came naturally to a dragon. She opened her maw and pushed the power out of her with her mind. A blue bolt of electricity struck out from her mouth and into the ocean below with a crackling bang. Her body sizzled with the surplus energy, and Silver was so surprised that she nearly didn't flap her wings. She could conduct lightning! This made her smile. Suddenly, the flashing blue streaks didn't scare her anymore.

The storm seemed to go on forever, and Silver felt the weight of her metal body against her wings. Every flap was torture as she forced herself onwards, not yet willing to let the world take her. Yet every moment seemed to bring that fate closer. Lightning continued to strike her at times, and every time she let it out through her gullet. She would have stored the power, but she had no idea how. In safer circumstances, she would have experimented, but now she was only focused on finding land.

More hours passed and—just as Silver felt as though she was about to give up—the storm broke. Her wings met with the cool night air of some different ocean. She smiled and closed her eyes, gliding for a spell to rest her wings. Her metallic shell retracted until it was again covering only her back, wings and tail. To make sure she had lost the planes, she glanced behind her, and there were no black dots in the sky anymore. She let loose a trumpet of joy. She had lost them, finally. As she gazed forwards once more she couldn't but roar again in relief. There, just a few kilometres ahead, was another stretch of land, one she intended to take advantage of.

She flew over the beautiful coastland of white beaches with a small smile. This land looked promising to the silver dragoness. Gazing around the green forests and grassland she tried to find food. The sun was steadily coming into the horizon once more, making her re-alise she had flown through both a day and a night. She was utterly exhausted, but first she needed to eat.

A herd of brown, four-legged creatures caught her eyes. She recog-nised that it was a strange type of cow, though she didn't know what type. They were near a human's house, but she couldn't care less about that. Instead she folded her wings and dived down towards them. The herd didn't even hear her until it was too late. The one she pinned to the ground let out a screech before it was silenced with a bite to the neck. The rest of the herd scattered away from the hungry silver dragon as she tore into her hearty meal.

Silver trilled in alarm at a sudden bang. A bullet ricocheted off her shell and into the sky. She quickly faced the source, covering her head with her wings. Another bullet bounced off them and flew in the opposite direction. Normally, she would have attacked the assailant, but at that moment she was too drained to even summon a threatening growl. And she was tired of fighting.

"Please," she heard herself say, "Please. I'm sorry. I was just hungry and needed something to eat. Please."

When no more shots rang out, she peeked past her wing to see a rough-looking human with a double-barrelled shotgun, looking at her in disbelief. She hesitated, not quite willing to trust the burly man, but when she noticed the gun was being aimed harmlessly at the floor, she withdrew her wings from her face. The man didn't even move, but continued to stare in fascination.

"Aah, hello," Silver tried, wondering if the man understood her. She knew that some humans didn't speak English. She wondered if this was one of them. "Can you understand me?"

The man's gun fell to the floor. "Holy sh… You talk!"

She hesitated, before nodding her head. She was somewhat used to humans acting like this.

"What are you?" he asked.

That question stumped her. She'd never had to explain her species to a human before. "Um … I'm a dragon. A metal dragon."

"A dragon? But aren't they a myth?"

She blinked at the stupidity of the question. "Well, if I'm not a dragon, what am I?"

The man blinked again, before turning to the house. He hesitated, then turned back to her. "Are you going anywhere?"

Silver shook her head, still a little confused at the human. The man seemed to nod to her, before sprinting as fast as his little legs could carry him back to the house.

"Honey! Wake up! You may want to see this!" His voice cried out into the open air.

CHAPTER 6:
A PLACE TO STAY

Silver felt herself relax in the hay-filled shed, shifting to get comfortable in her hurriedly made nest. Her tired wings sprawled out on each side of her. She didn't have the energy to fold them up. Her usually mirror-like shell was dimmer than usual and her tail looked like a dead snake.

She was glad the farmers had allowed her to stay the night with them, not being sure where she would have slept otherwise. It crossed her mind that they could have been in league with the humans who had attacked her, but she was too tired to care. Even if they did find her, she wouldn't be able to do much, so she opted to rest for the night and regain her energy.

In the shed last night, the farmer's wife had amused Silver a lot. She had screamed at the sight of the dragon and hid behind her husband. When both her husband and Silver assured her that Silver meant no harm, she slowly walked up to the dragon, beginning what became a fruitful conversation, at the end of which Silver had been offered a place to rest until she was ready to move on again. The dragon was more than happy to oblige.

As her eyes were about to close, the sound of footsteps forced her to lift her head. She blinked once as the farmer came into view holding another, smaller, human by the hand. This human was male, she thought, and had blond hair, not the bigger one's brown mane. He had an innocence about him, evidenced by his wide-eyed staring at the dragon.

"Wow."

The small human spoke with a voice far lighter than any human male she had met thus far.

Silver looked quizzically up at the farmer. "Who's this?"

"This is my son," he replied, "Greg."

She nodded. The human was just a boy, a hatchling much like herself. Smiling, Silver craned her neck downwards so her head was level with Greg, who gazed back at her in a mixture of fear and awe. He didn't know how to react to such an exotic creature.

"I don't want to sound rude," said Silver, "but I'm very tired. You can stay here, but I'm going to fall asleep."

The farmer nodded. "Of course. My son just wanted to see the dragon."

He carefully grabbed Greg's hand and led him back to the house. Silver watched them go, before laying her head down on the straw and closing her eyes. Sleep came quickly for her, and soon she was completely lost in the dream world, her body able to relax.

* * *

She woke up quite a while later. The night sky was dark but there was a hint of sun on the horizon. She nearly jumped in surprise when she realised where she was and what she was sleeping on. A growl escaped her as she pried away a loose bit of straw stuck between her scales.

Letting out a large yawn, she got to her feet and spread her wings, feeling her stiff joints crack and creak as the metal readjusted to movement. She groaned and shook herself, looking out into the sky again. She must have been exhausted to sleep the whole previous day and through the night. Then again, she had never flown for so long at such speeds. Instinctively, she looked into the sky for the planes that had chased her. They weren't there. She let out a long sigh, releasing all her stress in a single breath. She had managed to escape.

She let herself smile, looking around the farmyard in interest. It was very different to what she was used to. There were no mountains nearby, leaving a flat land with only the occasional copse of trees to break the view. The grass around her was green, and there was the scent of animal waste in the air.

Around the shed was a dirt patch, with a large machine to one side. A caged-off area housed strange red birds that walked around pecking and digging up the ground. In a round yard, a row of metal fences stretched out to her right. A number of tools were hanging all around her, the only one she recognised being a hammer. It all struck her as very strange, and she wondered how anyone could live in such a flat area.

"You're awake," said a familiar voice.

She turned to see the farmer walking towards her holding a thin, fawn-coloured wooden plank. He leaned it up against the far wall of the shed before looking at Silver once more.

"Are you feeling better?" he asked, seeming much more at ease now with the dragoness.

She nodded. "Yes."

She stretched out her wings and took a couple of flaps. They were still stiff and she wouldn't be able to fly as well as usual, but they would still hold her aloft.

"So, are you planning on leaving?" he asked.

"I guess so," was her slow, considered reply.

"Where do you plan on going?" he asked.

Silver hesitated. She hadn't thought about that question before. All she had wanted to do was to get away from the planes that had been chasing her. Now that she thought about it, she didn't even know where she was. For all she knew she'd arrived on the other side of the world. She had flown long and hard enough to do so.

"I ... I don't know. In fact, I don't even know where I am right now," she said, looking at the farmer.

"Oh, that's easy. You're in Australia," he said.

Silver blinked. She had occasionally seen maps of the world. She knew she lived in a valley somewhere in America, though exactly where she didn't know, but the names of the other countries had confused her. She remembered hearing about Australia, but didn't know where it was.

"Where is that?" she asked, a little embarrassed.

"Come with me. I'll get you a map," he said, "Do you know how to read one?"

"More or less," she said, following the farmer to his house.

It was bigger than Liam's house, with a tile roof and brick walls. Silver had never seen another human house before and was fascinated by its making. There was a chimney at the top, but no smoke. The windows were covered with glass, and a mesh door covered one of the main doors to the house; why they needed two doors, Silver didn't know.

The farmer entered the house while Silver stayed outside. She would have liked to see the interior, but she didn't think she'd fit, or be welcome in the house. So instead she sat on the front lawn, trying her best not to create too big an imprint on the grass.

The farmer came out a bit later with a large piece of paper. He set it down in front of the silver dragoness. She instantly recognised it as a map of the world. All the countries were set in different colours and she quickly spotted America. It was the only country she knew.

"Where's Australia?" she asked.

"Here," he said, pointing to a large country to the bottom right-hand corner of the map. Her eyes widened. She *had* flown halfway across the world.

"Where do you come from?" asked the farmer.

"Somewhere in America," she said, still gazing at the map.

She realised she had probably passed over Africa as well, and lost the planes over the Indian Ocean, before ending up on the west coast of Australia. It amazed her how only a few days ago she was wishing to leave the valley, and now she was on the other side of the world. A low sigh escaped her as she thought back to the valley. She wondered if her father, and her brothers and mother, had escaped. She had no idea where they would have gone.

"So … where do you think you'll go?" the farmer asked.

Silver stared at the map. "I … I don't know. I might find a … cave somewhere or look for anyone who escaped … or something."

The farmer frowned before asking a surprising question: "How old are you?"

"Six," she replied.

"Equivalent to human years?" he said.

She thought for a moment. Dragons tended to mature much faster than humans. They were able to have hatchlings at eight years of age, so it was difficult to tell what age that would be in human years. Liam had suggested that for the first ten years of a dragon's life, their age in human years is double their dragon age. After that, however, it became much more difficult to tell, considering dragons lived an average lifespan of five hundred years.

"Twelve, I think," she said, looking at him.

"So, you're still only a child," said the farmer, seeming surprised.

"I … I guess so. I hadn't left the nest yet," she said.

"What happened?" he asked.

"We were attacked, and I was forced to flee and was chased. That was how I ended up here," it was all she said, not wanting to give her life story to a human she barely knew.

The farmer nodded, seeming to consider something. "Sorry for not finding this out sooner, but do you have a name?"

"Silver," she replied, "What's yours?"

"Darren," said the human, before falling silent again.

The frown on his face told Silver that he was considering some sort of problem. His expression piqued her curiosity, but she decided to stay silent. Instead she looked down at the map, poring over the other continents. She knew how to read a little, but she wasn't good at it.

"Silver," said Darren, catching her attention again, "because you don't have anywhere to go, would you like to stay here for a while, just until you find your way?"

Silver was a little surprised, and hesitated.

"Of course, we won't be able to supply everything for you. You'll need to do your own hunting, maybe catch some of the kangaroos that have been pestering the neighbourhood, and clean up your own waste, but you can sleep in the shed and, as payment, you can help me work on my farm. It would be useful to have a creature like you to help round up the cattle when I need it."

She considered his proposal. It made sense, and would keep her busy while she figured out what to do next. It would also give her time to start to refine her skills. If the dragon hunters found her again, she wanted to be readier than she was last time. She could fly faster than one of their planes, but in a fight she was hopeless against one, and then there was that strange gun that the scarred human had used. She would need to find a way around that.

"Okay," she said, "but can you try to keep me a secret? I don't want the humans who attacked me to find me again. If we do meet again, it will be on my terms."

Darren nodded and smiled. He wasn't worried too much about the dangerous humans. It would be hard to get a force like that into Australia without them noticing. He hoped the dragon would be more of a help than a hindrance, and she seemed willing enough.

"Anything else?" he asked her.

"Oh, yeah," Silver smiled a little sheepishly, "What's a kangaroo?"

CHAPTER 7:
LIFE ON A FARM

S ILVER turned sharply and swooped low over the flat, green ground. She let loose a low roar, frightening the cattle towards a fenced-off area. She flew above them, watching them trample as fast as they could into the next paddock. The farmer came in behind them and locked the gate, boxing them in. She landed behind him with a small thud.

"Well done," said Darren, brushing off his hands.

Silver smiled and looked to the sky. "Is that all today?"

He nodded, "That's all. I have some computer work to do, but I don't think you can help with that."

"Okay. Seeya!" Silver took to the air with a grin, glad to be free for the day.

The few weeks she'd been farming had proved far different from her expectations. Mostly she was moving the cattle around to different paddocks. She also looked for breaks in the electric fence where cattle had got through, and for any dead beasts, which she was allowed to eat.

The work had kept her busy. She often found herself falling asleep early, tired after a day's work. It wasn't that physically taxing, but it wore on her day by day. At least it kept her fit, but every so often she wished for a break. She didn't complain, though; it gave her a safe place to rest while she figured herself out.

Sighing, she came to a landing near the shed and stretched her wings out. She had finished early that day and the sun was still high in the sky. It was probably around midafternoon, which gave her a few hours to herself. She looked around, searching for something to do. She had wanted to start working on her powers again, like her father had taught her, but there was no way to train and no dragons to practise with. She sighed, looking over at the small forest that stretched through the farm, and an idea came to her.

Smiling, she took to the air. She could use the trees as obstacles and practise flying. She was already quite agile, but training should never stop. She just hoped she didn't accidently cut down any trees in the process. Once above the forest, she folded her wings in and dove at the ground. As she passed through the trees, she spread her wings and collided with one of them. Groaning, she fell to the ground.

She lay there for a few moments, recovering from the shock, before getting to her feet again. The world swam for a moment and she closed her eyes, letting herself recover a little before taking a few more steps forwards.

"That wasn't the best idea," she said to herself as she stumbled back to the shed, not trusting herself to fly.

As she reached her shed she collapsed into her straw nest. A headache began to pound, and she knew she'd hurt for the next few days. Sighing, she shifted in her nest, looking to the half-finished metal nest beside her. While sleeping on straw was far better than sleeping on the ground, she preferred a nest.

Deciding she'd rather do something—anything—other than sit and worry about the headache, she began to work on her nest again. It was slow work, adding metal then shaving it away, and soon she was lost in her own world, so lost that she didn't notice the sudden appearance of Greg, the farmer's boy, walking towards her.

"Hey," he said, startling her.

She turned and lowered her head to look the boy in the eye and smiled. "Hey."

"Dad said you finished early," he said, sitting down on the straw bed.

The two had become good friends over the weeks she'd been there. They often talked when they had the time, and occasionally they would wander around the farm together. The few times the boy had asked for a ride on her back, Silver had instantly said no. He wouldn't have been that heavy, but she would feel uncomfortable with another human on her back, and she doubted he would be able to stay on.

"How was your school?" she asked, pushing her nest to the side.

"Oh, same as always. Boring," he said with a little laugh.

She smiled back. She had found the idea of this "schooling" very weird. Parents sending their children away to be taught things about the earth, and how to read and write. It all seemed a little pointless to her.

"You rounded up cows, I'm guessing?" he asked.

She snorted, but bobbed her head in a 'yes'.

"Hey, are you going to show me your powers today? You said you would when you had the chance, and I still have a few hours till dinnertime," he said eagerly.

She hesitated. She had never been much of a show-off, maybe a bit boastful, but never a show-off. The only times she used her abilities were when she was training or creating something, or fighting.

"Oh, come on, Silver, you promised," pleaded Greg.

"Aargh, fine. I probably need the practise anyway."

She got up from her nest and shook herself rid of the hay straws that had wedged themselves under her scales.

"Is there anywhere we can go where I won't be in danger of accidentally damaging any of your father's stuff?"

Greg nodded. "I'll grab my motorbike. Just wait here."

Silver did as she was told, watching the boy run back to his house. He came back a few minutes later riding a loud two-wheeled vehicle that she had learned was called a motorbike. His was small compared to his father's, but still ran quite well. It was dark red and had many dirt stains across its cover and wheels. Greg now had on a helmet, slightly too large for his head, and a long, hardy jumper that was also covered in dirt and grime.

Greg revved the engine a few times before saying to Silver, "Follow me from the air. I know the perfect place."

He slammed the visor down on his head and sped off on the bike, the noise grating on Silver's sensitive ears. She growled a little, but did as the boy said, her departure much more graceful than the motorbike's, and followed Greg across the large farm.

Greg led her into a small grove of paperbark trees about a kilometre away from the farmhouse. He stopped in the middle, at a small clearing that Silver could access. She did so gladly, gliding down and landing among the trees. Greg took off his helmet and turned off his bike, before looking back at Silver with a smile.

"This should be a good place. No-one's around for miles," he said.

She nodded, wondering what to show the boy first.

"Show me how you breathe metal. I've seen you working on that thing where you sleep, but I've never seen you shoot it," he said eagerly.

Silver chuckled, but nodded, "Okay, stand back. I don't want to hit you with this stuff."

She opened her maw and shot a glob of liquid metal at a tree. It hit the middle of the tree and instantly solidified. She smiled—a perfect shot, right where she'd aimed it.

Greg laughed a little at the display. "I was expecting more than that," he said, challenging Silver.

She looked at the boy and snorted. "Fine."

She opened her maw again and sprayed liquid metal at the tree, covering the entire length of the paperbark trunk with a silver husk. Silver sat on her haunches to admire her work. The sun caught the silver shell and scattered light throughout the clearing, making her smile. The shine was beautiful.

"Wow, that's cool," he said, walking up to the tree to inspect it.

He knocked on the trunk, creating a ringing that echoed among the paperbarks. The other side of the tree was still free of the metal.

Silver wondered if it would be able to survive its new shell, and looked forward to seeing how it did over the next few weeks.

"Can you do anything else?" asked Greg.

Silver nodded. She looked back to her tail and formed spikes on it, before flicking them at the metallic tree. Each spike embedded itself into the trunk, except for a few that flew wide. She grumbled. Her aim was a bit off.

"Spikes—cool!" said Greg, attempting to pluck one of them from the tree, only to find it was stuck.

"I can also do this," said Silver, expanding her metal shell to cover her whole body.

Greg's eyes widened with surprise and he walked over to Silver, whose exterior was now fully metal. He tapped her side, ringing another dull echo among the trees.

"I can also transform my tail into different things," she said, forming it into a razor-sharp blade, "but I still haven't learnt everything yet. I should be able to darken my shell, but I can't do that very well, and there are a few other things I haven't perfected yet. But I plan to."

"That's still so cool, though," said Greg. "When I was young I always thought that dragons could only breathe fire. But now I know you have so many different powers. It's awesome."

Silver flushed with pride at the compliment. "Yeah, it is pretty cool."

He looked up at the sky. "Hey, well, I need to head back now. Dinner should be almost ready. I'll see you tomorrow."

"Yeah, tomorrow," replied the dragoness.

She watched as the boy sped off on his motorbike before looking around the clearing again. This would be a great place to start her training. She needed to practise, given her sloppy performance that day. A few weeks without using her powers was taking its toll. Nodding to herself, she took to the air and followed Greg back to the farmhouse.

Chapter 8:
A Test of Strength and Will

THE months passed quickly at the farm. Every day followed the same routine. Get up early in the morning, work until the sun started to die on the horizon, and then train, if there was time. The seasons changed rapidly as well. As summer came, the heat rose till Silver found it uncomfortable. The grass changed from a healthy green to a brown-yellow. Rolls of hay were bundled up across the surrounding farmland and covered in a white cloth. They looked like giant white marshmallows.

Prey were still plentiful, however, as the kangaroo population seemed to increase over spring. Silver found herself growing quickly as well. She was now the size of a large packhorse, and didn't show any signs of stopping. And with her size, her power also grew. Bending metal to her will was becoming far easier. Her strength and speed increased with each week. The clearing she used to train was now covered in a bowl of metal that she constantly added to.

To her relief, few humans knew of her existence. The few farmers in the area knew of her, as did the farmhands who occasionally helped Darren with different pieces of machinery. Occasionally she was called on to work with the farmhands, rolling huge cylinders of hay into a shed. It was hard work for the young dragoness, and she often found herself too tired to train at the end of the day. But it was worth it in the end, because every night she would fall asleep with a sense of accomplishment.

Silver glided down over a large paddock and landed close to where one of Darren's machines was hauling a load of hay into a huge pile at the end of the field. She had just been out hunting, and the bloodied remains of a kangaroo were smeared over her maw. That day had been intensely hot, the sun's rays biting at her shell. Shifting slightly, she ignored it, then put her shoulder against the bale of hay and pushed, rolling it over to the pile.

As she finished, she noticed a sudden commotion at one side of the field, where the large machine was. Frowning, she padded over to the few humans around it, including Darren. He had his apprentice, Ethan, with him, as well as another human whose name escaped Silver. They grew silent as she approached.

"What's wrong?" she asked.

Despite her living at the farm for almost five months, most other humans found her terrifying. Maybe it was her size, or her intelligence, or the fact that she was a "mythical" creature, supposedly with magic powers. She didn't know, but whenever she was around them she did her best to make herself as non-threatening as possible.

"The hay baler's bogged," said Ethan.

Ethan was a strange human. He was short, far smaller than normal, and had dark hair that he let grow out and usually tied up behind his head. The first time Silver had seen him, she'd mistaken him for a female, and they hadn't started on good terms.

"What?" she asked.

"Stuck," Ethan replied, seeming a little frustrated. "We can't move it."

Half of the baler's giant wheel had rolled into a muddy trough in the middle of the field. It didn't look like it was going anywhere fast.

"Do you need help?" she asked.

The farmers looked at each other before Darren spoke up. He was the only one of the three who fully trusted her.

"That would be good. Thank you, Silver," he said, before turning back to the problem at hand. "Silver, could you try and dig up the tyre while the rest of us find some wood to lodge underneath."

The dragoness nodded and moved over the muddy ground to where the tyre was deeply bogged in the mud. With a sigh, she sunk her claws into the mud near the tyre, suddenly regretting her offer to help. She hated mud. It got in between her scales and dirtied her shining shell. While her shell's shine was annoying when she was trying to hide, she couldn't help but admit to liking the gleam.

With a snort she dug her claws into the soft ground and began to dig, scooping up the mud much like a dog would. She tried keep her underbelly clean, but in vain, and before long her legs and stomach were dripping with mud. At least it cooled her down.

She dug for what seemed like hours, but soon it seemed futile. The water in the ground collapsed the mud in on itself and filled up the hole. She growled in annoyance and doubled her efforts, but the earth continued to sink. Eventually she gave up and sat back. The mud slowly trickled down her underbelly and legs. She'd managed to uncover nearly all the tyre, but the water wouldn't let her dig any further.

The farmers came back a little later. Silver told them of her predicament and they just nodded. Darren came in with a long piece of wood and jammed it into the ground just in front of the tyre, followed by the other humans. Silver noticed a long coil of rope around the farmer's shoulder.

"Silver, I want you to pull from the front. I'm going to hop into the baler and try to drive it out. You got that?" he asked.

She nodded. "Is that what the rope is for?"

Darren nodded. "Hope you're strong enough. Let's go."

Silver padded around to the front of the tractor and opened her wings slightly to allow Darren to tie the rope around them. The farmer came up beside her and threw the rope over her neck. Ethan helped, grabbing the end of the rope on one side while Darren was on the other. They threaded it under her wings and to the tractor, where they tied it around the axels that held the two front wheels. Darren climbed up into the baler and started the engine.

"Okay, Silver, when I say pull, pull!" he yelled out over the sound of cranking machinery.

Silver nodded her agreement. She stabbed her claws into the ground and pulled. There was an instant weight at her back, like she was trying to pull a tree out of the ground. She had done that once, but she knew this would be harder.

"Pull!" yelled Darren, revving up the engines.

Silver's muscles bunched as she pulled forwards. The wheels of the baler spun, not gaining any traction. Mud flew, and the tractor didn't move. Silver's claws began to cut through the ground, leaving large grooves. This was a lot different from trying to pull a tree from the ground. The rope was beginning to push into her metal shell, but she barely felt it, and pulled harder. Then it slipped part-way down her wings, but she didn't notice and continued to heave.

As she pulled, Silver instinctively folded her wings, not realising the consequences until it was too late. The rope slipped over the elbow of her wing and she shot forwards with a growl of surprise, as if she were jumping involuntarily. With a grunt, she landed face first in the muddy ground a few metres away. The tractor stalled as the small progress they had made was undone and the wheel sunk back into the mud.

Silver growled and pushed herself from the ground. She shook her head, dislodging as much mud as she could from her jaw and neck. She turned and looked back at the rope, expecting to find it broken. It wasn't, and it took her a moment to figure out why.

Darren got out of the tractor and was making his way towards the muddied dragoness.

"Are you alright?" he called to her.

She nodded back, feeling a little frustrated. "The rope slipped over my wings."

She padded back over to where the rope lay in the mud. It was frayed slightly where it had met with Silver's wings, but it didn't seem close to breaking.

As the humans approached her, she said, "Try putting it around my neck this time, and over my wings. It won't slip then, hopefully anyway."

They did as they were told and slipped the rope under her neck and over her wings. She pulled again and, satisfyingly, the rope was taut. Shaking herself out, she prepared to pull again. Darren started the tractor up, and she hauled.

Instantly, pain sprung from where the rope was around her chest, digging into the soft scales. A metallic dragons' scales are far softer than the average dragon's, making them poor protection. She wished she had been in full-metal form before she started, but it was too late. Snarling, she ignored the pain and continued to pull.

A huge groan came from the tractor as it slowly began to move forwards and up the side of the hole. Now it was time for the hardest part: pulling it out. Darren revved the engine harder and slammed down the pedal. The wheel spun helplessly in the mud and began to slide backwards once more. Silver felt herself being dragged back and nearly roared in defiance. She stabbed her claws further into the ground and pulled forwards with all her might, trying to take a step. That was all she needed to free the tractor – one more step.

The rope was beginning to compress her chest cavity, and she knew if she pulled much harder her ribs may break, but they were so close.

"Silver, stop!" cried Ethan, relaying Darren's order. "It's no use. We'll have to find another way."

"No!" she growled, "I've almost got it … just … a little more."

The tractor groaned again. Silver reared on her hind legs, letting loose a stubborn snarl. She squeezed her eyes shut and flapped her wings, trying to use the wind to boost her efforts. She didn't know why she was so determined to free the tractor, but something inside her wasn't going to let her stop until the job was done. She needed to do this.

The tractor shuddered again and groaned as the wheel finally gained some traction. It lurched forwards suddenly. Silver fell back down on her four feet – and took a step forwards. It lurched and groaned again, before sliding free of the hole with a loud, wet squelch. Silver tripped and fell again into the mud, but this time didn't bother getting up.

She took big gasps of air as she tried to catch her breath. She was certain a few scales had been cracked or pulled out, and her leg muscles cramped slightly, unused to being worked so hard so quickly. It took a couple of minutes, but Silver got up and shook herself off. She looked back at the humans, Ethan and the other farmer, who were staring at her in awe.

"Silver, that was amazing!" called Darren, jogging over to where they stood after parking the baler in a safer part of the paddock.

Silver let a small smile cross her face. She had really done it, pulled a couple of tons of human machinery out of a ditch, by herself. Well, Darren helped, she guessed, but most of the effort had been hers.

"Are you okay?" asked Darren, as he got a better look at the silver dragoness and noticed a bloodied gash that spread across the unprotected part of her chest.

Silver craned her neck to see what the farmer was looking at, and winced. The rope had torn and broken multiple scales across her chest, like a great red smile. It scared her a little.

"Yeah," Silver said. But even as she said it, a sharp pain crossed over her, making her gasp, "I've taken worse."

"Good," he said, "but you must be exhausted after that."

She didn't deny it, and only nodded.

"Well, go back to the house and get that wound treated. Afterwards, if you're feeling up to it, come back and help us with the rest of the hay. Good work today."

Silver felt pride blossom in her chest, and smiled. She opened her wings and took to the air. The wound hurt every time she flapped her wings, but not enough to stop her.

Chapter 9:
Found

Abrown-haired man sighed with fatigue as he once again sat back at his desk. The screen in front of him flickered to life, bouncing its dull light off the man's glasses. He brushed back his ruffled mop as he set himself to, once again, get on with his job. He didn't know what the point was. A year had passed and still they hadn't found the target. He suspected she was dead.

He looked out over his desk to the other people who had been stuck in the same boring job. There were hundreds of rows of them, scouring the internet, wireless phones, satellite images, anything that was connected to the internet. Hundreds of dragons had been found throughout the world, from America to Russia and down into Africa, but the dragon they were supposed to find had disappeared.

Grumbling to himself, the man went to the bookmarks on his browser and opened Facebook. There was nothing better to do. He glanced around to make sure no-one would alert the bosses, though the man next to him was playing some old computer game and, over the partition, a woman was too focused on her task to notice. Smiling to himself, he began to scroll down his newsfeed, looking for any break from the mundane life of a hacker.

He continued to scroll when something caught his eye. At first he went past it, but stopped and scrolled back up, shocked at what he saw. It took a moment for him to comprehend, but when he did, an excited yell sounded across the room. He stood up from his chair with a quick movement, startling the few people around him.

"Sir! Sir!" he cried out to the man who was overseeing the operation, "I found her!"

An intimidating, dark-haired man slowly walked over to where the excited man had been working. His eyes narrowed at the screen, studying the image before him.

"Well done," said the man, straightening his body. "I will notify our employer immediately. You are dismissed. Have the rest of the day off."

The hacker couldn't believe his luck. He stood up, saluted awkwardly, and hurried out of the room before his superior could change his mind.

The leader ignored him, poring over the screen.

'Rare metallic dragon spotted on the south-west coast of Australia.'

Accompanying the words was a shot of the silver dragoness in the distance, flying over a field of crops. A smile spread across his face. They finally had her.

* * *

Silver landed next to the house with a small thump, stretching her wings and yawning. It had been a rough day for her, harder than usual. A herd of cattle had escaped their pen, and she had spent the rest of the day finding them and bringing them back to the paddock, and fixing the fence. She had been forced to carry a few over, which had been hard work. Cattle weren't light.

With a sigh, she walked over to her metal nest and curled up in it, the cool surface soothing her warm body. The bowl-shaped nest rocked slightly, making her drowsy. She knew there was still a couple of hours of sunlight left, but she couldn't be bothered to hunt when she was so tired, though she knew she'd be hungry in the morning.

"Silver! Silver!" A boy's cries echoed over her, and she moaned in annoyance.

She lifted her drowsy head, and looked at the now-thirteen-year-old boy. He seemed excited about something. She resisted the urge to growl at him. She was in no mood for an excited human.

"Wake up!" the boy cried again, even though she was obviously awake, "I saw another dragon! I saw another dragon!"

The words got her attention, and she tilted her head slightly in confusion. Greg ran up to her and bent down on his knees, puffing in exhaustion. Silver waited impatiently for him to regain his breath, and when he straightened up she asked her question.

"What do you mean?"

"I saw a dragon. It was out over the fields, flying slowly past. It was yellow, like you, but without the metal shell, and about the same size, or a little bigger," he said excitedly.

Silver was wide-awake by the time he had finished. "Where did you say this dragon was?"

"Just over the fields, over there," he said, pointing south over a large area of open ground.

"Thank you for telling me," said Silver, getting out of her nest. Her rest was going to have to wait.

"Oh, and Silver," said Greg before the dragoness could take off, "it had this strange thing on its head. I couldn't see it properly, but it was in between its horns."

Silver frowned, worry building up inside her. If what Greg said was true, then her time with the farmers may be over. Shrugging her wings, she took off into the air with a single flap and shot high into the sky, using the clouds as cover while she searched for the dragon.

For nearly an hour she scoured distant landscapes for any sign of an electric dragon that fit the description Greg gave her. Of course, the boy may have seen it wrong, but Greg's senses were usually accurate. Though the dragon may not have friendly intentions, Silver couldn't help but be excited. It had been nearly a year since she'd had any interactions with her own kind. The only people to celebrate her seventh hatch day with her had been humans with no idea of dragon customs, and she was missing her ability to fly with her own species. Birds were boring companions.

Eventually her hopes faded. Maybe Greg hadn't seen the dragon, or maybe it had just flown off before she could find it. With a sad sigh, she began to fly back to her nest. Tiredness began to weigh her down again. She had been looking forward to meeting the dragon.

As she came out over the house, something caught her view. Darren was standing on the driveway, stock-still as a yellow dragon stalked towards him. The dragon's stance was threatening. Its wings were raised slightly, making it seem bigger. Its tail swished behind it as it got ready to pounce at its prey.

Silver didn't hesitate. Her wings closed, and she dived headfirst towards the dragon. It pounced, and struck Silver in midair. With a wallop, both dragons collided with the ground. Silver was instantly on her feet, standing protectively in front of Darren, wings raised and teeth bared, snarling viciously.

The other dragon was slower to recover, rolling to its feet and backing up from the sight of the silver dragoness. Each stared at the other for a moment, sizing the other up, taking time to recover from the collision. Suddenly, Silver's wings dropped in recognition.

"Zepos?" she said in disbelief.

"Hey, Silver." The electric dragon smiled through his pain.

He had grown over the past year. He was bigger than her by nearly a full foot. A few new scars and scratches tattooed his neck. His horns and wings were longer, and his scales gleamed with health. But through it all he looked tired, like he was straining against something. Between his horns was a red device, the same type the scarred man had used.

"What are you doing here?" she growled.

"I've come for you," he said, though he didn't sound like he was trying to woo her this time. "I've been ordered to bring you in alive."

"Bring me in?" the dragoness snorted.

"The humans that attacked us have ordered me to, so I must do it," he said.

She could scarcely believe what she was hearing. No dragon would willingly follow the orders of a human, especially if the order would in some way hurt another member of the species. As much as Silver disliked the lightning male, she didn't believe even he would fall so low. Suddenly, a realisation hit her.

"You're being controlled, aren't you?" she said, worry filling her mind.

"Of course I am," he snarled. "I thought you would have realised that the moment you saw the thing on my head."

She gulped. As she'd suspected, the humans had found another way to control dragons, just like they had so many years ago before her father freed them all. This time, though, they could fire their contraptions at long distances, making it much easier for them to trap dragons. And they had probably made the devices harder to take off in the meantime.

"I'm sorry, Silver," said Zepos, "but I can't stop myself. You know that. I expect you to fight. I want you to, but I have been ordered to bring you in and nothing short of death will stop me."

Again, Silver growled. The device made reasoning with him useless. It was true – whatever the humans ordered, he would have to do. Nothing she said would change Zepos's mind.

She looked back at Darren. "Get inside the house. Things are going to get a bit messy out here." She turned back to the lightning dragon: "So be it."

A sad look passed over Zepos's eyes, before he steeled himself and snarled Silver's challenge back at her: "So be it."

He suddenly launched himself at her, flapping his wings once to power himself forwards. Silver hesitated; she could kill him. A single stroke of her wings would be all it would take, but as much as she disliked the dragon, he was still a dragon. To kill him would be to kill part of herself.

Her hesitation cost her. The electric dragon slammed into her, and the two rolled backwards, barely missing the farmer as he ran back to his house. Silver snarled, breaking out of her trance, and latched her jaw onto his leg, biting down hard. Her sharp teeth easily broke through scales, and blood filled her mouth. She then hit Zepos's underbelly with her hind legs, throwing him over her head and onto his back. She rolled to her feet and snarled, spraying a thin stream of metal at him.

Zepos blocked the stream with his wing, but the metal stuck and solidified. Putting his wings up blocked his view of Silver, which she took advantage of. She leapt forwards, landing on his back and digging her claws into his sides. A pained cry came from the dragon, and he bucked, trying to throw her off.

Silver melded the end of her tail into a blade and struck the joint of one of his hind legs, and Zepos collapsed, roaring. Electricity sparked from his body and up her unprotected legs and belly. She bellowed in surprise and pain, leaping from his back and into the air. She shot a glob of metal at him, aiming for his neck and hoping to pin him down. The yellow dragon dodged out of the way.

Zepos followed her into the air, one of his wings slightly lopsided from the extra weight of the metal. He opened his maw to spray her with lightning, but she moved quickly, flying up higher and over him, before plummeting back down. With a growl, he powered forwards, narrowly dodging the dragon.

Silver deftly turned on her back, and glided upside down, narrowly avoiding slamming into the ground. She shot another glob of metal at the dragon. This time it was a direct hit, splashing against his belly and solidifying, also knocking the air out of the dragon. He grunted in surprise and quickly readjusted to the new weight.

Now that Zepos had been slowed down substantially by the metal, Silver allowed her metal shell to grow over her. Her yellow eyes turned red, and the sun gleamed viciously off her new armour. A challenging roar echoed out from her, the metallic sound booming across the land. Zepos turned to face her, and froze at the sight. A metallic dragon with full-metal armour was extremely difficult to defeat.

The two stared at each other. Fear struck its way through Zepos as he gazed at the dragoness before him. He had been trying to resist the machine in his head, but it was useless. His orders meant he would take down Silver or die trying, and he seemed to be heading towards the latter outcome.

An idea came to him. Metal was a great conductor of electricity, and Silver was covered in it. A single blast of his lightning would strike through her armour and bring her down. He regretted even thinking about it, but he didn't want to die, not yet. Besides, the machine didn't allow his idea to escape.

Opening his maw, he charged a strong bolt of electricity as Silver began to fly towards him. She was building momentum, but her armour slowed her down. However, the metal on Zepos's body slowed him down a lot as well, and there was no use trying to outrun her.

As soon as he was sure she wouldn't be able to dodge the strike, he unleashed the power from his throat. Lightning arced through the sky, hitting Silver square in the chest.

The shock of the bolt stopped her in mid-flight. It ran through her metallic shell. Lightning struck outwards at all angles. It felt much like the lightning she'd flown through in the storm, though not as powerful. Closing her eyes, she took a deep breath, letting the ever-growing energy run through her. When she felt she couldn't hold onto the power anymore, she opened her eyes and the current rushed back out of her maw, towards the lightning dragon.

Zepos roared in pain, hurled backwards by Silver's power. Being an electric dragon didn't make him immune to electricity, so it hurt him just as readily as it would Silver. He cried out as he plummeted to the earth.

The machine on his head began to whirl with the sudden overload of power. It sparked before turning off. The pain knocked Zepos unconscious as he clashed with the ground, falling limp.

Silver flew down and landed in front of him, warily. When she realised he'd been knocked unconscious, she let her armour retract, padded over to Zepos and nudged him slightly, hoping he wasn't dead. Relief fell over her as she heard his heart beating in his chest.

She looked over his body to the machine attached between his horns. The red lights had died, making it look like a black, domed box. But what really interested her was that a small portion of the right side had slipped loose. Curious, she formed her tail into a blade and put it under the gap created by the crash, and yanked it off.

Zepos convulsed slightly before falling still again. Blood began to well up at the top of his head where the machine had been, and dripped onto the earth. Silver wasn't worried, though. A small wound like that would hurt, but wouldn't kill. She was more interested in the broken machine. She smiled. There was a way to break the machines, a weakness she could exploit.

With a flick of her tail, she threw the machine into the air and cut it in half with a single swipe of her tail, before turning to Zepos and his injuries. While they weren't life-threatening, they needed treatment. With a small snort, she padded back to the house to rouse the humans, knowing she couldn't help Zepos on her own.

CHAPTER 10: LEAVE-TAKING

A disgruntled growl awoke Silver from her sleep. It was early morning. The sun was just beginning to peak over the horizon, casting a dim blue glow over the fields that stretched out before the shed. Birds chattered overhead, announcing the arrival of the sun; their song did no good for the growing headache in her skull.

With her own growl, she moved her head over to what had woken her. It was Zepos. His body heaved slowly as he breathed. Blood-soaked bandages covered his flanks and horns, and cut grooves in his yellow scales. As Silver watched him, his yellow eyes cracked open slightly, the cat-like pupils inside wincing at the sudden light before quickly turning to Silver and widening in recognition.

"Silver?" he croaked, obviously not well.

She did her best to smile. "Morning."

"What happened?" He closed his eyes again and sighed deeply. "I didn't think they'd capture you."

It took her a moment to realise what he was talking about. Their location in a shed probably made it look like they'd been caged, to an extent. He probably didn't remember being freed either. He was unconscious when it happened.

"We're not captured," she said. "You attacked me. Remember? And I managed to free you."

Zepos's eyes cracked open again as the dragon frowned. He brought around his tail and tapped the wound between his horns, growling in pain. But the pain was nothing compared to the excitement that shone in his eyes, accompanied by disbelief. Steadily, he got to his feet, testing his body.

Silver smiled as the yellow dragon roared with joy, finally figuring out what had happened. He jumped and flapped his wings, flying right into the shed's ceiling. With a grunt, he fell to the floor again, collapsing. Silver couldn't help but snort with laughter.

"How did you do it?" he said, disbelievingly, ignoring her laughter.

"I think it was the electricity I hit you with," she said, getting up herself and stretching her wings. "When it hit the circuits of that thing, it got fried and stopped working. It was pretty easy to yank off after that."

Zepos let out a scoff and shook his head. "I didn't know you could breathe electricity."

"I don't," she replied with a grin, "but when I'm in my full-metal state I can conduct it however I wish, and you hit me with millions of volts, so it really isn't that surprising."

"I … I guess not." He let out another laugh and looked himself over. "Wow, you really scratched me up."

"I'm not saying sorry," she said. "You kinda deserved it."

"Hey!" he shot back, "I was being controlled. It wasn't my fault."

"I know. But you did try to attack a friend of mine."

"That wasn't my fault either. My orders were 'Do whatever you can to find Silver and get her back here,' word for word. I knew that farmer had something to do with you, so when I asked him and he refused to tell me … well, y'know."

She snorted. "I guess so."

He sighed, looking away from her. He seemed a bit guilty for doing so, but Silver was standing by what she'd said. There was one thing that bothered her: Zepos had found her. Did that mean others were coming as well? If so, it was time to leave this place.

"Are there others coming?" she asked him. "To capture me, I mean."

He looked at her and nodded his head. "Yes. Many others. I was part of a scouting force of a hundred dragons. In fact, I'm surprised they haven't found you already, especially after you destroyed that device. It has a tracker in it."

She growled. "Then we need to get out of here. Follow me."

She padded out into the open air. Zepos followed, a little reluctantly. He looked up into the sky, half expecting a storm of dragons to fly down. Now that he was free, he really didn't want to be captured again. The stories he had heard of what the machines did were nothing compared to the reality. Being controlled by the hunters felt as though a fog had descended on him, and his every movement seemed slow and sluggish. He had still been control of his body and his speech, unless he was ordered to do something. Now that he had control again, the relief was like being washed clean after a day spent wrestling in the mud.

"Zepos, can you tell me what happened to my family?" Silver asked.

The question had been on her mind for a while. She had last seen her father when she was fleeing the mountains after they'd been taken. The last she had seen of the rest of her family was in the first clash, during the battle.

Zepos hesitated before answering. "Well, as far as I know, Blaze and Elron have been captured by the enemy. In fact, they're probably out looking for you right now. I don't know what happened to Raize. I doubt he's dead, though. The last time I saw him was flying out after you."

She breathed her relief. Even if they were captured, her father had freed himself from the machines before, and could do it again. She had no doubt. And even if he couldn't, *she* knew how to free them now. She was a little worried about Raize, but knowing her brother, he'd probably managed to find a safe haven somewhere. He had always been hard to catch, even for her. It was then she realised that the electric dragon left someone out.

"What about mother?" she said, her heart in her throat.

Again, he hesitated. He looked down at the ground, "She … she was killed. When Blaze was captured, she went into a rage, burning everything and anyone. They decided she was too dangerous to capture, and a sniper … finished her. I'm … I'm sorry."

Silver looked away from him, the news hitting her hard. Though some part of her wasn't surprised. One of the last things Elron said to her was, 'I won't lose you too.' She had taken that to mean that one of the family had been killed. A tear slowly trickled from the corner of her eye. She blinked it away. She would mourn when she had the time. Now it was time to act.

"Do you have an idea what you are going to do? Once we leave, I mean," said Zepos, trying to get their conversation back on a happier note.

Silver thought for a moment. "Well, I was thinking we could try and find my dad and brother, and free them."

"Bad idea," he said instantly. "While Blaze might be easy to free, trying to go for Elron would be extremely difficult. He's the most important dragon in the force, and by now they'll know what happened to me, so they'll be guarding him closely. Plus, we wouldn't stand a chance against him if it came to a fight. Even you."

A snort escaped her as she looked back at the electric dragon. "Thank you for that. Well, have you got any ideas?"

"I do, actually."

"Then enlighten me."

"I've heard there's a dragon haven somewhere in China. I have no idea where it is or how to get there, but if I could have a guess then it would be in the north-west corner, where there's very little population."

"A dragon haven?"

Zepos nodded his head as Silver thought through the idea. It seemed logical, and far safer than what she had had in mind. It would also give her more time to train and increase her power. As much as she didn't want to admit it, she still had no chance against the humans. She might be able to make a dent in their plans, but it would be a dent that would be quickly fixed. On the other hand, her father and brother were still captured, living like slaves.

"Fine," she snarled, "but as soon as I'm strong enough to fight, I'm going to come back and destroy the hunters."

Zepos didn't reply.

Darren met them at the gate, and by his look Silver could tell he already knew what was going on. She stopped in front of him. The two of them looked at each other.

"Thanks ... for helping me," sighed Silver.

"No, I should thank you," he said, smiling. "You saved my life, and have been a great help this past year."

"It's been quite fun, actually," Silver grinned. "You'll say goodbye to Greg for me?"

"Why don't you say it yourself?" he asked.

"Because the longer I stay here the more danger you will be in. In the next hour or so some men will probably come knocking at your door, asking about me. Make up some story, because they won't believe you that I wasn't here. Say I was flying overhead or something when Zepos attacked, but don't tell them you housed me. It would be dangerous. Oh, and try to get rid of all the metal stuff I've made over the year. They'll recognise that as well."

Darren nodded.

She hesitated, feeling guilty about leaving the human to fend for himself. "And I'm sorry ... for all this."

"Don't worry yourself. Go and run. Don't look back. Maybe one day you can come back and see us again."

"One day," the silver dragon agreed.

She bowed her head slightly before looking back at Zepos. He nodded to her and together they shot into the air. She let Zepos take the lead because he knew the way better, and they flew into the sky, heading north. Behind them she noticed several trucks trudging down the highway in the distance, too far away for human vision to spot them, and she was relieved she and Zepos had left so early. Turning her head away from her home, she once more looked forwards, scorning the feeling that she was running yet again.

Chapter 11: On the Run Again

Silver and Zepos made their way north as fast as they could, dodging humans and hiding from any dragons they saw. The going was slow, and they mostly flew high in the air or close to the ground. Silver still hadn't perfected metallic dragons' camouflaging technique, but she was good enough to stop her shell from shining out their presence, which helped them a lot.

Zepos's injuries didn't help. He tired easily, and occasionally some of his wounds, which had been healing, reopened. They had long since abandoned the bandages that had wound around him, knowing that they were too bloody to be of use. But he never complained.

The difference in him surprised her. Back in Dragon Valley, he'd been a carefree nuisance. Always trying to flirt. Always trying to show off. Thinking he was the greatest dragon in the world. But now, as they flew, he seemed almost mellow. He didn't try to talk, or flirt, or annoy her in any way. Maybe it was the seriousness of the situation, but somehow Silver didn't think so. He had changed. She had too, but nowhere near as much as him. Through the blood on his scales she saw other wounds, scars from fights, and glinting, newly grown scales that suggested many had been torn off. The year had been hard on him, and she felt sorry for the lightning dragon.

They reached the sea eventually and stopped on a remote beach with very little evidence of human activity. Zepos cleaned himself in the ocean, sending clouds of red dragon blood through it, before stepping out and shaking himself. A dragon could handle a lot of blood loss, but she worried it might be too much. He assured her it wasn't, and the two fell asleep.

As morning came, they set out over the ocean. Silver hoped it wouldn't be a long flight. She hated the sea. Every time she saw it, she couldn't help but think of her desperate flight over the ocean a year ago, when she had almost given up. It scared her to think of such things, but the blue mass of ocean in front of her daunted her more than she liked to admit.

Zepos took the lead again, and they flew close together. His wounds had closed overnight, but every flap of his wings raised the chance that they'd reopen. Flying up alongside him, Silver proposed a plan.

"Once we get far enough out of Australia we should rest for a couple of days, just while you heal," she said to him, shouting over the wind.

He looked at her and nodded his agreement. It would be better than continuing the way they were going. If anything, they were lucky to still be free. As much as his body hurt, his mind was stronger than it ever had been.

To Silver's delight, it didn't take them long to spot land. Hundreds of islands appeared on the horizon, stretching out vastly over the earth's surface. The large island in the middle was populated, she could tell, but the many small ones seemed scarcely occupied.

The two of them quickly rose high into the air, hiding their bodies in clouds while gazing down at the archipelago. Their keen vision allowed them to spot the thousands of humans in the city on the main island, and in the countryside. There was no place to land that would allow them to hide safely. She looked at Zepos.

"Let's keep going," he said. "There's other islands out further we can try."

They flew on, keeping high in the clouds, but the altitude restricted their oxygen supply, exhausting them far quicker, and while Silver could deal with it, Zepos was having trouble. A small island caught their view, and she pointed it out to the yellow dragon. He nodded again, and together they descended.

For a minute or so they circled the area. There were no clearings to allow an easy landing. Eventually they flew down and landed on a rocky outcrop, which didn't cushion their landing. Silver's claws cut the stone as she landed, sending deep gouges into it. Then Zepos landed, thudding heavily on the stone. Landing hurt him more than it did Silver, and he snarled.

Among the trees was a bare but well-sheltered area. The forest's canopy filtered the sun, which was now low in the sky, and after Silver cut away some of the undergrowth it seemed like the perfect spot for an overnight stay. And better yet, the scents of numerous animals flooded the clearing, making known the prey that awaited the dragons.

Zepos was bleeding again, but not so much as before. It was a sure sign he was healing. Slowly. But still healing. He lay down on the ground, exhausted again from the flight. Silver lay down as well with a sigh, and for a moment neither dragon spoke.

"I think we should stay here for a couple of days," said Silver eventually, "It's a remote island. Plenty to eat … I think."

"I agree," said the yellow dragon, bobbing his head.

She smiled a little before laying her head back down. It had been a stressful couple of days. She hated running, but she had no choice. She wasn't stupid enough to think she could take all her hunters on at once, but she could have at least made a difference. And then there were Darren and Greg. She hoped whoever was pursuing her hadn't figured out she'd been at their farm. They would probably kill them if they knew. Or they might just capture them. It hurt her to think she had just left them.

"Silver," said Zepos suddenly. "What was it like living with humans?"

She hesitated, "Aah … It was good."

"Good? Just good? Come on. There has to be more to it than that," he said with a hint of a smile.

"Well. It was satisfying. They let me live with them, just as long as I helped them out. It was a farm, so there was a lot to do. I herded cattle, moved hay bales, fixed fences. A lot of stuff. They were friendly too, and occasionally I got to eat one of their cattle. They were honestly delicious, but most of the time I just lived off kangaroos and rabbits. There were no deer there, not that I saw anyway."

"Living off kangaroos for a year. Yuck!" said Zepos.

He had tried kangaroo once. The first night of their journey, Silver had gone hunting and brought back a few of the strange creatures. While he did eat them, he preferred meatier animals. Kangaroos were too stringy for him and the flesh got stuck in his teeth.

Silver chuckled. "They aren't too bad. Especially the bigger ones. I could live off one of them for a week."

"Yeah, but that's because you're female. You don't eat as much as us males do. I'd eat them if I really needed to, but that's it," he said.

She snorted. "How 'bout you? What was it like living at the human compound?"

"They actually took surprisingly good care of us," said Zepos. "We were fed well. Allowed regular exercise. The baths were amazing. But it was very controlling. We were checked up on every day, forced into regular routines. Our devices were checked often, especially Elron's. There was no greenery whatsoever, and the only time we could see the sun was when we went on missions. Really, the only good part about it was the baths."

Silver nodded slightly. "Hmm. It's not as bad as I thought it was."

Zepos snorted. "Honestly … it's worse. Not because of how they keep us fed and that, but because we were forced to fight dragons we're friends with. I captured three dragons myself, and it killed me inside. No, I would rather die than go back there."

The two looked at each other for a moment, before Silver looked away again. Her father had said something similar to her when she was a hatchling. He had told the story of how the dragons were captured and freed, and Silver had listened, intrigued. She had wished she was there to witness it … and now she was in the middle of it. It's funny how the things you wish for become the things you hate. Oh, how she missed the valley, her parents, her brothers. It was nearly too much for a young dragoness to handle. And she hadn't even seen the worst of it yet. All she had done was farm.

"Tell me about this dragon haven we're going to," she said to Zepos, trying to keep her thoughts on track.

Zepos thought for a moment. "As I said before, I don't know much about it besides the fact that A.O.D.H. hasn't found it."

"What's 'owed'?" she said confused.

"Not owed, a-owed. The Association of Dragon Hunters. A-O-D-H," he said. "They're the humans that are basically trying to capture us all."

"Oh, I didn't know they had a name," she said.

"Me neither," Zepos shrugged, "until they caught me. Anyway, they know about this dragon haven because of the number of dragons they've seen heading in that direction. At a certain point they seem to disappear. They don't know the numbers or the power of these dragons. Their searches have found nothing, and the Chinese government has refused to share any information."

She snorted. "Why are you so sure they'll let us find them?"

"Because we aren't working for the A.O.D.H. They'll be able to tell because we don't have those mind-controlling things," he said.

"If you're sure," she said hesitantly.

Relying on vague information made her nervous. What if it was all just a set-up? What if this Chinese government had their own mind-controlling machines that just weren't visible? She didn't voice her fears, because as wary as she was, this place was their only hope. If they didn't find a safe place soon, they'd undoubtedly be found.

As she pondered the few other options they had, a sudden movement in the bush caught her eye. She frowned, before crying out in surprise, then leapt up, spreading a metallic wing over Zepos's form. A small bullet shot from the undergrowth, attaching to her left wing. Electricity surged from the bullet, stunning her. Because she wasn't in her full-metal state, she couldn't control the power, and it flowed through her rapidly. She cried out in pain as her body convulsed, before falling unconscious.

Zepos launched to his feet, spraying a bolt of electricity into the forest and setting it alight. Cries of alarm echoed back, but as Silver fell unconscious one of her wings covered his head, blocking his view. He backed up with a snort, regaining his vision, but he wasn't fast enough. A tranquiliser dart shot from the forest and stung his neck.

The electric dragon instantly felt tired. He cried out in defiance and sprayed lighting over the forest, setting many fires. But it wasn't enough. His vision began to sway, and he stumbled, his power waning.

"No! I will not get … captured again."

But it was already too late.

He fell to the floor, and the last thing he saw was a squad of black-clad humans walking out of the fire, guns aimed at him and Silver.

CHAPTER 12:
COLLARS AND CHAINS

SILVER's world slowly regained its composure. First were the noises. Unearthly screams echoing in a yet unknown place. The dull murmur of voices. Then there were the smells. Dragon blood spilled on a wet concrete floor. Overworked machines and animal manure. Burning wood. An overwhelming human stench, not the clean type.

As the light crept into Silver's sight, she realised there were heavy weights on her shoulders, legs, tail and wings. Something was snapped over her muzzle, tightly, only allowing her to breathe through her nose. A grey wall stood in front of her, with a small metal door in the middle. The concrete floor was slippery and wet, and smelled of something unhealthy. Dim white lights shone from what she assumed was the roof of the enclosure, but as she tried to look upwards she realised her neck was also chained.

Silver squeaked as a scream penetrated the wall behind her. She instantly went to cover her head with her wings, trying to block out the sound, but her wings were trapped. The sound suddenly stopped, but this gave her little relief. As her mind began to function again, fear crept over her. What was this place? It couldn't be the A.O.D.H. because her mind wasn't being controlled. At least she didn't think it was. Her thoughts didn't seem any different from before. She couldn't check for the device, but why would they have her chained up if they already controlled her?

She shivered as she thought they could be doing it while she was awake, attaching one of those things to her head. It had happened to her father, and he said it had been the most painful thing he'd ever experienced. It had nearly broken him. And her father was the strongest dragon she knew.

Think, Silver, she told herself, trying to control the fear that was threatening to seize her. *You can get out of this. Just ignore your feelings. For now.*

She closed her eyes again, testing the bonds that trapped her wings, tail and legs. As far as she could tell, they were either iron or steel. Easy enough to cut through. She focused on the edges of her wings, and the metal around them began to shimmer and ripple like water. The blunt limbs began to reform, growing edges that could cut diamond. It was a trick her father had taught her. When she was born, her wings had been naturally sharp, but soon she'd learned to dull their edges. With limbs that could kill with a single swipe, wrestling another dragon was dangerous, so this was the first aspect of her powers she'd gained control of. Now it was effortless.

With a scowl, she moved her wings as much as she could, slowly sawing away at the bonds. It would be quicker if she could put more force behind her movements, but her restraints made that difficult. As long as they didn't check up on her before then, or have a camera inside the cage.

A sudden creak startled her, and she instantly stopped cutting away the bonds. Her wings rippled and became normal again, and she looked over at the intrusion. A man walked inside the enclosure with a notepad in his hand. An expensive blue suit covered him, with a gun holder on one hip and what looked like a TV remote at the other. A pair of spectacles sat neatly set on his face, enlarging his dark brown eyes. He looked up from his notepad and frowned, glancing at the bound dragon. The bounds around her muzzle suddenly loosened, allowing her to open her mouth slightly.

"Name?" he said in a monotone.

Silver didn't answer, too startled by the question. Was this an interrogation?

"Name," the man insisted.

An angry growl bolted from her throat. "Why should I tell—"

She didn't make it halfway through her sentence before pain erupted across her body. It was so sudden. So unexpected. It felt as if every nerve, bone, artery and blood vessel was being ripped apart by stinging needles. She screamed, unable to help herself. There was no way to stop it. No way to defend herself. Her metallic screech echoed throughout the room and into the enclosures around her. It was so loud even the man covered his ears with a grimace.

Then the pain stopped, just as suddenly as it had started. Her tensed muscles fell limp against the ground as she gasped for breath, taking in deep draughts of air. The man gazed critically at Silver, as if her pain had been her own fault.

"When I ask, I expect you to answer," he said threateningly. "Name."

"Silver," she said, the shock of the pain loosening her tongue.

"Age?" said the man.

"Why do you need to—" She screamed as the pain erupted again, then stopped.

"Age?" the man asked again.

"Seven-and-a-half," she gasped.

"Species?"

She hesitated for a moment. The man looked up from where he had been writing her answers on a sheet of paper. He raised an eyebrow, as if asking "do you want it to happen again?"

"Metallic dragon," she gave in.

"Powers?"

"Aaah … I can shoot liquid metal from my mouth, and spikes from my tail … um." She thought for a moment. If she gave these people everything about her, she wouldn't be able to surprise them in any way, nor escape.

"You realise if you hide anything from us, you'll get much worse then you have," said the man.

Worse? Maybe it wouldn't hurt to name a few more of her powers, she thought. "I can make my wings sharp, and transform my tail into stuff."

She hoped that gave her enough leeway. They didn't know she could darken her shell or that she could make it grow over her whole body. That would give her some advantage.

"Thank you," said the man, writing down the last pieces of information of his paper.

He began to walk over to her, pulling what she recognised as a measuring tape out of his pocket. He took the tape and began to measure different points of her neck. At one point, Silver suppressed a growl when he stepped on her paw. She didn't want to risk torture again.

He seemed to nod to himself, and stepped back from her. He called out some measurements into the air and some sort of machine began to move above her. Her head was lifted into the air, exposing her neck. Something descended from above her and wrapped tightly around her throat, just above her wings. It wound around both her shell and her bare scales. At first, she thought it was trying to choke her, and she tried to thrash, but another bout of pain defeated her. To her relief, it didn't choke her, but it was uncomfortable.

The chains around her feet, wings and tail retracted suddenly, leaving her free. At first, she didn't move, exhausted. Her body was tingling, traumatised from the torture. Her eyes were swimming, and everything seemed to fade in and out of sight. Yet as her vision cleared, her mind seemed to register that she was free again. She quickly jumped to her feet and gathered a clot of metal in her throat, ready to solidify the man who caused her so much pain, but as she was about to release her element the coil around her neck tightened, and then – agony. Instead of liquid metal, her maw released another piercing scream. She collapsed to the floor, he body seizing until the pain suddenly ended.

A small whimper escaped her throat. It was all too much. Her body and mind couldn't handle it any more. Darkness welcomed her.

* * *

She woke again to the sound of a bell being rung. She lay still, taking a moment for her mind to catch up with her body. Slowly she forced herself from the floor, getting up onto all fours. The collar around her neck was still there, holding her captive.

She looked around the room with interest. The chains that had held her were lying limply on the floor, but she didn't think she was free; they hadn't been attached during that final bout of torture. It was the collar that did it. She reached around with her tail, blading it and trying to cut the collar. But a zap surged through her body, and she jumped. It didn't hurt as much as previously, and lasted for less than a second, but it was enough to warn her away from meddling with the device.

The concrete wall in front of her screeched open. The blue-suited man stood there with a bored expression on his face. Silver's first instinct was to attack him, but she knew it would do more harm than good. Instead she restrained herself, staring at him as if trying to kill him with a look.

"Follow the path, second turn to the left," he sighed. "If you try to stray from it, you will be electrocuted. If you try to harm anyone on the way, you will be electrocuted. If you do anything that even looks like an escape attempt, you will be electrocuted. Got that?"

Silver nodded, choosing not to answer. Instead she padded out of the cage. It wasn't worth getting electrocuted again. At least until she found a way to escape. That they'd been torturing her with electricity made her think: all she needed to do was morph into her full-metal state and she would be invincible. The only problem was the collar was wound so tightly around her neck she doubted she cover her whole body with her shell.

Other dragons were making their way out of the cages as well. At least ten that Silver counted. Most of them were fire dragons, with two earth dragons and what looked like a wind dragon … and Zepos? Silver couldn't help but let a cry of happiness as she saw her friend.

Zepos looked up at her and smiled as she ran up to him. "Silver!"

"Zepos, they got you too?" she said, feeling a guilty kind of relief at not being the only one trapped.

"Yeah, they did." He looked around with an angry expression.

A collar wound around his neck as well. It looked like two metal ropes coiled around each other and tightened, a greyish black against Zepos's yellow scales.

"Where are we?" she asked, looking around.

"I don't know," replied the electric dragon, "But it isn't A.O.D.H."

"What?"

"Yeah, I know. It seems we've run into another dragon-capturing group, and, so far, I like these people less."

CHAPTER 13:
D.E.D.

Silver followed the path she had been told to, Zepos walking right next to her. They were silent, both thinking through what had happened. Silver had always been a free-spirited dragoness, loving to try new things and not afraid of danger, and now she was trapped. Silver had never considered herself claustrophobic—she had spent a lot of her time in caves—but as she walked through the tiny corridor she doubted she could open her wings fully, and she was scared. The bleak walls, lit intermittently in red, seemed to be descending on her, making her jittery at every brush of a dragon's wing or clack of claws against stony ground. She nearly missed the turn, but Zepos caught her and turned her in the right direction.

"Are you alright?" asked the electric dragon.

Silver nodded her head slightly and forced herself to take a deep breath. "Yeah … I'm alright."

He could tell she wasn't, but didn't press the matter. Instead they followed the small group of dragons down another dimly lit corridor. At one point, some humans with assault rifles joined them—two at the front and two at the back. The strong urge to attack and run coursed through Silver, but with her collar on she doubted she'd get far.

The humans led them through the base at a fast pace. Silver tried to memorise the layout, but before long her mind became muddled. It was like a maze. Everything seemed to look the same, and Silver swore at one point that they went in a circle. Maybe it was a trick to confuse the dragons about where they were.

Eventually, they stopped outside a large double door. Growls and groans were heard from the inside, followed by the occasional roar and, to Silver's surprise, laughter. How anyone could laugh in this place was beyond her.

The guards opened the door and told the dragons to walk inside. Silver nervously walked in last. She was the smallest of the group, probably the youngest as well, and even with her metal shell and fighting prowess she suddenly felt vulnerable. She tried to extend her metal shell over her body, but stopped as the collar tingled her. Encasing herself in her shell would break it, and the collar ruled that grab for freedom unacceptable. She had no doubt next time she tried she'd be electrocuted.

"And here are this week's newbies!" said a loud voice over the crowd. "Let's see what we got here."

It sounded like a dragon's voice coming through a microphone. She could tell because it was slightly more guttural then a human's, almost like it was growling. No human could make their voice that deep without hurting their throat.

"One … three, nope. Five more fire dragons," the voice continued, "Two earth dragons … a wind dragon; nice, we need a few more of them."

A few chuckles spilled from the crowd.

"An electric dragon, and …" The dragon hesitated, and Silver assumed it had seen her. "What seems to be a new species! Well, this just got interesting."

The place was crowded with dragons of every type. From common fire dragons and earth dragons to species Silver had never seen before. A dragon with skin a strangely light, almost fluoro, green was eyeing her up and down in interest. She glared at the dragon, which snorted and turned away. A blue-white dragon flew overhead, landing on one of this cavern's many ledges.

To Silver it looked like a cricket oval, but bigger. A series of large steps, all covered in dragons, ascended each side of the area. It was like one of the meetings her father sometimes called, but a lot more crowded. She was disliking this place more and more, especially since over the past year she'd had no dragon company. Though that had been lonely, she'd prefer it to this overcrowded prison.

A thud caught her attention. She turned around and nearly yelped in surprise as a large dragon looked down at her, his eyes taking in everything she was in one glance. He was an earth dragon with scars covering his body. Dragons only scarred when their scales were completely ripped off and given very little chance to heal. This dragon had seen a lot of that.

"And who might you be, dragoness?" He said it somewhat kindly, but his voice boomed above those of the dragons around them.

There was some sort of device on the side of his head that Silver guessed allowed him to project his voice.

"I … um … Silver," she said, seeing no harm in giving out her name.

"Silver, huh? A suitable name for a beautiful dragoness," said the dragon, with a grin.

Silver got flustered and stared down at her feet, shuffling slightly. It was awkward being the centre of attention, and right now she just wanted to be alone. All this was confusing to her. These dragons seemed almost … happy.

"What species are you, Silver?" asked the dragon.

"Metallic," she replied, "Metal."

A collective gasp ran through the dragons near her. She wondered whether they'd heard of metallic dragons. As far as she knew, she and her father were the only metal dragons on the planet.

The dragon seemed surprised as well. "A new species, huh? Well, this is a welcome arrangement. Some extra excitement in our lives. Welcome to D.E.D., the dragon education department."

For some reason, Silver didn't feel very welcome.

* * *

Zepos managed to find them a quiet spot towards one end of the cavern. Silver lay down on the ground and sighed. It was all getting to her now. Another headache was beginning to form in her head. The noise, the crowd, the place. She had spent the whole year wanting to find another dragon, and now she had found too many.

"That was strange," said Zepos.

"Agreed," sighed Silver, laying her head on the ground.

"No, I mean that earth dragon," he said.

"What about him? He did seem a bit too cheerful and all, but honestly, he didn't seem too bad," she sighed.

"Didn't you notice something about his collar?"

"What about it?"

"He didn't have one."

Silver's head shot up, and she stared at the electric dragon in surprise. For a moment she didn't believe him. That meant that the dragon was willingly here. Why a dragon would want to be here was beyond her. It seemed impossible. If she could get her collar off, she would shield herself in her shell and break out of this place within ten minutes. It would be easy. That the earth dragon wasn't wearing it told her a few things about the dragons here.

"It seemed there is a bit more to this place than chains," said Zepos.

"I know." Silver looked out over the crowd of dragons to the other side of the stadium.

The earth dragon was sitting at the top of a platform, just above the gate they had entered through, looking over the expanse below. He was with a few other dragons, an electric dragon, two fire dragons and a dragon whose species she didn't recognise. All were large, and none had collars.

"They seem to be the leaders of this place," she said to Zepos. "Maybe it's a reward for good behaviour or something."

"Probably," he agreed.

Then that might be her way out. If she could get rid of her collar for "good behaviour", she'd be able to escape easily, and maybe even rescue a few other dragons as she did. It would also make the humans trust her. A shiver of excitement ran through her at the thought. So this place wasn't invincible after all.

"Silver?" said a voice she didn't recognise.

Frowning, she looked around to see a wind dragon nervously approaching them. He was older than Zepos by a few years and bigger than both of them. He seemed frail, though. In fact, most of the dragons there seemed that way, as if they weren't fed quite enough. He was a creamy-white, like most wind dragons, but the colours seemed duller than usual.

"Yes?" said the dragoness.

The wind dragon trudged up to them. "I'm Eril. I don't know if you remember me. I left the valley, like, five years ago now."

"You lived in Dragon Valley?" said Silver in surprise, searching her memories for the wind dragon. His name did sound familiar.

"Yeah, your father rescued me from that other place, but I found staying in the valley boring, so I left. A week later I ended up here, and well … I've been here ever since."

"You've been here five years?" She felt sorry for the dragon; he must have been younger than her when he arrived.

He nodded glumly. "It's been horrible. The humans here are focused on … 'educating' us dragons, making us into pets. Every afternoon, Tetrad gives us a 'lesson' on how we should accept the humans as our superiors and how they will take good care of us, and that we should do whatever they say. It's a bit more than that, but you get the gist."

"Who's Tetrad?"

"That earth dragon who greeted you on the way in," he said.

Silver growled. She was beginning to like that dragon less and less. "Why would he do such a thing?"

Eril shrugged. "There's some sort of hierarchy here. The dragons that agree and do whatever the humans tell them get promoted higher and higher until they become 'collarless'. These dragons are the leaders of this place, and if you don't do what they say … well … I'm sure you would know what happens."

"I can guess," she said, looking up at the collarless dragons with a sudden hatred. How dare they torture their own kind. She felt herself wanting to fly up to where they were and give them a piece of her mind, but she was sure that would end up worse for her than for them. "We need to get out of this place. Can it be done?"

The wind dragon hesitated, "Yes … well, it's been done before. Some fire dragon by the name of Raize managed to break his collar and escape about a year ago, and there have been other attempts."

Zepos and Silver looked at each other in surprise. Raize had been here? And he'd escaped. She felt herself getting excited again. The collars weren't unbreakable. Fire dragons weren't as strong as metallic dragons, so if her brother could do it, she could too. She just needed to find a way.

"Did you know him?" asked Eril, seeing the look they gave each other.

"He's my brother," said Silver.

"Oh!" The wind dragon was suddenly excited. "Do you know how he did it?"

She shook her head. "No, but knowing him, he probably found some trick or something in the collars and managed to unhook it or something. He's smart like that."

"Okay." His wings drooped slightly.

"But we will find a way," said Zepos confidently, stepping forwards, "I know we will."

Eril smiled slightly at the electric dragon and nodded. "I'll help you guys as much as I can."

"Good. Can you tell us more about the collarless dragons?" asked Silver.

"Of course. First there's Tetrad. He's kind of like the leader of them. Then there's Irelia the fire dragon. She's the meanest and you really don't want to get on her bad side. Especially when she's gravid.

Then there's her brother Tirene. He mostly follows his sister's lead, and basically does whatever he's told. Then there's Cert. He's the electric dragon and probably the most dangerous of the bunch. He handles all the punishments, and seems to enjoy doing it. And lastly there's Krita. He's the mind dragon, and probably the most important of them all. He's the one who decides whether or not a dragon is 'improving' in their education."

"A mind dragon?" Silver was confused.

"Yeah. He can read and control minds, though he doesn't have a very strong will, so if he does try to mind-control you, it's easy to break. If you're anything like your father, you shouldn't have to worry."

Silver smiled slightly. She had heard of mind dragons, but had never seen one. They were a rare species, but far from endangered. Most were smart, and often used their powers to create illusions or help fix mentally broken dragons. The fact that a mind dragon was in the group instantly quashed her chances of joining them. A dragon who could read minds always knew who was an enemy and who was a friend.

"Well, I better go," said Eril. "My break is over. Call for me if you need me."

The wind dragon took to the air with an easy flap of his wings and quickly flew off. Silver watched him go, startled a little by the information Eril had shared. Dragons willingly going into slavery … for humans. Especially humans who tortured them. It was wrong. A growl escaped her.

"Don't make a mess of anyone yet," said Zepos, giving her a friendly nudge, "Make sure the collar is off first."

"No promises," she muttered.

"Silver, seriously. Look, do what you can to remain low-profile, or, better yet, get them to trust you. Doing that will make it far easier to escape."

She looked at him, knowing he was right. "I'll try, Zepos, but I'm furious. Even torture won't hold me back for long."

Zepos smiled. "Well, at least try to hold back, until you can make a difference. Can you promise that?"

She sighed and smiled back. "I can promise that."

Chapter 14: Potential Allies

"Humans … are the ones who will save us! From ourselves! Dragons are too dangerous to roam free on this planet. We are a danger to everything and everyone, including ourselves. Ask yourself how many times you have lost yourself to anger. Or lust. Or greed. We cannot be trusted, and we must accept humans' control over us, or we will perish and take the world with us. Humans can help us get control. They can help us find the pure beauty of this world and who we are. They can show us how to help each other and how to use our powers for good! Why can't you accept that? Give up your freedom, because we are too dangerous to be free. Give up your …"

"Is this how it is every afternoon?" Silver whispered to Eril.

Every dragon in the oval was standing in the centre, all looking up at Tetrad as he gave his sermon. No-one moved, and everyone listened. It was compulsory that every dragon attended these meetings, and that they listened. The earth dragon had been droning on for hours about why dragons didn't deserve to be free and needed to accept humans as their leaders. At first Silver was angry, but now … she was bored. It all sounded the same to her, and while she had to admit Tetrad was a good speaker, he just continued to come back to the same points over and over again. Give up this! Give up that! She felt like roaring at the earth dragon to stop, just so she could think. It nearly hurt.

"Yep, every afternoon," Eril whispered back.

Silver groaned in annoyance, attracting scornful looks from a few nearby the dragons. They probably thought of her as a young hatchling. She was young, maybe, but definitely not a hatchling. She felt like growling at them as well. The earth dragon had preached the same sermon the day before, and it was getting on her nerves. Maybe that was how they did it. He just kept giving the same speech over and over, drilling it into every dragon's head until they believed it. She couldn't imagine years of this gruelling propaganda.

"Just keep your head for a few more hours, Silver," Zepos whispered to her. "It'll all be over then."

She snorted at him and held down a yawn, or tried to. A few more irritated dragons glanced at her. She glared back before refocusing her attention on the dragons perched on the ledge, overlooking the cavern.

"And now, three of you have decided to come and prove yourselves worthy of our rank. Come forwards, Celestia of the light, Turrella of the earth and Shiro of the fire."

Three dragons flew up from the crowd and landed on the platform above. One was a pale lemon-coloured dragon who looked young, maybe ten. She had long horns and wings that looked like sheets of cotton, way too delicate for her to fly with them. The earth dragon was also female, but older than her two companions and a little thinner than the average earth dragon. The fire dragon, also young, was a male, and had a strange fire in his eyes that showed he was willing to do anything appease his superiors.

Tetrad spoke with a loud thundering voice. "Come forwards and present yourselves to Krita, and he will decide whether or not you are worthy of joining our cause."

Shiro bowed his head towards the mind dragon, who stepped up in front of him. Krita put his paw on Shiro's head and closed his eyes. They were like this for a few minutes while the dragons watched eagerly. Finally, the mind dragon stepped back. He looked at Tetrad and gave a small nod. The joy on the young fire dragon's face was so immense Silver thought she would be sick. He nearly skipped over to Tetrad, and bowed his head again. The earth dragon raised a claw and brought it down on the young dragon's collar, and it snapped, falling to the ground. Silver's eyes widened in surprise.

Next was Turrella. Krita stepped forwards, placed his paw on the earth dragon's head and closed his eyes again. This time he shook his head as he stepped back. Turrella nodded glumly and opened her wings, then with a single flap flew back into the crowd of dragons. They parted for her, some giving her sorrowful glances.

Celestia was next to have her mind examined. She also didn't pass the test, but this time she seemed angry at something. She cried out in rage and her body shook as light began to shine from her wings, and then she screamed. As one, the dragons flinched as the scream echoed around them. Krita leapt back with a small snarl of his own and looked at Tetrad. The earth dragon walked over to Celestia and pinned her neck to the floor with one of his claws.

"You are a disgrace, Celestia. Using your position to attempt escape is something we profoundly condone here. You are stripped of your rank, and may your mind one day find the right path."

He tossed the light dragon from his perch, and she landed with an audible thud on the floor below. Something cracked as she did, and she cried out again. Silver felt her heart ache for the dragoness, but she could do nothing to help her. Not yet, anyway.

"That concludes today's meeting. You are all free to go," said Tetrad.

Silver, Zepos and Eril walked back to where they had formed their little home in the back of the cavern. They had a plan for that night, and if all went well, every dragon there would be free by morning. The problem was it was based on a lot of assumptions. If even one of those assumptions was wrong, the whole plan would fall to pieces.

"That was interesting," said Zepos, laying down on one of the steps that surrounded the oval.

"More interesting than usual," agreed Eril. "Shiro is the first dragon to be chosen in a year. I'm surprised he made it, actually. When he first came, he had the hottest temper in the base, and got zapped about ten times before he realised that anger didn't get him anywhere."

"What about Celestia? Does that happen often?" asked Silver.

"More often than dragons get chosen," replied the wind dragon, "Some would do anything to get free, but it doesn't pay off."

She sighed and looked away. She noticed Celestia sitting by herself, nursing her injured wing. She seemed frail, and Silver was surprised such a weak-looking dragon had such a strong will. She hesitated and looked at Eril and Zepos.

"How long until we set the plan into action?" she asked the two males.

"A few hours. Why?" Zepos asked.

"I'm going to make some friends." Silver smiled at them and got up.

They watched her go before returning to their conversation. She padded through the throng of dragons milling around to where the light dragoness was sitting. Light dragons had always been strange to Silver. Apparently, they were quite powerful, with their element anyway. Their physical prowess was something of a mystery. Some were extremely good fighters, while others were weak when it came to claw on claw.

As she got closer to Celestia she realised the dragoness was weeping. Anger and sympathy dashed through her. This place was getting to her. She was going to snap soon. With a sigh, she walked over to her.

"Hey," she said, causing the light dragon to look up at her, "are you alright?"

Orange patterns, like ancient carvings, ran over her snout and body. Her wings were transparent, and any light that passed through them became a beam of yellow, almost like sunshine. Wet tears streaked down her maw, and the wing she had been nursing seemed to have snapped, half of it being bent at an odd angle.

"Yeah … Silver, was it?" she said, seeming to gather herself.

Silver nodded her head. "I saw what happened."

Celestia sighed, "It was worth a shot, wasn't it?"

"I guess, though I don't know how you planned to get past the mind dragon," Silver said.

"I heard he wasn't that strong. I thought I could hide those thoughts from him," sighed Celestia. "But it's done now. I may never have a chance to escape again … and … and my wing's broken."

Her voice cracked. Both dragonesses knew that a break like hers was unlikely to heal properly. She may never fly again, at least not properly, and a dragon without wings wasn't a dragon. Now Silver knew why she was weeping.

"Hey, I might be able to straighten it out for you," said Silver.

"No, you get hurt if you try to use your element without permission," Celestia sighed, "Besides, what could you do? All the healing dragons have refused to help. Said I was a disgrace."

A tear trickled from her eye, but she managed to hold herself together. Silver looked at Celestia mournfully, trying to think of a way to help her. An idea suddenly reached her head. She had done it before, once, and it had worked. She just hoped that it would this time.

"I think I can fix your wing," said Silver.

"How? You're a metallic dragon, aren't you? Or something like that? Don't tell me that includes healing powers as well," said Celestia.

"No, well, not exactly. But I can set your bones so they heal straight," she said.

Celestia blinked in surprise. "Really?"

"Yeah. It'll hurt a bit, but it's worth it."

"Great! But why? We hardly know each other." The dragoness seemed to be getting suspicious.

"You didn't deserve it," replied Silver, "and you'll need a good wing for what's to come."

Celestia frowned and tilted her head in surprise. "What?"

"You'll find out soon enough. Now, where do I get permission to use my element?" asked Silver.

"You have to ask Tetrad," she snorted. "He usually wants to make sure that the dragon in question doesn't do anything that will 'harm others'."

Silver grinned, "Doesn't sound too hard."

"Oh, and he will probably ask a favour from you," she said.

"What type of favour?"

Celestia shrugged, "It varies."

"As long as he doesn't ask too much," she said, opening her wings and taking to the air.

She flew over to the platform where the collarless dragons were, landing at the edge, hesitantly, not knowing how she was expected to approach them. They had all gathered around their newest member, and the young fire dragon looked like he was about to explode from pride, listening intently to what the other dragons had to say. At first, they didn't realise she was there, but it didn't take long for one of them to spot her. Namely Krita. The mind dragon was on the outside of the group, seeming to scorn Silver. When he saw her, he frowned and padded up to her.

"What do you want?" he asked.

"Aah … a friend of mine has been injured. I was just wondering whether or not I would be able to use my element to heal her," Silver said.

"I was not aware you had healing abilities," Krita frowned.

"I don't," she said quickly, "but I can use my element to join the two bones back together."

Krita narrowed his eyes, and she shivered slightly. It seemed that the mind dragon was boring his mind into hers, searching her. Her mind suddenly wrenched to the plan they had to escape. What if he found out? This was a stupid idea. Krita narrowed his eyes and turned from her.

"I will talk to Tetrad," he said, walking over to the earth dragon and leaving a nervous dragoness waiting, guilt gnawing at her. There was no way he hadn't noticed her idea of escape. Oh, she had stuffed up big-time.

Krita came back with his leader. Tetrad sat in front of her with a friendly smile. Silver didn't smile back. This dragon was nothing but trouble, and she would give him the respect he deserved – none at all.

"Silver, my favourite dragoness," he said. "What would you like to speak to me about?"

She nearly growled, but instead spoke in as friendly a voice as possible. "I would like your permission to heal a friend of mine. Her wing's broken."

"Am I right to assume that this friend of yours is Celestia?" he asked.

She hesitated, before nodding.

"I would have to advise you on the company you keep, young dragon," sighed Tetrad. "First Eril, and now Celestia. Both these dragons are freedom-seekers. Dangerous. Untrustworthy. May I suggest you befriend some more agreeable faces. Maybe Turrella and her daughter."

She shuffled on her feet. "I'm fine. All I'm looking for is your permission."

Tetrad snorted. "Not granted. That dragoness got what she deserved. Trying to attack dear Krita, and having the nerve to try to become collarless to get free. No, Silver, she deserved what she got."

Silver froze, looking down at her feet. Anger began to bubble up to the surface again, and she couldn't help but let out a low growl. Oh, how she wanted to lash out at the dragon in front of her right now, to rip that grin from his maw and coat his insides with liquid metal.

Don't lose yourself now, a voice suddenly said in her head. *Gain control. And then speak. Be polite. He wants something from you. You can compromise.*

She nearly jumped in surprise but managed to hold herself. Who had said that? Was it just her imagination? She looked over at Krita to see him staring at her intensely, as if concentrating.

Stop looking at me! This is hard enough as it is without you trying to fight me off. Now ask again, and say you're sorry for growling. Ask what you can do.

She hesitated before turning her attention back to the earth dragon. He was staring at her, unimpressed.

"I'm … I'm sorry," she said, trying to sound sincere, "I just want to help my friend. Please. Is there anything I can do to get your permission?"

She hated every word that came from her mouth. It was false, and put forwards with a façade of helplessness. She felt bad for merely saying sorry. She was anything but sorry. If she could, she would rip his legs off, fly down to Celestia and use her element anyway, but her collar stopped her from resisting at all.

Tetrad snorted. "As you should be. If you growl at me ever again, you will be punished. Now, I may grant your request, on one condition. When is your eighth hatch day, Silver?"

She was surprised at the question, but answered, "Um … a few months away. Why?"

The earth dragon merely smiled. He turned back to the rest of his friends. "Shiro, will you come here a moment, please?"

The young fire dragon looked up from what he was doing and glanced at Cert, who had been telling him something. The electric dragon nodded, and Shiro trotted over to the two of them. It was then Silver realised just how young the fire dragon was. He wasn't even as old as Zepos, maybe just past his eighth hatch day. And when he looked at Silver he suddenly seemed transfixed.

"Shiro, meet Silver. I assume you recognise her from the new batch of dragons yesterday?" Tetrad asked.

The fire dragon nodded his head. "Pleased to meet you … Silver." He bowed.

Bow back. And for goodness sake, please be polite, Krita growled in her head.

She felt like growling back but instead bowed her head. "Likewise."

"You two are about the same age," Tetrad grinned, "So I think you would be a great match. My condition is that, coming your eighth hatch day, you will accept Shiro as your nest mate."

Both dragons looked at him, Shiro in surprise and Silver in horror. Dragons could bear hatchlings only after their eighth hatch day. No-one knew why; it was one of nature's mysteries.

"I … but … what?" Silver stuttered.

"It's a simple request," said Tetrad, "and it will increase your rank among your fellow dragons, bringing you that much closer to being collarless. And I think you two would enjoy yourselves."

Agree, Krita urged.

Silver didn't say anything, her mind awhirl. Again, that anger began to creep up on her. How dare they make her choose between her friend and a potential mate? She didn't want this. Far from it. She wanted to wait a few years after her eighth birthday to find her other half.

Look, if your plan works the way it should, you don't have to worry about it. You'll be free in less than a month, said Krita.

She looked at the mind dragon with surprise and sudden worry. He knew about it? Then why didn't he say anything? With a word, he could ruin any chance of her escaping. She knew the earth dragon would trust his word.

I want to help you. Now, if you want to help your friend, then agree, said Krita, *I will be your overseer and we can discuss anything as we fly. Okay?*

She took a shaky breath and looked at Shiro. He was watching her carefully, as if afraid of rejection. He hadn't even asked her. She barely knew him, and what she did know she didn't like. But what Krita had said was true. If their plan did work, then her word at this moment wouldn't matter.

"Fine. It's a deal," she said, regretfully.

"Good. Krita will oversee your work. Maybe tomorrow you and Shiro can get acquainted," Tetrad stated.

He turned and walked away, Shiro following him, glancing back at the silver dragoness. He smiled slightly. She didn't smile back. Instead she turned and opened her wings.

"Let's go," she said lowly to Krita. "And you better explain yourself."

Chapter 15:
Escape Plan

Your plan won't work, said Krita as they flew over the dragons below them. Several looked up at Silver's glinting form as her shell caught the light, but she didn't notice them. She felt anger and fear at the dragon beside her. He knew a lot about what the dragons were planning that night. They were at his mercy.

"What do you mean?" she asked, seething quietly.

Speak with your mind, Silver. We do not want to risk anyone catching our conversation.

Oh, like this?

Yes. Thank you. And I mean exactly as I say. Your plan won't work.

Silver glanced at the dragon, frowning. *Why are you helping us?*

I will tell you later, if your plan succeeds.

A low growl formed in her throat. She didn't trust Krita, but she had no choice considering he could blackmail them if he wished, even if for some reason he hadn't. He was collarless! He had accepted humans as his leaders. Why would he want to help them?

The two of them landed beside Celestia, who studied Krita suspiciously. Silver had no doubt that the light dragon blamed him for her broken wing. He was the one who had read her mind, after all.

"Can you flatten out your wing?" Silver asked her, wanting to get this over as quickly as possible.

Celestia lay on the ground and spread her flimsy wing as far as the broken bone would allow. She was obviously in pain, but Silver admired her for keeping silent. She probably did this to show defiance in front of Krita, though the mind dragon could likely hear Celestia's voiceless screams.

"Now, I'm going to need to cut open the broken part of your wing. It'll hurt, so brace yourself," Silver said to Celestia.

The light dragon didn't say anything, but her muscles tensed, and she clamped her jaw shut. Silver was surprised, and grateful, that she didn't question her. If a dragon wanted to cut her wing open, she'd want to know exactly why. This show of trust warmed her heart.

Being as careful as she could, Silver formed the end of her tail into a blade and carefully cut a small slit just above the broken bone. The cut was clean, owing to the blade's sharpness, and a little blood began to well in the wound. The bone was revealed, and Silver sighed with relief. It was a clean break, and would be easy to fix.

"You might want to bite something. This is going to hurt … a lot," said Silver, meeting the light dragon's eyes with her own.

Celestia hesitated, looking around for something to grab. Stones lined the ground, and she pulled one over to her, before nodding her readiness to Silver. She looked down at the bone. Dragon bones were hollow, so it looked like a giant white reed.

Silver gathered a small amount of metal on the tip of her tongue and manoeuvred the bone, so the broken halves were attached perfectly straight. Celestia whimpered as she clawed the ground and bit down on the rock. The silver dragon quickly squirted a thin stream of metal around the bone, sealing it in place. With the blade of her tail she cut of the rugged edges of the seam before closing the skin back over the bone and sealing it with another layer of metal.

"There we go. Once we find a healing dragon willing to help, you can heal it properly, but for now that should do," said Silver, stepping back and licking the blood off her paws.

Celestia let go of the rock and looked at her wing. The silver suture gleamed slightly. She took a couple of flaps and beamed.

"Thank you! Thank you so much!" Celestia said with the excitement of a hatchling, flapping both her wings. "How can I ever repay you?"

Silver smiled. "Don't do it again. That'll be enough."

Celestia nodded, marvelling at how straight her wing looked now. It was if there hadn't been a break at all. Though it was a little heavier, she could easily grow accustomed to this. Smiling, she took to the air, wanting to test out her newly healed wing. The frail dragon bugled with joy, flying as high as she could and beginning to circle the others.

You said our plan wouldn't work, said Silver, looking at Krita.

No, it won't. Two of your assumptions are wrong, the mind dragon said, watching Celestia fly. *First, there are human guards outside the main gate, so sneaking out would get you captured. And second, you assume you will be able to deactivate all the collars at once. While that is possible, it requires a pass code, one you will never be able to guess.*

Silver hesitated. If what he was saying was true, then she doubted they'd be able to escape at all. Just getting past the gate was impossible. If they didn't have the collars, Silver wouldn't hesitate. Defeating humans in a fight was as easy as swishing a claw, but with their collars on, one look would be the end of it.

Is that what you wanted to tell me? she growled mentally. *To dissuade us from trying, because you know it's impossible?*

No. I want to help. I know the access code that unlocks the collars. And I'm a mind dragon. It would be simple to trick the guards into thinking you weren't there. But I cannot spread my mind throughout the whole base, so after the guards at the front, I will be unable to help you.

Silver studied the mind dragon, confused. He was willingly serving the humans, so everything he was saying could be a trap, one that he may even enjoy seeing her fall into. But maybe he really had turned on the humans.

I don't trust you, she said.

I know. I can read your mind, sighed Krita. *Think of it this way: I am the only one who was able to infiltrate the collarless, because I am a mind dragon. They couldn't hope to read my mind, and they needed someone they could trust. So I allow them to trust me, and do their dirty work, but I secretly help dragons escape. No-one suspects me, because I am part of the collarless group and I keep up a façade of a heartless dragon who follows orders. Sometimes I have to do some terrible things, but it's worth it if I'm able to free even one dragon from this miserable place.*

She was beginning to believe Krita. He probably could have escaped himself, but he stayed behind to help other dragons escape. Of course, his story could be made up, but Silver couldn't help but feel a grudging admiration for the dragon.

You try escaping tonight with Zepos. If the guards at the gate ignore you as if you aren't there, you know you can trust me and follow the rest of my directions. If not, well, there is really nothing you can do.

I guess I have to trust you. Silver sighed, realising that they may attract suspicion because their conversation had been going a little longer the necessary. *Just one last question. With the collar on, will I be able to form objects with my tail?*

Yes. The collar only reacts to elemental powers around the neck, since that is where it's fastened. If a dragon tries to breathe their element, their collar will zap them. However, if you use your tail, or even your wings, there shouldn't be a problem. I will place the directions in your mind, so you will be able to find the control room easily. It will be night-time, so there shouldn't be too many humans throughout the hallways or even in the control room. But make sure you are careful.

Silver nodded and thanked the dragon. A series of images suddenly flashed through her head. They were directions, leading through the base and into a computer room. A word also flashed before her: "Derula". She didn't know what it meant, but she assumed it was the password to unlock the collars. She just hoped she would be able to type it on a human keyboard.

Did you get it all? asked Krita.

Yes.

Good. Now look chastised. I will need an excuse for talking with you for so long.

Silver nodded and hung her head, dropping her wings. A snarl burst from Krita's maw before he turned and stalked away from her. Silver was careful to keep up her act until the dragon left, before gathering herself and walking away, back to where Zepos and Eril were waiting. She couldn't help but smile a little. Krita was a smart dragon.

* * *

That night, around midnight, Silver and Zepos woke from their sleep. She had told her friends of Krita's offer to help. At first, they had been very reluctant, but eventually they accepted that they would never escape without the mind dragon's help.

Zepos and Silver had been chosen for the mission because the silver dragoness was the only one able to cut through the door at the front, and Zepos didn't want to let her out of his sight. All the other dragons were sleeping soundly on the floor. Some were curled around others, while a few slept by themselves off to the side. They moved as silently as possible. Silver had darkened her shell as much as she could, so it didn't reflect any lights in the base.

Krita was sitting atop the collarless dragons' perch. He gave them a small nod as they walked by. Taking a deep breath, Silver formed a blade with her tail and looked at the chain that held the door closed. It was a simple device, one that any dragon could break with enough elemental power.

Silver swung her tail downwards, hard, cutting through the metal bars with a single stroke. Zepos caught them before they clanged against the floor. He gently lay them down and nodded to Silver. The dragoness smiled at him before pushing open the door slowly. It creaked, as if in vengeance, and both dragons winced. They quickly looked back over the sleeping dragons, and while some stirred, none woke. With a relieved sigh, she slowly pushed the door open, allowing just enough room for the two of them to get through. Zepos went first, and Silver followed.

They both froze at the sight of two humans, standing backs faced to the doorway. They didn't even look at the dragons as they crept out. A greyish sheen covered their eyes, suggesting some sort of trance. Relief washed over her; they could trust the mind dragon.

Zepos looked at her with surprise, and she grinned and mouthed, 'Told ya so.' Silver took the lead as they began to make their way through the base and towards freedom.

CHAPTER 16:
HALFWAY

DRAGONS weren't made for stealth. Even the lithest of them were too big, too cumbersome, especially in small areas. And as the two dragons made their way through the base, they couldn't help but wince at the occasional clack of their claws against cement, or the scrape of Silver's metallic tail against a wall.

"There better not be any humans around," muttered Zepos, taking extra care to walk with the pads of his feet.

They were pretty certain that Silver could fling her tail spikes if worst came to worst, but that was the only weapon the two of them had. They couldn't attack with teeth or claws—if they got too close to the humans, their collars shocked them—and they couldn't use their elements at all.

Silver stopped at a corner and looked around, before continuing. It was difficult to navigate such an area, but with Krita's memories of the place, she knew it like the back of her paw. As long as they didn't take a wrong turn, she was pretty sure she could get them to the command centre. And, scanning Krita's memories, she knew that the hardest part was yet to come.

They stopped at an intersection of corridors. The hall they'd been following continued ahead, while another branched to their left. Silver took a deep breath, glanced around the side, and quickly pulled her head back. It would be so useful to have a mind dragon with them now. Two human guards stood in front of double doors that blocked the path that Krita had planted in Silver's mind.

"Two guards," she whispered quietly to Zepos.

The electric dragon narrowed his eyes. "And that's the only way?"

She nodded her head.

"Okay, I'll distract them, and as they approach, you get them with your tail spikes," he said.

She nodded again and let spikes grow from her tail. The collar didn't zap her, much to her relief. She took a couple of steps back from the corner and nodded to Zepos. The electric dragon gathered himself and tensed his body, before suddenly pouncing past the turn. A grunt of surprise followed, and the sound of guns being cocked.

"Did you see that?" asked one of the humans.

"Yes. It looked like a dragon."

As soon as the men walked into the corridor, Silver struck, lashing out her tail and sending a dozen spikes in their direction.

One man cried out as a spike caught him in the chest, while the other fell silent, two spikes embedded in his neck and head. The rest of the barbs missed and headed directly for Zepos. He growled in surprise and ducked, but not fast enough. One of them scraped along the top of his head, drawing a trickle of blood, and lodged itself in his collar. It broke the metal, springing the collar open, before collapsing to the ground. Zepos's collar soon followed, falling beside the spike. Both dragons stared at it in surprise, silent for a moment.

"Okay, what was that?" Zepos whispered, startled.

Silver walked over to him and touched the broken collar with her tail. Severed wires shot electric bolts onto the floor, which spewed sparks in response. She let out a small laugh of disbelief. It seemed the spikes were able to cut through the collars easily. They weren't as strong as she thought. She voiced her theory to Zepos, who agreed.

"Now try with your collar," Zepos said. "Maybe not with spikes, but try to cut it off with your tail or something."

"I'll try," she replied, blading the end of her tail.

She aimed it at the collar and swung as hard as she could, angling the blade so it wouldn't cut through her scales. It hit the collar and stuck. Pain rushed through her as the collar punished her for the attempt at escape. She opened her maw to scream, unable to hold it in, but Zepos had seen what had happened and clamped her muzzle shut. A whimper escaped her instead as she collapsed, convulsing slightly as the electricity ran through her. The pain died, and she relaxed again. Zepos slowly freed her muzzle, allowing her to gasp for air.

"Are you alright?" he asked worriedly.

"Yeah," she coughed. "But let's not try that again."

"Agreed," Zepos replied.

Silver slowly got to her feet, shaking slightly. That pain was something else. It was probably the worst feeling she had ever felt. The electricity targeted every nerve in the body; at least that was what Eril had said.

She was a bit confused as to why her tail hadn't cut the collar open. Maybe the spikes were sharper than her bladed tail? Or maybe they just had more force behind them, which allowed them to cut easier. It didn't matter. Her collar would be off soon and then she was likely going to destroy this base.

Once the two dragons had gathered themselves, they walked over to the door, this time Zepos leading the way. Now that he had his collar off, he would easily be able to kill any human who got in the way. Though they still wanted to be as stealthy as possible. Even with Zepos's freedom, any alarm would bring squadrons of soldiers who the electric dragon wouldn't be able to handle.

"Behind this door is the main hangar," whispered Silver. "From memory, there will probably be at least five human guards in there. The control room is on the other side. It's a large open area with a sidewalk surrounding it. Once we get inside it will be simple to hide, but opening this door may alert one of the guards. There's usually one walking along the sidewalk at this side. If we can open the door as he passes, and grab him, it will be easy to slip inside."

Zepos nodded, impressed by her knowledge, even if it wasn't hers. "How does it feel to have memories that aren't yours?"

"Strange," she admitted, "but worth it."

Silver pushed open the door slightly, leaving a gap they could just see out of. It was a small door, much to her annoyance, and her bulk would take up most of the doorway. They would only be able to get through one at a time, so she let Zepos take the lead. With his collar destroyed, he was the only one who could get in close quarters to humans without being zapped.

"Here he comes," he said.

Silver took a couple of steps back to allow the electric dragon room. Seconds passed as both dragons waited anxiously for the man to get close enough. The human's footsteps could soon be heard as he neared the door. He seemed to be grumbling about something, murmuring under his voice. A second later, Zepos opened the door, snatching the human before he could make a noise, and stabbed him through the chest. He died quickly.

They leaned him against the side of the wall and passed the doorway slowly, in case any other humans saw them. None did. They quickly opened their wings and glided down to the floor of the hangar, hiding behind numerous boxes. Silver took a breath of relief. The hardest part was over.

The hangar was gigantic. Its ceiling reached high, at least a hundred metres. Hundreds of different vehicles, from planes to tanks, were parked in the hangar. Crates were also spread throughout, full of weapons and ammunition. It was like these people were ready to go to war. Throughout the hangar, torchlights were swinging around, searching through the crates and vehicles. There was an exit sign at the other side, lit up green, showing the way out. Silver took a mental note of it, knowing it would help them later.

"There's more than five," whispered Zepos.

"I said at least five," replied Silver. "There could have been more."
"I count ten. That's double," the electric dragon said.

"Shut up," snorted the dragoness, letting her shell darken to a dull grey.

She began to move through the crates and vehicles. Zepos followed close behind her. This place was much easier to sneak through than a corridor; they could hide among the crates as the lights passed over them. The wider space didn't make them any quieter. The constant clacking of claws against the ground sent loud echoes across the hangar. Lights followed wherever they went, but the humans assumed the sounds were made by one of their fellow guards. The dragons knew, though, that they couldn't fool them forever.

"We'll never get past them at this rate," hissed Zepos as they hid behind an armoured vehicle they were nearly as big as.

"I know," Silver replied, seeing their problem. "But we can't just try and break through."

The two dragons sat in silence for a moment. The dragoness looked at the roof as an idea came to her. If they were able to fly, they could get high enough that the torches wouldn't reach them. It was risky, but once they were near the ceiling it would be safe. The only problem was taking off and landing.

"We could fly," she suggested to the electric dragon.

Zepos looked to the roof, seeming to ponder the plan, and nodded. "Good idea."

They began to move again, wanting to get to an area where they could lift off easily without being seen. As they walked, they didn't notice a beam of light pass over them, but they did notice the shout that echoed out over hangar, and the gunshot that followed.

"Dragons! Dragons in the hangar!" yelled one of the guards, firing his gun down at them.

Silver cried out in surprise as a bullet pinged off her right wing. The two dragons didn't waste another moment. They spread their wings and leapt into the air, Silver slightly ahead of Zepos. They flew higher and higher, trying to get out of range of the gunfire, and then Silver's collar activated.

She screeched in pain as her wings seized and she plummeted from the air. She crashed into a plane, skidding sideways. Her body convulsed as the collar tortured her, leaving her incapable of anything but screaming. Lightning arced through the sky as Zepos flew down to help her. An explosion ruptured the air as the lightning bolt hit a pile of oil barrels. An alarm sounded, and red lights began to flash through the hangar, lighting it up.

"Silver, get up!" yelled Zepos as he landed in front of her.

The collar had stopped zapping her, but Silver felt lightheaded after the crash, everything flashing in and out of focus. Zepos snarled and gave her a quick jab to the leg with his claw, the pain focusing her vision. She growled and rolled to her feet. The explosion had bought them some time, but it wouldn't be much.

"We need to get out of here!" yelled Zepos. "There's an exit on the other side of the hangar!"

Silver nodded. She turned and began to run, not trusting herself to fly again. But it didn't help her. The collar activated again, sending her stumbling from her feet and crashing into the ground. A scream escaped her throat. They couldn't fight like this. She sent a number of tail spikes back the way they came, hoping she managed to hit something, and tried to get to her feet again, but her collar electrocuted her a third time.

Her vision began to swim as unconsciousness beckoned her into its shadows. The collar activated again, and another scream racked her throat. She coughed up blood and closed her eyes. The pain was unbearable. Oh, she just wanted it to leave her alone. Why wouldn't it just disappear?

"No Silver! Don't give up yet!" Zepos cried.

He slipped his neck under her and hauled her onto his back. He wasn't going to leave her behind, not after all they had been through. But it was hopeless. An explosion knocked him off his feet as he ran, throwing Silver into a nearby truck. She whimpered, not having the strength to scream, as her collar activated again. Her muscles clenched, and a tear trickled from her eye. It was all too much. Too much.

"Leave me," she murmured.

"No! We have to escape! I'm not leaving you here!" Zepos began to struggle to get her up onto his back again.

A bullet flew out of the fire caused by the explosion, ricocheting off the floor and skimming the electric dragon's flank. He growled in pain and sent a lightning bolt through the smog, electrocuting a party of men. But there were more coming.

"Please, Zepos," cried Silver as another volt of pain attacked her body, "Please. Just get out of here! I'll buy you all the time I can."

"No, Silver. I can't leave you. Don't make me do this." He tried to get on her onto his back again, but she pushed herself off.

"You're no use to me if you're captured! Go! Find an escape plan, more dragons even, and come back. Please don't get captured because of me. Go! Please go."

Zepos gulped and watched as she convulsed again as the collar waged its war on her. His heart ached. He knew she was right. There was no way he could get out of this place with her. It was impossible. But he couldn't just leave her. She had freed him, twice.

With a mournful whimper he took a step back, sending a bolt of lightning at a group of humans who ran through the smoke. The bolt caught the first one in the chest, sending him flying back into his comrades. Silver's scream echoed through the hangar again, but she forced herself to her feet. Her tail sprung up with spikes as she whipped them forwards, impaling another squadron of guards.

"Go, Zepos!" she yelled.

With a wail of remorse, he turned, opened his wings, and dashed into the air. As he flew, he sent a wave of electricity into the trucks, causing a massive eruption to blast the hangar. It wouldn't kill a dragon, but humans were another matter, and it distracted the guards enough for him to fly down towards the exit. Silver's scream followed him, before it was cut short.

The dragoness's head fell to the floor as the collar finally won. Unconsciousness pulled her into its comforting darkness. There was no fight left in her. Her body went limp.

CHAPTER 17: AN EXAMPLE

THE silver dragoness was chained, again. The chains strapped her wings, tail, head, neck and muzzle tightly. There was no chance she could move, or even attempt to move. Cameras were zoomed in on her, the humans behind them not taking any chances. They were still confused as to how she had escaped. They had seen the security footage of the dragons walking through the base, but it didn't explain how they walked right past the guards.

Silver's form began to move, and a small groan escaped her as she was dragged into the conscious realm once again. It didn't take her long to realise that chains wound around her body, and a low growl escaped her throat. The collar beeped, and a small electric shock passed through her. Not enough to hurt but enough to warn. She resisted the urge to growl again.

The cage that held her was much like the one she'd found herself in when she had first arrived. There were large grey walls and a small metal door, and what she could see of the roof looked the same. This time, however, cameras lined the walls, seeming to watch her from every angle. It was like they didn't want her to move an inch.

She waited there for what seemed like hours, her mind replaying what had happened in the hangar. The guards had seen them! How could they have been so careless? A simple mistake had ended their nearly successful mission, and she had ended up in this mess. She shuddered at the painful electrocution that was sure to come.

The metal door suddenly creaked open, and her heart pounded with surprise. A human walked in, followed by two others. She recognised one of the humans as the man she had first seen in this place. He had the same blue suit and eye-enlarging glasses. There was also a woman in similar attire, although instead of a suit she wore a deep blue business dress and a dark scowl.

The last man, however, looked strangely calm. He wore a black suit, and a scar streaked down one side of his face. His hard eyes bore into her, studying the dragoness in front of him. He didn't say anything; he simply crossed his arms and glared at her. Silver shifted slightly, as much as her bonds allowed, and met his gaze. An advantage of being a dragon was no matter how intense another species' stare, the dragon's would always be fiercer. But this man was an exception, and Silver broke eye contact first.

"Silver," said the man, simply stating her name.

She looked at him again, unable to speak through her tightly bound muzzle.

"It has come to my attention that you and a friend of yours broke into our main hangar in an attempt to escape. Unfortunately, your friend succeeded. We have patrols searching for him right now. But I would like to know why. There was no way for you to get out—you still had your collar on. It has a tracking mechanism on it, you know, something that tells us exactly where you are at all times. So why?"

She nearly sighed in relief. Zepos had escaped! At least something good had come from the mission. It also gave her hope of escape. She knew Zepos would not stop until she was freed. The bounds around her muzzle loosened slightly, allowing her to speak.

"What do you mean, 'why'? I was trying to escape," she snorted.

"Don't lie to me, dragon. You're not stupid enough to try to escape with your collar on. So tell me, why? There were three other places you could go besides the exit—the barracks, the common room and the main control room. I suspect you were heading towards the control room. But why? The collars are password-protected, and there is no way to unlock them."

"I … I didn't know that," Silver lied. "I thought there would be a way to free all the dragons, so me and … my friend, decided to head there and see if we could. Even if we couldn't, we thought there might be a way to at least get our collars off."

She couldn't let him know that she knew the password. It would make him suspicious, or at least more suspicious than he already was. He probably suspected that a mind dragon was involved, but she couldn't let him suspect who. The humans still trusted Krita, so the dragons may be able to attempt escape a second time.

The man narrowed his eyes at her. "I don't believe you, but I have other things to worry about now. Namely the destruction you caused to the hangar last night. It will cost a few hundred million dollars to repair the damage you have caused, and I have instructed Tetrad to punish you severely."

He turned to walk away, nodding to his two associates.

"Why are you doing this?" Silver suddenly growled. "What have we ever done to you?"

The man turned back to her with a surprised look on his face. "Don't you listen to Tetrad's speeches? Dragons are too dangerous to be left to do as you will. Too powerful. You need us to control you. Last night proved this."

She snorted. "I'm only dangerous to those who harm me or those I love."

The man laughed, "Well, good luck being 'dangerous'. You belong to me now. You don't have a choice in what you do."

Silver narrowed her eyes, not backing down from the human's gaze. This time, he was the one who looked away, a hint of uncertainty flashing across his eyes. He walked to the door and opened it.

"Have fun with your punishment," he said, and closed the door.

The chain around her snout tightened once more, preventing her from saying anything else. The two other humans walked over to her.

They unlocked the chains around her wings and tail, and grabbed the chain that held her maw to the floor, pulling her head up. She snarled lowly, and the two of them hesitated.

"You will follow us," said the male. "Any attempt to resist will result in punishment."

Silver nodded. She knew the procedure. She had done it before. They led her like a dog to the wall with the metal door. The wall opened like before, and the humans pulled her through. There was no use resisting, so she didn't.

They walked through the base, taking the same twists and turns they had taken before. It didn't bother Silver too much this time, though. She knew her way around the base, or at least some of it. They came up on the outside of the door. The two guards who had been there the previous night had been replaced with others, and they glowered as she walked past. The gates opened with the same ear-piercing screech, and they walked inside.

Inside, the dragons all looked at her in surprise as she was led through them. They quickly got out of the way of the humans, fearing the power of their collars. A few even bowed slightly as they walked past. Silver caught Celestia's questioning glance. She gave a weak smile in response.

A shadow passed over the dragons, and Tetrad landed in front of them. He gazed down at Silver, anger and surprise in his eyes. It was like Silver had disappointed him somehow. He turned his stare to the humans and bowed low, spreading his wings in an exaggerated gesture of obeisance.

"My Lord and Lady," he spoke in his usual deep voice, "I will take this troublemaker and make sure she is punished appropriately."

"Make sure that you do, Tetrad," scorned the female. "We do not want this happening again."

Tetrad bowed his head again. The female human reached up and untied something underneath the muzzle that held Silver's mouth shut. It loosened, and then slipped off. She took a step back, opening and closing her maw as she regained some feeling. While the top of head was metal, the bottom part was soft scale that the tight bounds dug into.

The humans turned and quickly left the dragon area, leaving Silver at the mercy of the earth dragon in front of her. She glared at Tetrad as he took a step towards her. The anger she had for him began to rise again, and she wondered if she could throw a volley of tail spikes before the collar could electrocute her.

"Silver," Tetrad sighed, disappointed, "why did you do it?"

"Because no dragon deserves the treatment we get here," she growled. "We deserve to be free just as much as humans do, and nothing you say will change that. You're a fool if you think that we are meant to live under a leadership as cruel as this! A fool!"

Her reflexes saved her as Tetrad's paw suddenly whipped around at her maw. She ducked, the claw passing harmlessly over her, and jumped backwards, out of range. Her collar suddenly activated, and she screamed, collapsing to the floor. The dragons around her backed away as she suffered, her screeches echoing through the cavern. It stopped, and she gasped for air.

"Get up," snarled the earth dragon.

Silver slowly got to her feet, her legs wobbly beneath her. She didn't see the claw coming this time, and her head was wrenched backwards as Tetrad hit her hard on the side of her jaw. The metal-coated upper part of her jaw only clanged dully, but the fleshy lower part tore, sustaining long claw marks. Blood began to run down her mouth and drip from her chin.

"You do not speak to your superiors in that way," he growled.

"You're not my superior," she snarled back, her anger bubbling.

This time, as his claw came down on her, she tilted her head, allowing him to hit the top of her skull, which was well protected by her shell. A screech rang out as the earth dragon's claws scratched down the metal plate. She stumbled back, the shell not protecting her from the force of the blow. Tetrad hissed in pain as one of his claws broke on her head. She smiled grimly. Though it hurt, this was pain she could deal with.

Instead of hitting her again, the earth dragon spoke. "Your punishment for attempted escape is every dragon here will touch your collar, electrocuting you every time, until none of us are left." Turning to face the rest of the dragons, he continued. "This is what will happen to any of you should you attempt to follow this treacherous path."

Silver gaped. There were over a hundred dragons here. Over a hundred times the collar would zap her. The pain would kill her. No dragon could withstand this sort of punishment. She looked around at the dragons, seeing remorse in their looks. They didn't want to have to do this either, but it was that or get zapped themselves for disobeying orders.

"You're not a dragon," Silver growled. "You're a monster."

"I'm more of a dragon than you are," he snarled. "You're lucky Shiro has chosen to forgive you. He is horrified at what you have done, and if I were him I would let you go, but he has chosen to stick by you."

"Go to hell," Silver snarled.

"Enough of this! You come forwards!" Tetrad yelled, pointing his claw at a random dragon in the crowd.

There was a small ruffle of movement as the dragon he had called came forwards. Silver didn't turn to see who it was, keeping her gaze fixed on the earth dragon who had caused so much pain and suffering.

"Well what are waiting for!" he growled at the dragon, "All you need to do is this."

He brought down his claw on Silver's collar in a glancing blow. Pain suddenly needled through her and she screamed again, struggling to stay on her feet. The wound in her jaw was nothing compared to this. It tore apart her whole body, ripping it up as though it were a piece of foam. Her form convulsed, and a tear trickled from her eye.

"There, come on! It's not hard!" Tetrad said.

"No," said a familiar voice. It was Celestia.

"No?"

"She's my friend. I would never hurt my friends," the light dragon said.

"You fool! Would you rather take her place?"

"If that is what it takes." Celestia stood strong, spreading her wings in defiance.

There was silence throughout the crowd of dragons. This was all new to them. No dragon had so openly defied Tetrad, and now two of them were. The earth dragon shivered in rage, unused to having his leadership questioned.

"Would you like me to break your wing again? This time I'll shatter it so there is no chance for it to heal." Tetrad was breathing heavily.

Celestia didn't answer.

"Don't you dare," Silver growled in a low, threatening voice.

"Or what, Silver? What are you going to do? Blast me with liquid metal? You can't do that. You will get electrocuted." Tetrad suddenly pounced at Celestia, knocking her to the ground and pinning her. "You will do as you're told! Or you will suffer the consequences!"

Celestia struggled against the earth dragon's grip, but he was much stronger than her. Earth dragons were considered the physically strongest of the species, and often grew the biggest, though metallic dragons were nearly their equal in strength.

Tetrad pinned Celestia's right wing to the floor and raised his mace-like tail, ready to smash it to pieces, when Silver's scream of pain filled the room. Every dragon froze, watching the dragoness's muscles clench as she battled the collar. No-one knew what was happening. There was no obvious reason for her pain.

Silver had snapped. The rage she had been holding inside for the earth dragon had suddenly broken through, and her armour pushed at the collar, struggling to cover her once more. The collar fought back, trying to stop itself from being forced apart, but the rage overtook the pain and Silver continued to push. The metal shell slowly began to grow outwards, and the collar strained against it.

"You … will not … hurt … anyone … else." Silver growled past the pain and the rage.

She screamed, rearing up on two legs and pushing the armour downwards with as much force as she could muster. The collar couldn't take it anymore … and snapped, spinning away on the floor. Silver landed on all fours, the armour quickly surrounding her body. Her now red eyes glinted as she turned to the earth dragon, who stared at her in disbelief.

The broken collar lay discarded on the floor. Dragons backed away from the full-metal dragoness in fear. No-one had ever done such a thing before. No-one had ever defeated the pain that was caused by the device. Tetrad staggered backwards, freeing the light dragoness. Celestia quickly got to her feet and backed away from him, casting a glance at Silver.

"You are going to die," Silver stated simply, before pouncing.

CHAPTER 18:
SILVER'S RAGE

Silver collided with the dragon, claws outstretched, tail blade pointed forwards, wings razor-sharp. Her claws dug through the scale like tissue paper, and she raked them downwards. As Silver's force knocked him sideways and onto his back, a piercing scream erupted from Tetrad's mouth, throwing Silver off him and into the crowd of dragons, who darted aside as the metallic dragoness rolled to her feet.

Tetrad rose, blood seeping from the wound Silver had wrought in his side. He stumbled backwards, away from the dragon who glared at him in hatred. She advanced again, the metal pads of her paws clanging ominously as she walked. Her vision narrowed onto her enemy, ignoring all else.

"Silver, look out!" Celestia cried, a second too late.

A large weight crashed into Silver's back, throwing her on her side. Before she could recover, it landed on her again, pinning her to the floor. Heat blasted into her face, blinding her and tickling her metal. She growled with annoyance and waited for the flames to disappear, then opened her maw and shot a stream of metal upwards, into the assailant's face. A roar followed, and the grip on her loosened. She stabbed with her tail, catching the dragon above her in the hind leg. Her father had taught her how to weaken larger dragons by stabbing at their pressure points. It loosened grips, caused a lot of pain, and she didn't charge it like the last one—but it still pained its victim. Tirene roared.

While the collarless dragons were distracted by the new threat, Silver attacked. She pounced at Tetrad again, knocking him over, and sent a tail spike into Cert's leg, piercing flesh and bone. She ripped scales and skin with her claws before leaping away as Tetrad threw a boulder directly up at her. The end of her tail turned into its blade and she stabbed the dragon in the side, puncturing his body. The earth dragon howled in pain as Silver jumped back, slipping her tail free.

Another bolt of lightning caught her in the side. She absorbed it and, instead of hitting Cert with it, she turned it on Tetrad, electrocuting the dragon like he had done so many times to her, and he screamed. His body seized in pain. Blood dripped from his wounds and onto the floor. There would be no way that he would survive. Satisfied, she turned to Cert, who limped away from her with as much speed as he could muster.

Silver's rage was beginning to fade, and instead of attacking the electric dragon, she turned towards the still-collared dragons, who were watching at a distance. Another scream rang out as Celestia blasted Tirene with another light beam, knocking him unconscious from the pain. Only two collarless dragons were uninjured now: Krita and Shiro. Both perched on the platform, and while Silver had no intention of fighting her ally Krita, Shiro was another matter. He cowered behind Krita, who was making a show of protecting him. Snorting, she decided she would let the coward be.

Celestia landed beside her, looking at her full-metal form in wonder. She had no idea a metallic dragon was capable of so much. The fight being over, the light in her body faded back into her golden yellow scales. She stretched out her wings and let out a roar of victory, one that Silver joined. The dragons around them looked at the two young dragonesses in fear. The two of them had slaughtered four old and powerful dragons as if they had been but nothing.

"For those who want to be free," Silver spoke, "come to me. I will cut open your collars."

The dragons went silent, gaping at her. Now that the prospect of freedom was staring them in the face, they were hesitant. Many of them had been there for most of their lives and couldn't imagine anything beyond the walls that encaged them. The dragons shuffled as a wind dragon stepped out from among them. Eril.

"Heck, yeah!" he grinned, bounding over to them, "I want to be on the badass dragoness's side!"

A few in the crowd laughed, and Silver chuckled slightly, shaking her head. She could see what he was doing. By making a joke he had loosened the tension between them and the dragons, who were intimidated after seeing what they were capable of. Eril's levity reminded the stunned dragons of what had just happened: This was their chance at freedom, and they should take it!

Silver rolled her eyes at the wind dragon, before sending a tail spike at the collar around his neck. She was careful to aim it so it wouldn't hit any other dragons as it went through. Elation began to take her as she realised what she had just done. They were free! Finally free! Oh, it felt amazing, and she could see the feeling spreading among the dragons around them. No more fear of electrocution. No more pain. They could leave this place, preferably destroying it as they went, and make their own lives, without humans deciding for them. For some it was overwhelming, and as collar after collar fell to the floor she saw tears on some of their faces.

She was about halfway through the dragons when a loud shriek caught her attention. The metal door that trapped them inside began to creak open. Silver caught Celestia's eyes and the light dragon nodded. She opened her wings and took to the air, light filling her again as she prepared to battle the humans trying to enter the dragon enclosure. One human walked through, and was incinerated by a blast of white light. A few of the other newly collarless dragons followed Celestia's lead, sending blasts of wind, earth, water and fire towards the humans trying to get through the door.

Silver began to work quickly now, occasionally freeing two dragons with one spike. The collared dragons were getting worried. Any moment now a shock could run through them. They had all experienced the pain of the collars, and to have it happen now when they were about to be free was something they feared. Finally, the last collar was cut off from a young water dragoness. Silver took to her wing, keeping her full-metal form, and landed where the door was.

"I'll go first," she said to the dragons around her. It was safer that way. Besides, she was bulletproof.

Stretching her wings and letting out a grin, she opened the door slightly, popping her head through. Almost instantly, bullets showered her, ricocheting off her head and maw. She growled in surprise and backed up quickly, shaking her head with a snarl. The dragons around her looked at her in expectation.

"Okay, there are quite a few of them out there," she snarled. "In a second I'm going to open these doors. I want there to be a large gap behind me so that the bullets that miss will hit no-one. No dragons are going to die on my watch today."

They quickly followed to obey. They all crowded to either side, each dragon ready to grab quick revenge on the humans who had held them. With a deep sigh, Silver walked over to the door, stabbing her spear-tipped tail through it. The metal yielded easily under the point of her tail. There was silence, before the silver dragoness yanked the door open, quickly slipping her tail free. Bullets showered her, bouncing off. Growling, she put her wing up. It wasn't necessary, but it stopped the bullets from annoying her so much. A thunderous roar sounded behind her, followed by the sounds of draconic elements as they washed past her, and then by a massive explosion, whose force she braced herself against. And then there was silence.

The walls around the entrance of the dragon enclosure were crumbled, some collapsed. Burnt human bodies were lying around the floor, some with missing limbs. The remnants of elemental attacks – fire and broken pieces of earth – were scattered around the floor. It looked as if the place had been hit with a bomb.

"We're free!" The cry rang from a dragon in the crowd and, as one, they surged forwards.

Silver leapt upwards with a snort of surprise, taking wing. She hovered with difficulty above them as they surged through, crying and roaring out their freedom. She smiled and let her metal shell shrink back to its normal state, to more easily stay airborne. She looked up at the two dragons on the collarless podium, and tilted her head.

Are you coming? she asked Krista, hoping the mind dragon was listening to her thoughts. The answer surprised her.

No. I will stay. There are still things that need to be done here, and just because you have freed us all doesn't mean this operation won't continue. There are other D.E.D. bases throughout the world, and they will fix this base. No, I will stay and help more dragons be freed as they are brought in again. This victory is not D.E.D.'s defeat. It is only a nuisance. They will recover. Shiro, however, will be coming with you.'

She looked at Shiro, who had emerged from behind the mind dragon. He looked down at his feet, shuffling nervously. Silver sighed. She didn't like the fire dragon, but she felt sorry for him. He had probably been doing what he thought was best for him in an impossible situation, as many dragons do.

"You can come, Shiro," she said. "But I will not be your mate. That promise was something I made because I knew that I would escape before I had to see it through."

The fire dragon nodded sulkily. "I know."

Silver sighed before turning as the last few dragons ran through the exit. She landed and began to walk through. Shiro landed as well and hurried after her as they went to their freedom.

* * *

Zepos stood atop a mountain, gazing down at the base that lay before him. About ten minutes ago every soldier who had been searching for him had been called back into the base at some sort of emergency. He was struggling to figure out what it was. He hadn't slept the previous night because of them, and now they were retreating. It didn't make any sense, unless they were trying to draw him back in. Though why they would go to such trouble for an electric dragon was beyond him. His species weren't exactly rare.

Sighing, he was about to take to the air when something in the base caught his attention. It sounded like an explosion. Suddenly, the roof blew apart, and he growled in surprise. What came next surprised him even more. A torrent of dragons, of all species, flew out of the hole in the roof, rising into the air with roars of elation. Zepos watched in disbelief—they were free?

He jumped into the air and began to glide over to them, tiredness forgotten. This was impossible, yet as the last dragon flew through with a characteristic silver glint, he couldn't help but roar with them.

"Silver!" he cried, flying down towards her.

The dragoness looked at him in surprise. "Zepos?"

He caught her in midair, and the two spun slightly as they tried to regain balance. Her shell sparkled in the sunrise as she gazed at him with confusion, before she smiled.

"You're free!" he said. "How?"

"Long story," she grinned.

He looked at her incredulously. The dragoness was full of surprises. He felt a sudden urge to kiss her. The moment passed, though, as a dragon flew down towards them and asked Silver, "Where are we going?"

Silver hesitated, "Why ask me?"

"You're our leader now," said the dragon. "For many dragons, that place was the only home they knew; now they don't know what to do with themselves. So they will follow you."

Silver blinked, and glanced at Zepos. "Well, I guess we're heading to the dragon haven."

CHAPTER 19:
THE DRAGON HAVEN

SILVER sighed as she looked over the dragons travelling with her. They had settled in a small valley that was mostly hidden from the outside world. A rocky stream wound through it, allowing the tired party to drink their fill; by the time they were done she doubted there would be any water left. They had been flying for a while, and many of the dragons weren't in the best shape.

With a yawn, she lay her head down, basking in the sun that had come out an hour ago. China was a lot cooler than she expected, and her metal shell had nearly frozen her. The colder she got, the harder it was to move, her metal losing its usual elasticity. Occasionally, her shell would groan a complaint about the cold. It was annoying, so she was warming it up in the sunlight.

It had been three days since they had broken out of D.E.D., leaving the base in a smoky ruin. Little had survived the dragons' wrath. A few humans had managed to flee, the leader of the base, sadly, being one of them, but it would be a long time until they managed to get it up and running again, if they ever did. She was glad she'd managed to help the dragons, but she was unsure what to do now. In the three days they had travelled, there had been no sign of the haven, and she was beginning to suspect that the place was a myth.

With a weak groan, she stretched out her wings and sighed her relief. Maybe she should get back to flying again, to warm up her joints more. Sometimes being a metallic dragon was tiring. With a huff, she got to her feet and flapped her wings, entering the realm of the sky once more. The few dragons around her looked up in confusion, but she gestured for them to stay down with a shake of her head. They knew what she meant.

She flew higher into the sky, and landed on the peak of a mountain overlooking the valley they were resting in. It had been hard to hide such a large group of dragons from the human population in China, and they probably hadn't been totally successful, but so far, no other humans had tried to hunt them down. No-one they'd encountered in their travels had even mentioned the A.O.D.H. hunters. This made her a little suspicious, but it couldn't be helped.

Silver looked down into the valley of dragons. Their sparkling colours whisked up towards her, reminding her of a gem-riddled cavern, but outside. It had been such a long time since she had been with so many dragons, and free. Oh, how she had missed it. Mountains, valleys—there were even a number of caves strewn throughout the range. It reminded her so much of the place that had once been her home.

A feeling of sadness washed over her. Home. The very thought of the valley she had grown up in made her wings droop and her shell dim. Dragon Valley had been the one place where she had been safe. She didn't have to constantly look over her shoulder, or worry about whether she would wake up in the morning still free. And if she were there, she'd still be with her family. She hadn't realised how much she would miss the annoying habits of Blaze, or the constant nuisance of Raize. Her father's counsel had helped her through so much, and her mother had always been there to help her in a mostly male family. Scarlet, the red fire dragon who was her mother; oh, she missed her the most. And now she would never get her back.

For the first time in her life, a trickle of sadness ran from her eye in a droplet of water. It spilled onto the snow-covered peak below her, and she watched it, surprised. She was crying? She sucked air into her lungs, trying to stop herself from thinking about home. She needed to be strong. Not just for the dragons around her but for herself. She was strength itself, one of the most powerful dragons on the earth. She shouldn't cry.

Dragon tears were rare, and dragons only shed them when they had experienced too much emotional trauma. And right now, that was how Silver felt. She was still young, very young. The weight that had fallen on her shoulders was crushing her, and at times she felt as though she was struggling to stand. For a year she had pushed the emotions down and focused on improving herself, but sometimes, even for a dragon as strong as herself, it was too much.

"Dammit," she said to herself, as more tears began to fall.

She shook her head and closed her eyes, holding back before the flood of emotions overwhelmed her. Doing this hurt, physically, but that was better than the emotional suffering it replaced. The pain cleared her head as she finally won the fight. Later. Not now.

Opening her eyes again, she gazed around the open sky, taking deep breaths. She opened her wings and lifted herself into the air once more. Flying always cleared her head. It always helped her not to think. That was what she needed now, to not think. Or at the very least think of something else. Trying to distract herself, she found a strange dot on the horizon. Fear shot through her as the thought of planes finally tracking them down came to her mind, but as it got closer she realised it wasn't a plane.

Frowning, she narrowed her vision and gasped in surprise, wavering in the air. It was a dragon. Definitely not one of hers—it was too far away. There was nothing on its head or around its neck, not that she could see anyway, and from its dark blue colour she guessed it was a water dragon. She frowned and began to wing her way towards it. The closer she got, the more certain she became that it wasn't one of hers.

When they got closer Silver recognised it as a male, and bigger than her, between twenty and thirty years old, so not the youngest of dragons. The two circled each other suspiciously, sizing the other up. Silver was still wary of the dragon, but excitement began to build in her. This dragon wasn't imprisoned, collared or controlled. He was free. And if this dragon was free, he may be able to show her to the dragon haven.

"Hello," she tried with him.

The dragon stopped, and Silver hovered as well. They faced each other. He frowned at her, narrowing his eyes. He opened his maw and spoke in a different language, causing her to return the frown. It sounded like Mandarin, though she couldn't be sure.

When the dragon saw that she didn't understand, he snorted and released a grunting growl. Silver blinked. It had been a long time since she had spoken in the dragon language, Drakin, preferring to speak English. The language consisted of grunts, hisses and growls. It was a little rough, and lacked the complexity of most human languages, but every dragon knew it innately.

"Let us speak in Drakin," snorted the water dragon.

Silver agreed. "That's better. Who are you?"

"I would ask the same question. I haven't seen your species before," he growled. "I would say that you were electric with some sort of armour, but your scales aren't those of an electric dragon."

"I'm metallic," she said.

"What?"

"A metal dragon. That's my species."

The water dragon faltered in the air, before looking at her in surprise once more. He had heard of metallic dragons, but had never seen one. Apparently, they were quite powerful, and from what he had heard, they were nearly impossible to defeat in a fight.

"What's your name?" he asked.

"Silver. You?"

"Kai."

Silver nodded. "Do you happen to know where the dragon haven is?"

She was being direct, and she knew it, but that was all she was wondering. If this dragon did know, then her work would be finished and she could relax a bit. The dragon tilted his head at her, seeming suspicious.

"What do you mean?"

"A place where there are lots of dragons. Where we can be safe."

"There are more of you?"

"Well, not of me, but I'm with a group of dragons."

"How many?"

"A few less than a hundred," she said.

"What!" the water dragon gaped at her in astonishment. "We had heard of a large group of dragons moving through our territory, but not that many. You have a small army."

Silver shrugged, "We escaped from … one of the dragon-hunter bases, destroying it as we went. They had quite a lot of us there, so when we got free we made a group and went looking for the haven."

"We could use a large group like that," Kai nodded. "Show me."

Silver hesitated, not knowing if she could trust the dragon. He could easily be another one of the human-corrupted dragons from D .E.D., or even just some lone beast who worked for whoever payed him. She had heard of dragons like that, but had never met one.

He saw her hesitation, and sighed. "I'm not going to turn you in or anything. If anyone should be worried it's me, especially if you have a hundred dragons on your side."

She shrugged and nodded in agreement. "Follow me."

She turned and began to fly to the encampment. Kai followed her, and she could feel him watching her back. He seemed trustworthy, and her gut was telling her he was, but she also knew he was a fighting dragon. That was evident from the scars he had running down his left flank, and the way he had held himself in the air when they had been hovering.

"How old are you?" he suddenly asked.

"Why do you want to know?" she shot back.

"No reason, but I'm just unused to seeing such a young dragoness by herself. Most dragons your age haven't even have left the nest," he said.

"I'm seven," she said. "And our valley was attacked. My father and one of my brothers were captured. My other brother escaped, and my mother … she died."

"Oh, I'm sorry," Kai said.

Silver didn't answer him, and flew around the peak of the snow-capped mountain she had landed on before. Just beyond it lay the valley where the dragons were resting. A small gasp came from behind her as Kai saw them. She could tell the water dragon was excited.

As she landed, the dragons greeted her and cast wary glances at the dragon behind her. She quickly reassured them that he could be trusted, or at least she thought he could. She was glad the dragon didn't speak English, for she was able to talk without worrying that he would understand.

"Who's this?" asked Zepos, walking up to them.

"Kai. He's from the dragon haven we've been looking for," Silver explained.

"Really?!" The electric dragon looked at Kai, fascinated.

"Yeah. He can lead us there."

"Told you it was real."

Silver rolled her eyes and turned to Kai, speaking in Drakin. "So can you take us there? To the dragon haven, I mean."

"If you mean Sky Mountain, then yes, I can take you there," the water dragon said.

"It isn't run by humans, is it?" asked a light green healing dragon who'd been listening.

Kai turned to her and shook his head. "No. While it is required we cooperate with them, we run our own operation."

"You cooperate with humans?" she snarled.

"It is necessary. We have a deal with the government of this land. They leave us alone if we give them scientific data. Also, humans help us build and give us updates on our enemies' movements," Kai explained. "You are still free to do as you wish, as long as you obey and respect our laws and leaders."

"Sounds just like another prison," the green dragon said, looking at Silver.

"You may not like it, but I agree with cooperating with humans. It's better than going it alone," Silver told the dragoness. "Even with our numbers, we won't survive much longer out here, especially with the number of enemies we have, who doubtless have many more dragons at their disposal than we do. We won't last the week."

"But, Silver," said a male fire dragon, "what if it's a trap? What if this dragon is just like Tetrad and his dragons?"

"He isn't," Silver said, looking at Kai. "He's a fighter, a dragon who's used to hardship, and a dragon like that wouldn't accept humans as his leaders."

Kai tilted his head at Silver in surprise. She smiled at him. She had always been a good judge of character, and often knew whether to trust someone or not. Occasionally she got it wrong, but this time she was nearly certain she hadn't.

"If you don't want to come, that's alright. Go. Find your own way," Silver said to the healing dragon. "But this is our best hope at the moment. For once, I'd like the opportunity to sleep a night without worrying whether or not I'll be in chains when I wake up."

The healing dragon hesitated, before nodding. "Fine. We trust you, Silver."

Silver smiled and nodded before saying to Kai, "Lead the way."

* * *

The dragons flew for about ten minutes over a large mountain range. The further they flew, the higher and wilder the mountains got. Freezing air made every breath they took look like smoke, creating a small cloud. Snow had started falling around them, making even the fire dragons shiver.

Silver looked over at Kai jealously. He didn't seem to be affected at all by the cold, and continued flying as if there was nothing to worry about. The shell on her back was so cold it nearly hurt, but she went on, hoping they were nearly there.

Suddenly, Kai took a sharp turn to the left and dove towards the ground below. Frowning, Silver followed, as did the rest of the dragons. They levelled out in a valley that sheltered them from the cold winds. Kai didn't slow, and turned a sharp corner into another valley. Gritting her teeth, Silver followed with the rest of the dragons, who tried not to crash into each other in the limited space.

The valley opened up, revealing more mountains stretching to the horizon. Silver sighed, wondering which one was Sky Mountain, and if they were even close yet. With a snort, she continued to follow the water dragon. Suddenly, the air rippled, and the endless mountains in front of them fell away into nothingness. Silver gasped, coming to a stop.

Ahead, hidden by whatever had made the sky ripple, lay a large crater spreading for kilometres in every direction. Sunshine pierced the clouds, lighting up the largest mountain any of the dragons had seen. It shot up from the crater's centre like a giant spike. The mountain's very width was something to be amazed at, covering the area of a large human city. The peak pierced the clouds ranging around the top, obscuring it from view.

Murmurs ran among the dragons as they entered the area, finally seeing what Silver was seeing. It was astonishing, and more so because it could be hidden so well. She wondered how they did it. It probably had something to do with mind dragons.

Other dragons milled around the mountain, some in groups and others by themselves. There were hundreds of them, far more than the group Silver was leading, and probably more than there had been at Dragon Valley. She looked at Kai, who was waiting for them, shock written on her face.

"Welcome to Sky Mountain," he said with a grin.

Chapter 20:
A Reunion

Silver gaped in amazement at the entrance to Sky Mountain, forgetting to flap her wings for a moment. With a grunt, she stumbled to a landing on the beautiful yet hard stone floors, her talons scratching lines in the ornate carvings.

The half-dome entrance reached hundreds of metres into the air. Its arch was hewn from the same stone as the floor, and depicted a tableau of battling dragons and their elements. The top of the arch formed a front-on image of a dragon with spread wings.

As the group followed Kai through the entrance, they attracted many curious glances and stares from the dragons occupying Sky Mountain. The interior was just as spectacular as the exterior. Small groups of trees, and even whole forests, spread across a vast area that reached high into the mountain. A waterfall fell from one side, filling a stream that split the floor in two before it babbled through the entrance. Dragons crowded the area in their hundreds, representing all the thirteen known species, from the common fire and water dragons to the extremely rare light and dark. Seeing them all in one place astounded Silver, especially the few she had never seen before.

"Well … this was unexpected," Zepos said, looking around in astonishment.

"I know. I never knew there could be so many dragons in one place," Silver gaped. "How many do you think there are?"

"A lot more than in Dragon Valley, that much is sure," he replied.

Kai turned to them and smiled, before speaking in Drakin. "This is The Centre, the largest area of Sky Mountain. It is where dragons come to socialise, where some classes are taught, where assemblies are held. The Centre is one of the five main sections of Sky Mountain. The others are The Training Centre, The School, The Nest and The Lab. They are each rather self-explanatory."

The dragons hardly heard him, still dumbfounded at The Centre. It was bigger than anything any of them had seen before. Compared to the D.E.D. base they destroyed, it was at least twice the size, but there were many more dragons here.

"How many dragons are here?" Silver asked Kai.

"Including you? Now we have 2,398 dragons, and fourteen species," said Kai with a proud grin. "Our leader, Iraliene, is one of the oldest dragonesses in the world. She celebrated her four-hundred-and-eighty-fifth hatchday last week. She is a life dragon, one of the world's most powerful."

"Life dragon?" Silver questioned.

"The proper name for a healing dragon," explained Kai.

"Oh." Silver turned her eyes back to the dragons roaming around her.

Some of them gazed at her. She wondered if they had other metallic dragons here, or if she and her father were truly the only ones. She hoped not, though it was likely. She could hear the dragons whispering to each other, staring at the new group before them, particularly at the rarer dragons like Celestia.

A fire dragon caught her eye, and she frowned. They made eye contact, and she froze. The fire dragon froze as well as they stared at each other in disbelief. He was bigger than last she had seen him, seeming to have grown leaner, much like her. A new scar lined his snout and his eyes shone with an intelligent glint that hadn't been there before. But it was still the same dragon.

"Raize?" she said incredulously, more to herself than anyone else.

Her brother excused himself from his conversation and began to walk towards the new group of dragons, staring at Silver in disbelief. He began to trot, still watching his sister. He had thought her dead, or at least gone to one of the dragon-hunting organisations.

"Silver!" he called over the murmuring voices.

"Raize, it is you!" Silver laughed, breaking away from the group and running up to her brother.

The two embraced, wrapping their wings around each other in a dragon's hug. Stepping back, they stared at each other for a moment, still struggling to believe who they were seeing. Raize was slightly taller than her now, maybe by a foot or so, but she was thicker, which surprised her.

"What are you doing here?" Raize asked.

"What am I doing here? What are you doing here?" Silver said.

The fire dragon laughed. "A long story I'll have to reserve for another time, but wow. I guess I expected you to get here eventually, but after almost a year of waiting I'd given up hope. You're smaller than I remember."

"Smaller?!" she growled playfully. "Is that what you think? I could still kick your butt."

"Still the fiery attitude, I see," her brother grinned back, flashing his teeth. "You'll have to tell me your story as well, y'know. I've looked everywhere for you."

Silver looked away, a bit ashamed she couldn't say the same thing. "I thought you were captured."

He smiled at her gently. "Well, I'm not."

They shared a gaze, and she smiled back. Oh, how she had missed him. She was finally reunited with another family member.

"Raize! How did I know we would find you here?" Zepos came padding up to the two siblings.

"Zepos! Wow. I didn't think I would see you here. I thought you got captured by A.O.D.H.," the fire dragon said, surprised to the see Zepos.

"Silver managed to free me," Zepos said, "and we've been helping each other out ever since."

"You freed him?" Raize looked at his sister in surprise.

"I found a way," she said, smiling. "If you overload one of their devices with electricity, it breaks."

"Wow, that's great news. You'll have to tell Iraliene as soon as possible. We've been looking for a way to do that for a long time," Raize smiled.

They turned to see Kai looking at them in confusion. The water dragon was suspicious of them, unused to seeing such familiarity between two dragons who had seemingly just met. He had a paranoia that came from scouting for a powerful enemy, and was suspicious of anything unusual. He walked over to them.

"Hey, Kai." Raize grinned at the water dragon, speaking in Drakin. "Remember my sister I told you about? Well, this is her."

The scout's eyes widened in surprise as he looked back and forth at the pair. It was uncommon to see two siblings of different species, but not unheard of, especially among the rarer dragons.

"You didn't tell me your brother was here," he said to Silver.

"I didn't know," the dragoness shrugged. "It was a welcome surprise, though."

The water dragon smiled. It was good to see younger dragons, especially siblings, getting along so well. Sometimes siblings caused havoc, and he had to deal with it. Though from what he knew of Raize's troublemaking, the two of them getting on so well didn't seem like a good omen.

"You came in with quite a crowd." Raize looked towards the hundred dragons she had rescued. "What happened?"

"We escaped from D.E.D.," Silver said, "and took them with us."

"D.E.D.! Wow, you seem to have had a bigger adventure than I had."

"I heard you escaped as well. You'll have to tell me how you did that."

"I did," the fire dragon said with a grin, "though now it doesn't seem as good, 'cause you did it too. Once I found you, I was planning on that being my boasting point."

"Well, now it's mine," Silver chuckled.

"Hey, Kai, do you mind if I take Silver from you for a few minutes, just to show her around a little? I'll give her back when Iraliene talks to them."

"I don't see why not." The water dragon sighed and turned away from them, walking back to where the rest of the dragons were waiting.

"I'll be back," Silver called to her group, seeing their worry and confusion. "I'm just catching up with my brother."

They sent a few understanding and surprised nods in her direction, before turning back to Kai, who led them away.

"You should go with them," Silver said to Zepos.

"Why?"

"Just to keep them together," Silver said, "and answer any questions they have."

The electric dragon hesitated. "But ..."

"I'll be fine. Just go."

Zepos snorted before trotting back to the group. She watched him go and sighed. As much as she wanted not to, she was beginning to like the electric dragon. He had changed so much since Dragon Valley, and it seemed for the better.

"Zepos seems different," Raize said.

"I know," Silver replied, "I think it's good. He's more ... grown-up."

"Are you beginning to like him, as in ... you know?" Raize said, his eyes bulging.

"No!" Silver blushed, before turning away. "Maybe a little."

He laughed and shook his head. "My sister has a crush."

"It's not a crush," she hissed.

"Okay, okay, whatever you say, sis," he said, still laughing. "Follow me."

He flapped his wings and rose into the air. Silver grumbled before following him, and together they soared high above the dragons below. The dragoness couldn't stay mad for long, though, as the wonder of the place below filled her once more. She realised the many plants and trees spread throughout the area were arranged in the image of a dragon with its wings spread. The waterfall was at its head and the stream flowed out from its tail.

Raize flew up beside her. "Amazing, isn't it?"

Silver only nodded.

"It's a wonder how they made this place," her brother continued. "It required a bit of help from some powerful life and earth dragons and an intelligent human architect."

The two flew in silence for a moment, gazing down at the dragons below. They welcomed each other's company, for as much as they didn't want to admit it, finding each other had filled a hole in themselves. Now they were together, they felt as if they could do anything.

"Hey, Silver," Raize said. "Do you know … did you hear what happened to … Mum?"

Silver only nodded her head.

He sighed. "I miss her."

"Same," Silver smiled sadly. "I guess we'll have to make sure it doesn't happen to another one of us."

"Yeah." He went silent again.

A black dragon passed below them without even looking up, its dark scales absorbing the light around it. Silver shivered at the sight. Historically, many dark dragons had been evil, though now it seemed different. There had been another dark dragon at Dragon Valley, though she had often kept to herself.

"Hey, I better get you back," Raize said. "Iraliene will want to see you."

"Yeah, of course." Silver shook herself out of her thoughts.

Her brother led her back down to where her dragons had congregated. They landed, and he gave her another hug. She smiled and nudged him.

"I'll see you later, okay?" he said. "I've got a class I need to get to."

"See you later … brother." Silver grinned and poked him with her tail.

Raize rolled his eyes before running off into the crowds of dragons. Silver watched him for a moment, before turning her gaze to Kai, who was speaking to the dragons.

Chapter 21:
The Hierarchy

"As with all new dragons, our leader Iraliene will want to meet you in person," Kai said in Drakin. "Now if you would just … wait, here she comes."

He looked over the group to a light green dragon who flew towards them at a leisurely pace. She was a healing dragon, or life dragon, with glittering emerald scales that shone with an odd brilliance that would make females jealous and males swoon. She was easily the biggest dragon any of them had seen, even larger then Tetrad. Her wing beats seemed slow and calculated, like every movement was purposefully flawless, and she flew with a grace only experience could grant.

As she flew over the new group of dragons, their gazes followed her, transfixed by the glory she represented. She had always done this, every time a new group of dragons, especially a large group, came to Sky Mountain. It was easier to talk to them then, and they were much more likely to accept her as their leader. She smiled at them, her flashing teeth sharp and shaped to perfection.

With a graceful sweep of her wings she came to a well-rehearsed landing, not even shaking the ground despite her bulk. Her domineering yellow eyes struck the dragons in front of her, and she was delighted when they looked away. They could see how powerful she was, how brilliant she was. They could see she was the leader, and no-one would dare challenge her authority. Iraliene thought this a brilliant start, but an expected one given she had been performing this same act for over four hundred years.

One dragon, though, didn't fall for her entrance, or the choreographed movements that put on show her confidence, strength and leadership. A dragoness with a silver shell that sparkled gloriously in the flickering light stared right back at her, matching her piercing gaze with one just as dominant, something that was unexpected from a dragon so young. Iraliene had met with dragons like this before. They were trouble at the beginning but afterwards they fell into line.

She turned her gaze to the other dragons, searching for any willful enough to challenge her rule. None. Satisfied, she bowed—not too low, not too high—adding a graceful sweep of the wings for effect.

"Hello, my new subordinates," she spoke in the most eloquent Drakin the dragons had likely heard. "I am Elder Iraliene, leader of Sky Mountain for nigh on two hundred and seventy-six years. And I welcome you with open wings." She spread her wings regally. "We are glad to have you here, for every dragon that arrives strengthens us, every dragon gives our species a greater chance of survival. So yes, welcome, welcome."

A few of the dragons in the crowd murmured their appreciative thanks.

"Am I right to assume that you have escaped from the ruthless organisation D.E.D.?" Iraliene asked.

There was a nod and a murmured "yes" from the crowd.

"I notice the collar marks around your neck. I see you are malnourished, your scales are tattered, your claws dull. Here you will grow. Here you will become great. Here you all will have the life you have wanted, free of D.E.D. Here, you will have an opportunity for revenge."

At that, heads looked up. It was a winning point.

"Here we fight to rid the world of corporations like D.E.D. and A.O.D.H. Here we fight to rid the world of the tyranny of dragon hunters, and we will find a way to destroy them all, so we can live in peace once again. The only thing I ask is you respect the dragons that are your superiors. In perhaps a few years you will ascend the hierarchy, but until then do your best to help us in Sky Mountain, and we will see you set free from the fear of humans."

She looked over the dragons for a moment, seeing if they had accepted what she had said. A few nodded their heads. Others looked excited, and still others seemed hesitant. She wouldn't blame them. This place was a strict society, one she had worked hard to build. It only worked if every dragon did their part, and she hoped this large group would do what they were told. But there was still one thing she had to clear up before she left Kai to show them where they were going to be staying.

"Now, I would like to know which dragon your group considers their leader," she said.

The dragons seemed to hesitate for a moment. It was only natural. After seeing her they would think their current leader was a little less magnificent then they first thought, but as they turned to look towards the back she realised this wasn't true. Their gazes showed reverence, nervousness and even a little bit of fear. And they all pointed towards the young silver dragoness at the back of the crowd. The one who hadn't looked away. The dragoness walked through the crowd to the front.

Iraliene frowned as she looked at this dragon. The shell on her back wasn't armour. It was part of her. A metallic dragon. But as far as she knew, there were only two in existence. One captured by A.O.D.H. and the other lost. Unless …

"Silver, I thought I recognised you from somewhere." Iraliene smiled kindly at the young dragon.

Silver frowned. "How …?"

"Oh, don't you remember me, darling?" the large life dragon said. "We met when you were but a hatchling. A few weeks out of the egg. I travelled to Dragon Valley to speak to your father."

The dragoness didn't know what to say, so she stayed silent. She didn't remember their meeting, but then again, she remembered little from her infancy.

"And now you have ended up here. After A.O.D.H. attacked your valley I feared you were dead," Iraliene continued. "But I see you are not, and you are no less than a leader of a large group of dragons. You must feel proud."

"I rescued them. I'm not their leader," Silver said, standing up taller and looking the older dragoness in the eye. "They are their own dragons."

"But still, you command their respect," Iraliene smiled. "That is quite an accomplishment for someone your age. Would you not agree?"

Silver stayed silent.

"Hmm. How old are you, Silver?"

"Eight in a few months," she replied.

"My, my, you are young. It seems like such a long time ago that I saw you last." Iraliene sighed, as if thinking back to the time.

Silver shrugged. "Doesn't mean I'm inadequate. I'm just as strong as any other dragon at this place."

"What makes you so sure about that?" Iraliene said.

"Because I know what I'm capable of."

Iraliene snorted. "We'll see about that."

Before Silver had a chance to answer, the larger dragon turned away from her towards the rest of the dragon crowd. "Kai will lead you to your nests. I will be seeing you around. You will be given schedules of what is expected of you and will be expected to stick to those schedules. For those who cannot read, I suggest you learn fast."

The green dragoness nodded to Kai, before launching herself into the air once more with a wing stroke powerful enough to blow a human from their feet. She looped once over the crowd before soaring off into The Centre. Silver couldn't help but let a growl escape her throat. Maybe it was a mistake to come to this place.

* * *

As promised, Kai led them straight to The Nest. It didn't take long. They walked through a short tunnel, filled with more dragon carvings, before they entered another large area. Unlike The Centre, The Nest wasn't made to perfection. A large rocky cavern stretched high into the mountain. Jagged cliffs formed walls that were dotted with caves. Dragons entered and exited the caves in swarms. The younger dragons seemed to be at the bottom of the cavern and the older dragons were at the top.

"Okay, dragons under eight, please stay here. You will be taken care of by Gretta, a fire dragoness who handles younglings. She should be here any moment. The rest of you follow me," said Kai.

"What about me?" asked Silver.

"Are you under eight?"

"Yes, but …"

"Then you stay here," Kai sighed, "I'm sorry. But it's the rule."

"A stupid rule," she muttered to herself in English, but she obeyed.

The rest of the dragons left, leaving a mere five behind, including Silver. Zepos gave her a mournful look, but he was approaching nine now, so he was forced to leave. The few dragons that remained were an ice dragon, with freezing blue scales and sharp daggers along his spine, two winds dragons who couldn't be more than three and a water dragoness who was slightly younger than Silver.

With a grunting sigh, she sat on her haunches and angrily waited for Gretta. She was no longer a hatchling, having lived by herself for over a year, and could take care of herself. It was insulting, but she didn't want to anger Iraliene. As much as she hated the thought, they needed the protection of Sky Mountain, and if she had to do this to get it, she would. Though this would change as soon as she was powerful enough to take A.O.D.H. by herself.

A fire dragoness, who Silver guessed to be around a hundred years old, landed before them. She was large, but not muscular. Silver had never seen a fat dragon before, but that was the only way to describe this dragoness before her. Of course, when a dragoness was gravid, she got bigger, but never as big as Gretta.

"Are … you must be the new lot," the fire dragon said in English, "Come this way, my darlings. I will show you your new homes."

Silver suppressed a growl. She didn't like mollycoddling, though she was sure this dragon had the best intentions. She was no longer a hatchling. That life was far behind. It was insulting to be treated like one. But best to set an example. The other dragons were looking at her, willing her to lead. Though they were separated from the rest of the pack now, she was still the one in charge. With a nod of her head, they followed Gretta.

The fire dragoness noticed the exchange and frowned. She knew that this dragoness was a new species to Sky Mountain, but didn't know who she was or what she was capable of.

As they walked, the ice dragon fell in beside her. "I didn't know you weren't even eight yet."

"Surprised?" Silver smiled weakly. "I'm eight in a couple of months."

"Me too," said the ice dragon with a grin, "Though you're much more amazing than I am. "

"I just had the opportunity to be," replied Silver. "Where I lived, I had to be tough. And being a metal dragon helps as well."

The ice dragon chuckled. "Name's Ion. And I know you're Silver."

Silver laughed as well. "Yes, forgive me if I haven't memorised all of your names."

"Eh, didn't expect you to," said Ion. "I'm just surprised you managed to lead us the way you did."

"I wasn't really leading," Silver replied, "I just managed to free you guys. You don't need to be a good leader to be an excellent fighter."

"I know, but the way you handled those dragons was amazing. Many of us were actually scared of you after that, though not so much anymore."

"I think I scared myself, honestly," Silver sighed. "I didn't know I was capable of that."

"Yeah? Well, I only wish I could. You defeated two dragons who were at least a hundred years old, and fended off four," Ion said, vexed at his own lack of power. "I want you to teach me how to fight, 'cause that was amazing."

The dragoness flushed at the compliment. "I was trained by the greatest dragon in the world. You should see him fight. I couldn't land a hit on him."

"I doubt that. Who is this dragon?" Ion asked.

"My father, Elron, the first metallic dragon," Silver said. "He taught me all … no, most of what I can do."

"So you must be an extremely rare species then," Ion said.

"There's only two of us," Silver said. "My father and me."

Before Ion could say any more, Gretta stopped them at two large caves at ground level. The few dragons Silver saw coming in and out of them were very young, many younger than her, which was strange. She was used to most dragons being older.

"Okay, females into the left cave and males into the right," said Gretta, "Your programs should be waiting for you, though you won't have time tonight to do anything. So I will see you tomorrow morning. Bright an' early!"

The two younger wind dragons groaned before heading towards the male dragons' cave. Ion went with them, glancing at Silver before moving on. Silver and the water dragon entered the female section. It was somewhat relieving to finally be away from all the other dragons who had become part of her life, though she wished she could have a nest outside the cave.

The females' cave was a smaller cavern with about a hundred nests spread throughout the floor. Not all of them were filled, but it was obvious which nests were taken and which were not. A sudden tiredness filled the dragoness and she quickly found an empty nest towards the back of the cavern, falling into it with a grunt. It was time she had a good sleep. She would worry about building a metal nest later.

CHAPTER 22:
WEAKNESS OF METAL

"WAKE up, my darlings!" came Gretta's annoyingly mothering voice as she poked her head into the females' cave.

Groans of complaint rose from the sleeping dragonesses, but one by one they got to their feet, slowly making their way out of the cave. Silver opened one eye and sighed. She hadn't slept well. Straw from the nest had worked its way under her scales and poked into her skin. She had woken up many times during the night to remove them. It sucked having softer-than-normal scales.

Grunting, she hauled herself to her feet, fanning her wings to steady herself. She felt so tired. Her claws clacked against the ground, irritating her as she stumbled out of the cave.

I need to cut my claws, she thought as she saw how long they'd grown.

Shrugging, she decided to take care of it later. She walked into The Nest and winced as unnatural light shone throughout the cavern. A few of the other young dragons did the same, a hiss escaping a fire dragon at her left. Once her eyes adjusted, she looked around to see dragons leaving their caves along the jagged cliffs. There were thousands of them, and Silver couldn't help but feel a little nervous at seeing so many.

"Silver! So you did make it!" Raize's familiar voice came from the crowd of youngling dragons.

Silver smiled faintly when she saw her brother. He leapt over the crowd with a flap of her wings and landed next to her, giving her a friendly shove. She growled at him but shook her head, refusing to retaliate. She would get her revenge later.

"Have a good sleep?" he asked.

"Nope," she grunted. "The nests have too much straw and I didn't have time to make my own."

"Oh, that's right. You don't like comfortable sleeping quarters."

"They're not comfortable. They're annoying, painful and incredibly difficult to get a good night's sleep on."

"Ha! Well, deal with it, 'cause until you make your own, you'll have to."

"Shut up."

The crowd jostled their way through The Nest and into The Centre. It was even brighter there, as the sun shone directly at the entrance of the mountain, beaming its rays at the still-waking dragons. It glinted off Silver's shell, which lit up the room even more. A few dragons around her shied away at the sudden light. She growled in embarrassment and dulled her shell quickly.

"Where to first?" she asked her brother.

"Didn't you bring your program?" Raize chuckled. "Don't worry, I'll help you. We got combat training first."

"Cool!" Silver's mood instantly brightened. "Is that fun?"

"Yes, it can be. Though with you … just try not to kill anyone," he said, knowing full well what she could do.

"I'll go safe." She shrugged, and let the metal on her wings ripple into a blunt edge. She had kept it sharp ever since she had been captured by D.E.D. "What can I expect?"

"Well, at the moment I'm the best, that's with the rankings, but there are a few who are probably better than me," said Raize, "So, you'll basically smash everyone."

She laughed. "You've probably gotten better, you know."

"So have you," Raize said. "I made friends with … Ion, I think, one of your dragons, and he told me what had happened at D.E.D. I tried to fight Tetrad when I got free, and was slaughtered. You defeated all four of their fighters without much trouble at all."

"I had help," Silver insisted.

"I know, but still, that's amazing."

She sighed, tired of being praised for her success. If she hadn't been a metal dragon she doubted she would be able to overcome many of the challenges that had been thrown at her. A metal shell is a good shield against anything, even fear. She didn't know what she would do without it.

The dragons began to split up into groups. The hatchlings followed Gretta while the older dragons, being six and seven, made their own way to The Training Centre, another large cavern with smooth stone walls and a flat base. The remains of dragon elements were scattered around – a patch of ice, a stone spike stuck in the wall. It didn't look that amazing to Silver, but it seemed suited to its purpose. Artificial light filtered into the room from globes hanging on the ceiling. It wasn't sunlight, but at least it didn't make Silver's shell shine.

The adolescent dragons all assembled at a small ground at the edge of the arena. There were about fifty of them, with a near even split between males and females. No rare dragons were among them, besides perhaps the single mind dragon on the edge of the crowd, and Silver of course. Most were fire dragons, as usual, but a few more interesting dragons stood among them. A brown-scaled telekinetic dragon was sitting at one side of the group, talking to a dark green acid dragon and an ice dragon – probably the most diverse group in the class.

Soon their teacher arrived. He flew down from somewhere above The Training Centre and landed in front of the dragons. He was an ice dragon, around fifty years old and bigger than any of those in front of him. The spikes characteristic of ice dragons seemed longer and sharper than usual. Icy scales seemed to steal the heat from the room, and a few of the dragons shivered. He had a strong build, not too big, but not small, and was quite handsome. An all-rounder in a fight, Silver thought, and quite powerful, judging from the cold radiating from him. The more powerful a dragon, the more at one with their element they were.

"Good morning, my pupils," said the ice dragon in gruff Drakin. "I hear we have a few newer students here today, three, to be exact. Would Waylene, Ion and Silver come forwards, please."

"This is going to be interesting," Raize muttered to his sister, before pushing her towards the ice dragon.

She snapped playfully at him, causing him to roll his eyes, before walking to the front. She gave Ion and Waylene, the water dragoness, a polite nod. They nodded back before turning their attention to the ice dragon in front of them.

"My name is Frezron," he said, studying the three new dragons and paying close attention to Silver. "But while you are in my class you will call me 'master' or 'mentor'. My aim is to teach you to be the most powerful dragon you can be, and make you battle-ready for your fight against A.O.D.H., D.E.D. or the other dragon hunters out there. Understand?"

The three of them nodded.

"Now, before we start today's class I want to test each of you to see how you compare to your fellow students," Frezron said. "You others can either watch or spar with a partner."

A life dragon entered The Training Centre from one corner and walked over to them. She was another large dragon, maybe a little younger than Frezron. Her scales didn't shine like Iraliene's, but she was beautiful in her own way.

"This is my mate, Reha. You will respect her like you will me. She will heal any major injuries you sustain from fighting. If you are injured, stop immediately and ask for assistance. Dragons have died during this training before." The ice dragon was serious.

The three of them nodded. Silver sighed quietly to herself. She was going to have to hold back or she could kill someone with a single stroke of her tail. This meant using blunt spikes and dull breath attacks. Maybe she could use a few sharp edges, but nothing too dangerous.

She was intrigued to fight Frezron, never having faced an ice dragon before. She had never liked the cold, mainly because it slowed her movements, so she was curious about how she would cope against the winds of ice that this dragon would summon.

"Now, the first of you will be … Silver. I have never faced a metallic dragon before, and am looking forwards to see what you are capable of," he said with a grin.

Silver returned his grin and nodded eagerly. She still didn't know the full capabilities of these dragons, but they didn't know how powerful she was either.

Frezron led her onto the training field. They took positions a few metres away from each other. The rest of the dragons surrounded the edge to watch, wanting to know how this new species of dragon fought. They had all heard stories about her—word travelled fast in Sky Mountain—and a few of them didn't believe them. There was only one way to find out.

"Three … two … one … fight!" Reha yelled, seemingly the referee of this clash.

Neither dragon moved. Silver recalled something her father had said to her: "If you don't know the capabilities of the being you are fighting, let them attack first. That first attack shows how good they really are." Frezron seemed to follow the same rule. He smiled at her. The new dragoness wasn't stupid.

Frezron attacked first with such blinding speed Silver nearly missed it. His tail flicked towards her, sending a volley of ice spikes in her direction, one of her own favourite attacks. With a hiss, she swung a wing at them, the spikes shattering harmlessly against the metal shield, before she launched an attack of her own. She would try to go close range with this dragon, knowing that his elemental attacks were probably more powerful than hers.

She leapt forwards, spraying a stream of metal at him. The ice dragon rolled out of the way and the liquid metal froze where it landed. She was smaller than Frezron, and that made her quicker. She adjusted her leap with a flap of her wings and clashed head-on with the ice dragon. Her sharp claws made quick work of his scales, slashing, scratching and scraping at his sides. He snarled in pain, slashing back at her. He caught the top of her head, where the metal shell was, knocking it away with a loud clang as claw met metal.

Silver stumbled backwards, the other dragon stronger than she thought, and blinked to clear her sight. But her hesitation allowed Frezron to counterattack. He took the opportunity, and fiercely, swiping at her with his tail. But he made the mistake of hitting the shell on her back. The ice blade on his tail shattered into a thousand pieces. Startled, he fumbled.

Silver quickly drove herself at him, stabbing her horns upwards at the dragon's underbelly. The ice dragon anticipated the attack and caught her neck with his paw, ramming her into the ground. She grunted in surprise as the wind was knocked out of her.

Frezron stood back, keeping a hold on her neck, and blasted her muzzle with a breath of freezing wind. The dragoness whimpered as the cold froze her muzzle to the ground. He then froze her neck, trapping her against the floor. She growled and tried to struggle out of the ice, but it resisted. She attempted to inhale, but nothing flowed into her lungs. Her eyes widened in fear. She couldn't breathe. Her tenacity grew as she desperately tried to break the ice around her neck.

Silver bladed her tail and struck a hole in the ice, allowing air to flow in. She took a few deep breaths before cutting the ice with her tail. With a cry, she broke it, raising her head and glaring at the ice dragon who had come so close to defeating her. Frezron, having begun to walk back to his pupils, spun around.

"How ... no dragon has ever broken that ice," he growled.

"It's quite easy to cut," Silver replied with a grin, before ploughing forwards once more.

Frezron sent a powerful stream of ice in her direction. She jumped and flapped her wings, pulling herself into the air and shooting a stream of metal at Frezron, aiming for his right foreleg. Instead she hit his wing as he raised it in defence. The metal splattered against it harmlessly. Silver snorted in annoyance. At least he would find it harder to fly.

She twisted in the air as another volley of ice spikes flew her way, this time from the ice dragon's maw. With a growl, she flicked her tail, sending her own—far more dangerous—spikes in his direction. She didn't bother blunting them. The spikes wouldn't kill him immediately, giving him enough time to be healed by the life dragon.

Frezron snarled and leapt out of the way, but one of the spikes glanced off his leg, taking a number scales with it. With a roar, he leapt into the air with a clumsy flap, weighed down by his unbalanced wings. Taking advantage of his fumble, Silver dived on him and crashed into his back. But to her surprise, he flipped as she did, and growled as she crashed onto the ground, landing on her back with him on top.

Not wasting his opportunity, he carved a long gash in her chest, and Silver roared in pain. The soft scales on her unprotected stomach didn't provide much protection against the ice dragon's claws. With a snarl, she fired a stream of metal up at his maw. The stream wrapped around his muzzle, trapping it shut. He snarled, surprised by the move. Silver then attacked with her own claws, viciously driving them into the dragon's underbelly. He moaned and leapt backwards with a sweep of his wings.

Silver rolled to her feet and let out a wheezing cough. Blood oozed from her chest. But Frezron was worse off, numerous cuts marking his body. Both dragons breathed heavily, trying to block out the pain that now racked their bodies.

"Stuff this," snorted Silver. It was time to get serious.

The shell on her back grew, crawling down her legs and under her stomach. She exhaled with relief, closing her eyes and letting the metal do its work. She was invincible. Nothing could destroy her. Nothing.

Now in her full-metal form, she opened her glowing red eyes, which stood out against her armour, gazing at the ice dragon who was the cause of her pain. He stared in surprise, his muzzle still held shut by the metallic stream. Silver limped towards him. Metal armour didn't heal wounds, and the one that Frezron had dealt her hurt horribly.

The ice dragon growled as he backed away. Silver moved carefully, knowing she was slower with full-metal armour. It wouldn't take much for the ice dragon to dodge her. She needed to trap him and then strike.

So focused she was on the dragon that she didn't see the ice that had been thrown around the clearing begin to move. Frezron's scales began to glow an odd blue colour as a freezing wind gathered around them. The dragons who had been watching the fight backed away from them, knowing what was going to happen.

Silver stood, oblivious to the cold wind and whipping ice. All she noticed was her armour growing cooler. On her next step, the shell let out a creak of complaint, the coolness of the wind making it much stiffer and harder to move. Silver grunted in surprise.

A grin formed on Frezron's muzzle and, roaring as much as he could with his muzzle shut, he thrust his wings forwards. The ice, wind and cold assaulted the metallic dragon at once, battering hard into her in a swirling hurricane. Silver roared in surprised and held up her wing to shield herself. It hardly helped, the wind surrounding her.

But she staggered forwards defiantly. Grunts, creaks and groans sounded as her motion grew harder and harder, until she struggled to move even a leg.

"No!" she growled, forcing herself to take one more step, then another, and then … nothing. She couldn't move, not matter how hard she tried. Ice coated her limbs. Her metal shell was so cold its usual malleability was lost. She was trapped in her own armour.

The ice, wind and cold disappeared as Frezron limped towards her, victorious. He nearly laughed when he realised the dragoness was frozen stiff in the sub-zero temperatures. He was surprised she was still alive. Her metal shell proved a force to be reckoned with. He doubted he would have survived another clash with her. He stared into her eyes, silently telling her to admit to defeat.

Silver stared back, before lowering her eyes in defeat. There was no way around it. Not when she couldn't move. Frezron nodded and gestured to the dragons around them with his head. Raize quickly left the crowd and ran to the two dragons.

"That was awesome!" he said to his sister.

Silver rolled her eyes in response.

With a quick breath, her brother bathed her in fire. It took a minute or two, but the heat eased the stiffness in her armour and before long she could move again. She let her shell withdraw to its normal length with a shiver, the cold still in her bones. A trickle of blood ran to the ground as the metal armour retracted.

Frezron pointed to the shining metal strip that had trapped his muzzle, and tilted his head. With a grin, Silver bladed her tail and sliced the band off with a single stroke. The ice dragon opened his maw, testing it for any other damage. Satisfied, he returned Silver's grin.

"My, my. I don't doubt those stories now. That was the best fight I've had in ages," he said.

"I know," Silver said, still a little disappointed at being defeated so easily.

"We know what your weakness is now," Raize said.

"What?" she looked at her brother.

"Ice. You couldn't even move!"

Silver shrugged. "I guess so."

"I never would have guessed. And we thought it was electricity or something."

"Definitely not that."

Frezron watched the exchange with interest, before butting in. "Raize, let your sister be healed."

Raize nodded and stepped back, allowing the two dragons to walk over to where Reha was waiting for them. She nodded her astonishment at the silver dragon before opening her maw and bathing her in a splash of green energy. A gasp left Silver as a strange sensation ran through her. The wound on her stomach closed easily, as did her other small scratches. She was completely healed. She stepped back in amazement as Reha did the same thing with her mate.

Silver's first day at this place seemed to be going well so far.

CHAPTER 23:
THE GRAVITY DRAGON

THE days went by quickly for Silver. Soon they turned into weeks, and then months. It was all the same. Wake up early with a call from Gretta, and then on to a couple of hours with Frezron. After that the dragons went to The School, where they were put through gruelling hours of lectures about dragons and their different species, their abilities, strengths and weaknesses, and other dragon miscellany.

As much as she didn't want to admit it, Silver learnt quite a lot. There were fourteen species of dragons alive now, with a rumoured fifteenth. These species were split into three different categories: energy, physical and mental. And each species was on a scale from common to practically extinct. Silver was surprised to learn that her species fit into the physical category, and was practically extinct, as there were only two known metal dragons in the world.

After a while, though, it got boring and often she tuned out of her lessons, lost in her mind. She wanted to create her statues again. It had been so long since she had done something with her powers other than fight. At least she had managed to build her nest.

But it dismayed her that she hadn't been able to see her older friends that often. Occasionally she and Zepos managed to get together, but often only for a quick greeting before they were whisked away to their next lesson. She got to see Celestia even less, the light dragon being in special training somewhere in the mountain. Apparently, the rarer dragons got special treatment once they turned eight. That was another two months away for Silver.

She sighed as she lay her head down on a soft pillow-like thing on a long bed. She was in The Lab, the part of Sky Mountain where dragons were "studied" by human scientists. The data was sent to the Chinese government, where it was analysed somewhere that Silver didn't pay enough attention to know about. Now she was lying on her stomach with her right wing stretched under a microscope, with an excited young Asian scientist hurriedly scribbling down notes, glancing through the microscope occasionally.

"Amazing," he kept on saying in English. "Simply amazing."

Silver rolled her eyes in response. She wanted to get out of here as soon as possible. After this was done she had free time for the rest of the day, and she didn't want to waste the opportunity. She already knew how amazing she was.

"It's like it's alive," the scientist said, taking a longer than usual glance into the microscope.

"Of course I'm alive," Silver couldn't help but say sarcastically.

"No, not you. The metal. It's alive. But that's impossible," the human replied, getting excited again. "It's like a whole different type of ... creature. Different from fungi, plant or flesh. It has its own unique set of cells, different from anything we've seen before."

"And why should I care?" Silver muttered to herself, studying one of her newly sharpened and trimmed claws.

The scientist didn't hear her. "And you control them. Do you think I could grab a sample? Just for scientific reasons, of course."

"If you can cut a piece off," replied the dragoness.

He nodded eagerly and reached into his pocket, taking out a small knife. He gently pressed the knife against her wing and drew it along, creating an annoying shriek. Silver hissed and drew her wing back, and the knife clattered to the ground.

"You really thought that would work?" she said.

"What ... I don't understand. That knife is one of the sharpest things known to man."

She sighed, "Here, let me do it."

She formed the end of her tail into a blade and gently pressed it against her wing. She ran it along the edge, cutting off a thin strip of metal from the edge. The metal on her wing instantly rippled, replacing the piece that had been cut off in less than a second. The human watched in pure amazement, before reaching down and picking up the piece of metal that had been cut off. He placed it in a bag.

"Amazing," he muttered. "Simply amazing."

"Can I go now?" asked Silver, eager to leave.

"Yes … yes of course," said the scientist. "We'll make an appointment for a later time."

"Of course." Silver faked a smile before getting off the table she had been laying on and rushing out of the room before he could change his mind.

With a small sigh, she wound her way through The Lab until she got to the hole that led to The Centre. The Lab was the smallest section of Sky Mountain, followed closely by The School. It had taken a while for her to figure out how everything worked, but she eventually found out that the three biggest sections took up the base of the mountain and the smaller two were situated at the top. Most of the mountain had been hollowed out and reinforced with steel so it didn't collapse on the dragons inside it. It was well made, and Silver doubted she could create something like it even if she wanted to.

With a grin, she dived down the hole, not bothering to open her wings. She was going to enjoy herself for the rest of the afternoon. Maybe even find a place where she could start a new collection of metallic statues. That would be liberating.

She came out of the tunnel right above The Centre and opened her wings, bringing herself to a stop. It had been so long since she had flown for pleasure. Even back at the farm she had only ever flown when she needed to, spending most of her time on the ground to reduce the risk of being seen. Of course, it hadn't worked that well, but she simply had to fly.

With a flap of her wings she propelled herself to the large exit of Sky Mountain, eager to be in the air again. While the dragons at Sky Mountain occasionally went outside during their training, it was a rare thing, so Silver had made a mental note to go out whenever possible. There were boundaries that she wasn't allowed to cross, but she accepted that. It still gave her a few square kilometres in which to play.

As soon as she was outside she shot straight to the top of Sky Mountain. The valley around her was beautiful. Green trees spread across it and on one side was a lake that many dragons sometimes bathed in and drank from. It reminded her of Dragon Valley, though that was a fair bit smaller than this, and was more linear than this circular dale.

It was a clear day with a chilly wind, a little difficult to fly in, especially for a metal dragon, but Silver could make do. She had flown in worse. As soon as she got to the top of Sky Mountain she folded her wings to her side and let herself fall into a dive. The wind whipped around her wings like a hurricane, forcing them open somewhat. She closed her eyes and smiled. This was what a dragon was supposed to do, not be trapped in a mountain learning about what was what.

She let loose a small roar and opened her wings, pulling herself up out of the dive a couple of seconds before she would've crashed into the trees and using the momentum to cross from the centre of the crater to the edge without even flapping her wings. Laughing to herself, she came to a landing on a small ledge at the crater's edge. It had been a long time since she had done that.

Shaking with exhilaration, she studied her surroundings. There was a small cave to her left, maybe big enough for a single dragon, and a small clearing below her with another body of water. There were no dragons near her, most of them flying around in groups near the entrance of the mountain or hanging out at the larger lake. Shrugging, she leapt from her ledge and landed at pond's shore.

Smiling to herself, she slowly waded in. It had been a long time since she had been swimming. Dragons weren't huge on baths. Flying in the wild winds high above the ground usually got rid of any dirt or debris stuck in their scales, but she never had the opportunity for that, so a bath would have to do.

Silver murmured slightly as the cold water washed her scales, and she shivered before diving into the water. It was surprisingly deep, deep enough that she couldn't see the bottom. Smiling to herself, she swam a bit deeper before coming up for air. A dragon could hold its breath for a fair while, but Silver didn't want to risk swimming too deep now. Instead she lay in the shallows, enjoying the water.

She was just about to doze off when an unfamiliar voice spoke above her.

"Hello there." It was male.

Silver jumped and growled, looking up at the dragon. At first glance she thought he was a mind dragon, but she quickly realised he wasn't. The blue of a mind dragon's scales was a little darker on this dragon, and he had a set of spikes running down his back that mind dragons didn't have.

She quickly got to her feet, shaking herself free of droplets, and glared at the dragon who had disturbed her rest. He was a gravity dragon, an extremely rare species that fell under the mental category. They were said to be quite powerful, being able to control the effect gravity had on all earthly objects, but usually weren't much for physical fighting.

"What do you want?" Silver asked, trying not let distaste show in her voice.

The gravity dragon flew down and landed near her, watching her with an unreadable expression. He was a little larger than her, maybe around nine or ten years old, with a muscular build. The two horns on his head had been sharpened recently and his scales didn't have a scrap of dirt on them.

"Oh, I saw you fly over here and decided to follow you. We haven't made our acquaintance yet. I thought it was time we did. My name is Gravon." He bowed his head.

"Silver," replied the dragoness, watching the drake with suspicion.

"I know. I don't think I could forget the entrance you made," he grinned. "Apparently you were the leader of that group of dragons."

"I wouldn't call myself the leader. I freed them and they chose to follow me," Silver said.

"Still, it was quite an accomplishment," he took a step towards her.

"That's what everyone keeps saying," she muttered to herself. If this dragon just wanted to congratulate her, she wished he would have done it later.

He smiled at her. "So … do you like it here at Sky Mountain?"

She hesitated. "It's alright, I guess."

"Hmm. Bogged down by classes, are you?"

"Yes."

"Yeah, they suck. I often just skip them and come out here. Much better to be out in the fresh air."

Silver tilted her head. "You can do that?"

"Of course. The advantage of being a rare dragon is that they really can't control you. They need you, so they'll do everything they can to keep you here," he said.

"Really?"

"Yeah. I get in trouble so often I probably would've have been kicked out by now if I were a normal dragon, but being as rare as I am they can't afford to do that."

"Ha." Silver thought through what he had just said. If that was true, maybe she should start making some demands of her own, like moving out of that infernal cave where the females under eight slept. Maybe to a cave of her own.

"Though with what I've heard about you they probably wouldn't kick you out no matter what species you were. I heard about that fight you had with Frezron, about how you nearly defeated him. The only reason you didn't is that ice is your weakness."

She shrugged, "I was trained by the best dragon in the world; it's really no surprise."

"Your father, right?"

"How did you know?"

"There really is only one dragon that could have trained you to control your powers. Elron's kind of a legend around here. The first dragon to ever escape A.O.D.H., and the first metal dragon. Too bad he's been captured again."

"Yeah," Silver sighed, a little surprised her father was held in such high regard.

"Gravon!" a loud angry voice rung throughout the sky.

The gravity dragon winced and sent an apologetic look in Silver's direction. "Sorry, better go. That's Mum. See you around?"

"See you around," Silver replied, watching him as he took to the air, flying as fast as he could away from the source of the voice.

She frowned as she watched, trying to figure out what that was all about. He had seemed a little too friendly for first conversations, but then again, he could just be a friendly dragon. Somehow she doubted it, though. Shrugging to herself, she decided to worry about it later and lay down in the pond again, letting the water relax her. She closed her eyes and slept.

Chapter 24:
A Matter of Species

"Today's topic is a dragon's equilibrium. While many of you have heard of this, not many dragons know what it truly is." A wind dragoness stalked across the front of a large room with steps heading up to a door that led to the rest of the school. "There are only two known dragons—alive, that is—who have reached this milestone. Both reside at Sky Mountain, so if you wish to ask them questions after this lesson, feel free. Now, onto the lesson."

Silver was listening this time, learning something new, though she would still rather be outside flying. Back at Dragon Valley she had gone flying every day. It was a great way to keep fit and an enjoyable pastime. Now, she only ever flew when she sparred, and that was for less than a couple of seconds at a time.

"The equilibrium is when a dragon becomes 'one' with their element. Usually it only comes about during a time of great strife, when a dragon is pushed to its limit and beyond. This is why it is so rare. During this time a dragon has utmost control of their element. For example, when a fire dragon reaches their equilibrium they become pure fire, which they can manipulate however they want, changing their shape, expanding and contracting from the smallest spark to an inferno savage enough to engulf a mountain.

"However, a dragon in equilibrium is also very dangerous and unpredictable. Usually they cannot tell friend from foe and wreak havoc until they settle down, turning back to their original state.

"Once a dragon has reached their equilibrium the first time, they can do so again relatively easily, though it takes an enormous amount of energy. Also, the second time they do so they are usually in control of their bodies, though still a little more prone to rages and losing control. So should any of you reach this point, make sure to be extremely careful when using such power. Yes, Tylia?"

"What are the different types of equilibrium?" asked a studious acid dragoness.

"I was just about to get to that," said the teacher. "Let's start with fire."

Silver sighed and lay her head down on her paws as the teacher droned on again. An equilibrium did sound pretty cool, but she would worry about that later. After this lesson she would try to find one of the higher-ranking dragons to make some changes to where she was staying. Often at night she was kept up by the other females talking about different problems in Sky Mountain. And about the males; that annoyed her especially.

An hour later the class finally ended, and a small headache nagged at the base of her skull. She was only interested in what the metal dragon's equilibrium was, but they didn't know. She wasn't surprised, though. Besides her, her father was the only other metallic dragon, and as far as she knew he hadn't reached that point.

She was the first to rush out the door as they made their way back to The Centre. She needed to get out of there, and with the light fading quickly she had only about an hour until they could eat, and then they were sent to their nests, like hatchlings. She wished she could hunt by herself, but it was "illegal" to kill anything in the valley. Instead food was brought to them, most of the time cooked. While cooked food had more taste, Silver liked the raw variety better, having grown up with it.

"Silver!" The voice rose above the crowd.

She turned to see an older dragon struggling towards her through the crowd of young dragons. He was a telekinetic dragon, around twenty years old, with a regal build and a hard scar on his shoulder. Not exactly a strong dragon, but someone who had been through a lot.

Silver frowned and waited for him. She had never seen him before and didn't know what he would want. Raize had stopped as well, wondering what was happening, but Silver quickly waved him on. Frowning, he left.

"Who are you?" Silver asked when the dragon was close enough to talk to without yelling.

"My name is Cragin," he said, "I was sent by Elder Iraliene. She wants to talk to you."

"Iraliene?" Silver mentally grinned; getting to speak with a high-ranking dragon was going to be easier than expected.

"Yes, you are to follow me immediately," he said.

Silver didn't argue, only nodding her head. It was time she had a proper conversation with the leader of this place anyway. That last one didn't count. Cragin turned and began to walk in the opposite direction, seeming to expect the dragoness to follow. With a snort, she padded up behind him.

The two of them walked through The School to another tunnel that led straight into The Nest. Without a word, the two dived into the tunnel, flying slowly beside each other. Silver had never flown through a tunnel with another dragon at her side and was surprised to find that it appeared big enough to fit them both side by side with their wings fully outstretched. But she didn't trust the tunnel enough to test that theory, and stayed behind the dragon. He was supposed to be leading the way anyway.

They exited at the top of The Nest, flying down into the cavern. Silver rarely flew up here, so it was an interesting experience. Up here was where the higher-ranking dragons usually lived, and most of them were far older than her. Once, she had spotted a young dragon, no more than nine, fly into one of the caves, but other than that the minimum age was probably around twenty.

Cragin turned and flew up to the highest cave, and probably the largest as well. The opening was easily big enough to let almost five dragons fly in at once. Silver wondered why it would need to be so large. From what she remembered Iraliene could fit comfortably in a cave entrance twice as small. Deciding not to worry about it, she followed the brown dragon up to the cave.

The inside of the cave was no less massive. It split off into three sections, two of which Silver didn't get to see, as she was led through one on the far right. The room they entered was large, not as large as the females' cave she slept in, but big enough for a number of dragons. It was well used; there was a light dragon in the corner, sending out small beams at increasing intensity towards what looked to be bags of chaff, searing through them . A mind dragon was sitting at some sort of screen, watching words flash across it. A group talked in one corner and still more worked with a human, showing off their respective elements while the human wrote on a noteboard. They had one thing in common: all were rare species, from gravity dragons to life dragons.

And at the centre of it all was Iraliene. She sat atop a perch, her tail coiled around the edge, watching the proceedings with her ever-intense glare. Her scales reflected the light across the room, much like Silver's shell, and she had the expression of a dragon deep in thought. When she saw the two of them, she grinned. Her tail unwound from the perch and she carefully stepped down.

"Silver! Just the dragon I've been wanting to see." The leader of Sky Mountain spoke with grace.

"Elder Iraliene." Silver bowed slightly, thinking respect may get her what she wanted.

"You are settling in well, I presume?" she asked.

"Yes," Silver nodded, lying.

"Good. I have heard you are doing well in your fighting classes, but that is only to be expected given what you've been through," said the life dragon.

"I guess I am," she shrugged.

"Aaah, you're too humble, Silver. I watched what you did to Frezron, the leading battle trainer in Sky Mountain," Iraliene sighed. "If only our other trainee dragons were so good."

"I was trained by my father, the greatest dragon in the world. He taught me most of what I know."

"As to be expected. A shame that he is captured."

"Yes … it is."

"Which brings me to the reason for your visit." The green dragoness looked over the room. "If you would please join me."
Silver complied, sidling up to Iraliene's side. For some reason this dragoness seemed to be able to make her feel … weak. Her size, her beauty, her manner, even her eyes. They outshone Silver in every way, and she couldn't help but be angry. Never had a dragon inspired such awe in her, besides her father.

The two of them began to walk around the room, saying nothing. The silence was beginning to drive Silver crazy. She glanced around the room. Her gaze fell on a young gravity dragon lazing on a bed of pillows. The two of them made eye contact, and Silver blinked in surprise. It was Gravon. He winked at her and grinned. She smiled back before averting her eyes, frowning.

"Now," Iraliene finally spoke, "as I'm sure you've already noticed, every dragon in this room is of a rarer species, whether mind, darkness, light, life or gravity. Here at Sky Mountain we like to make sure that rarer dragons do not fall extinct. Do you know how many gravity dragons there are in the world, Silver?"

She shook her head.

"Eight. Soon that number will be ten, as a female of the species has recently laid two eggs. The father was also gravity, so their offspring will be of the same species," Iraliene said. "But your species, Silver, your species is far rarer. There is only your father and you, if I am correct."

Silver nodded her head, beginning to fear where this conversation was leading.

"Your eighth hatch day is coming up in two months," continued the life dragoness. "And we need … excuse me … the world needs more metallic dragons to be hatched. That is if A.O.D.H. hasn't already managed to 'convince' your father to produce more offspring. This would be a tragedy. So, until we manage to free your father it is up to you to increase the number of metallic dragons in the world."

"You're asking me to find a mate?" Silver gaped. "But I'm not even …"

"Not at this moment," snorted Iraliene. "I know full well you can't bear any eggs at your current age. No. I want you to bear eggs as soon as possible. This means I want you to choose a mate, if not on your eighth hatchday, soon after. If you don't feel ready to make that commitment, I hear it is commonplace that many of you younger dragons mate before actually making a final decision."

A low growl escaped Silver. "And why would I do such a thing?"

"To spread your species, my dear. Why else?" Iraliene sighed. "Not many know this, but I was the first life dragon. My father was an earth dragon and my mother, water. They were pleasantly surprised to find a completely new species hatch from their egg. However, they raised me as equal to my siblings. When I reached my eighth hatchday I chose a mate, and by the time I was ten I had given birth to five clutches of my own, with a sixth on the way. It would be wonderful if something similar happened with you."

Silver had never felt so embarrassed or angry. "I will not be your brood mare!"

"Hmm, fiery indeed. Maybe it would have been better if your brother had been a metallic dragon," sighed the life dragon. "But back to the problem at hand. Perhaps you need some persuasion? I presume you remember your friend, Celestia?"

The two of them stopped before a plump light dragon that Silver at first didn't recognise. When she did, she gaped in surprise. It was Celestia, although a far bigger Celestia than she recalled. This wasn't the type of "large" that came from being fat. Her friend was gravid.

"Celestia?" Silver said in disbelief.

The light dragon opened her eyes, lifting her head to look at Silver. A small, tired smile crossed her maw. She gave a small nod in greeting.

"Silver, I was wondering whether or not I would see you again," she said.

"You look … well endowed," Silver said, unable to find the right word to match her thoughts. "Who's the father?"

"A shadow dragon named Durin," Celestia sighed. "He's a little older than me, and quite the charmer. You could almost say it was love at first sight."

"But … it's only been a month!"

"And a month well spent," she gestured to her swollen stomach. "I'm due to lay in a week or so. And after that they'll take another three or more months to hatch."

"Are you ready for hatchlings?" Silver asked.

Celestia hesitated. "I don't know. But Sky Mountain will help me take care of them, so I'll still have my free time whenever I wish. Besides, isn't it worth it? I mean, both shadow and light dragons are extremely rare, so the more hatchlings of the species that are born the better."

"If you think so," the metallic dragon hesitated.

"Don't worry about me, Silver. I've never been happier in my life," she grinned, laying her head down. "But it is exhausting."

"She is right. We should let her rest." Iraliene led her away from her friend and they continued to walk around the cave. "You see, my dear, it isn't all that bad. Making them is fun, and having them is satisfying. Aren't you tired of being the only metallic dragon here?"

"Well … yes," Silver replied, "but that doesn't mean I want a mate. Taking care of my own hatchlings? … I don't think I'm ready for that."

"You don't need to be. As Celestia said, Sky Mountain will do it for you. We do it with many young parents who 'accidently' fall gravid," Iraliene smiled gently. "And as I said before you don't have to choose one dragon. You can always make that decision later."

"No. I would prefer to be with only one dragon," she shivered.

The life dragoness frowned. "If you say so. I won't hold you to that. Now, may I offer a suggestion? My son. I'm pretty sure you're already acquainted—Gravon."

"You're his mother?" Silver was shocked. She didn't think the older dragon was still having hatchlings.

"Yes, don't sound so surprised, my dear; of course I still have the occasional clutch." Iraliene seemed to think for a moment. "Any rare dragon would do, though if you want to go for the more common ones, I won't stop you. I hear you and a young electric dragon have a liking for one another."

"Zepos?"

"Aaah, is that his name? A promising young drake, I must say, but then, he has been through both A.O.D.H. and D.E.D. relatively unscathed. I fear that he may be even more headstrong than you are." She smiled. "So you see, dear, it won't be that difficult."

Silver sighed. "I'll try."

"Good. Because if you don't ..." Iraliene's kind demeanour grew sinister, "I will choose for you."

Chapter 25: Specialist Training

SILVER woke early the following day, far earlier than usual. Soft snores echoed through the cave, signalling that it wasn't time to get up. She shifted on the metal surface of her nest, enjoying the cool, smooth touch, and closed her eyes again, trying to fall to sleep. But sleep didn't come. Her thoughts circled back and forth, trying to make sense of each other. It all came back to what Iraliene had said.

She shifted in her nest again. On one hand, it made sense. There were only two metal dragons left in the world, and Silver doubted her father had mated again, or ever would now that her mother was gone. So the responsibility fell to her to increase the metallic dragons' numbers. She didn't want them to go extinct, probably more so than Iraliene, and knew that someday she would produce hatchlings. But now?

On the other hand, she didn't feel ready for it. Many dragons waited a long time until they finally found a mate, some even to nearly fifty. Silver knew she wouldn't wait that long, but she didn't want to choose one as soon as she was able. It was … wrong. She wasn't even in love. Well, there was Zepos, and Silver couldn't deny the strong feelings she had for the drake, but was that love? It was all so confusing for her, but the thoughts continued to run around and around in her head like a drunk dragon.

Knowing she wouldn't be able to sleep in her current state, she slowly got to her feet, shaking herself off. A water dragoness, still barely two years old, shifted, but didn't wake up. Silver opened her wings and quietly took to the air, flying towards the cave's exit. She landed at it, only to be surprised by a dragon sitting tall on a rock, seeming to guard the cave.

"You there!" he yelled as soon as he saw Silver. "What are you doing?"

She stopped, surprised, and didn't say anything.

He was an earth dragon, maybe fifteen years old, with a strong complexion and hard eyes. There was a hole in one of his wings and a long scar created by a dragon talon running down his side. His forest-green scales were dulled, mixing with the brown scales that ran down his chest.

"Answer me!" he growled at her.

Shaking out of her stupor, she snarled back, "I woke up early, couldn't sleep, so I decided to go for a morning flight before I lose the chance."

"Dragonlings are not allowed out of their caves before called," the earth dragon stated.

Silver blinked in shock. She was far from a 'dragonling'. Anger began to bubble in her, but she suppressed it. Now was not the time to be rash.

"And you're going to stop me?" she threatened, giving her voice a dangerous edge.

The earth dragon hesitated, seemingly surprised by her resistance. She suspected that he hadn't dealt with a dragon like her before. She was so close to eight that he wasn't sure if she was supposed to be in the cave or not.

"Let her go, Baraki!" came the familiar voice of Gravon. "She's with me."

The earth dragon, Baraki, looked up to see Gravon descending from above. Though Baraki was the older of the two, he shied away as the rarer dragon landed in front of him, letting him take control.

"Silver! What a coincidence. I was just coming to get you," he said with a charming grin.

"What do you want, Gravon?" asked the metallic dragoness. Since she had learnt that he was Iraliene's son, she was a lot more cautious of him, even more so given Iraliene had suggested him as a potential mate.

"Oh, come on, Silver, don't be like that. I would have told you she was my mother, but you never asked." He shrugged.

She snorted. "Whatever. Answer my question."

He rolled his eyes, infuriating her more. "Well, Mum wants you to start on your speciality training a bit earlier than usual. A.O.D.H. has been on the move lately and we thought it might be safer if you learnt how to defend yourself."

"I know how to defend myself," she growled.

"Oh, I have no doubt about that. But this is more teaching you how to control your powers," he said. "Before you say, 'How can anyone teach me something like that?' follow me and I will show you."

Silver sighed before nodding. Gravon smiled and launched into the air. She followed, still a little wary. They flew up to Iraliene's cave and glided inside. Again they took a right turn and walked into the same cavern as the previous day. There were far fewer dragons this time, maybe around ten, ambling around. Iraliene was nowhere to be seen, much to Silver's relief.

"Aah, here we are. I'm sure you remember Professor Daquan," said Gravon, gesturing to a human scientist Silver knew only too well.

He smiled at her, bowing his head. "A pleasure to meet you again, Silver."

"Likewise," grunted the dragoness.

He frowned slightly but continued speaking. "As you've surely wanted to know, the analysis of your metal has yielded some interesting results."

He pulled out a book from his coat and began to flick through it in the same excited manner as before. For the life of her, Silver couldn't understand what was so bizarre and interesting about a piece of metal cut from her wing.

"The metal on your shell is indeed, well, living. An organic material never been seen before. It has its own unique cell structure, which transports nutrients all around your body." He flicked to the next page. "The metal is … astounding. It is a compound we have never seen before, comprised of every metallic element, from iron to silver to mercury, combined to create the strongest material on the planet. It melts at no less than thirty thousand degrees Celsius, or over fifty thousand degrees Fahrenheit, and responds to electric stimuli in a way we have never seen before …"

"Woah, woah, woah," Silver said, stopping the flood of information that she barely understood. "Can you please repeat that in a language I'm able to understand? I'm not a scientist. I'm a dragon. So please."

Daquan hesitated, an embarrassed grin on his face. He scratched the back of his head and took a deep breath. "It means you can control the metal however you want. You can grow, manipulate, expand and contract it with a single thought. You can make your tail nearly as long as you want. You can get rid of your shell altogether if you wish, and grow it back at a moment's notice. You can form different parts of your shell into different things; whatever you want it to be, it'll become. It's incredible. All this is theoretical, you understand. We have no idea if it's possible in real life."

Silver only nodded, looking back at her shell with a frown. She could already form her tail into nearly whatever she wanted, but had never lengthened it. And the shell had never been smaller than it was now. Curious, she attempted to shrink it. To her surprise, the armour retracted from her sides readily, revealing the dull yellow scales that lay beneath. The metal on her wings, tail and neck also began to retract, until only a silver line ran from the tip of her snout to the end of her tail.

She shivered, her scales sensitive to the light. In many ways she looked almost like a light dragon. Her wings were transparent and flimsy, the amber scales not reflecting the light at all, and she felt extremely vulnerable.

"Oh, wow," Gravon said, staring with surprise at the completely changed metallic dragon.

"Are you still here?" snarled Silver, letting the metal shell expand to its normal state. She decided not to do that again.

"Of course; I'm overlooking your training," he grinned. "And I suggest you do that again. You never know when it might come in handy."

She snorted at him before turning to the scientist. "What else did you say you think I could do?"

Daquan shuffled through his notes and cleared his throat with a cough. "Well, you should be able to expand and condense different parts of your shell."

"And lengthen my tail, right?" she asked.

He nodded.

Silver grinned and looked back at her tail. She focused on it, much like she did when she wanted it to turn into a blade or mace, and watched as the metal began to ripple and flow like water. The end of her tail slowly began to lengthen, snaking out like a rope, only narrowing at the point where Silver made it stop.

Interested in this new power, she lifted her tail, only to move the part of it that had flesh underneath. She frowned as the extra length hung limply from the end. "Useless" was the first word to come to her head, but then another thought came to her mind and she grinned.

"You may want to take a step back," she told the dragon and human watching her.

They did as they were told, staying well out of range of the metallic appendage. Silver snaked her tail around, pulling the extra length with it. Her tail was a little more unwieldy like this, the extra weight dragging on her movements. It probably wouldn't be a good idea to use this while she was flying. On the ground, though …

Silver smiled and leapt forwards, swinging her tail up above her head. The whip-like part of it followed quickly and struck out with a metallic crack, sending a dull ring through the room. A few of the dragons looked over at her in surprise, wondering what had just happened.

"Can I practise on anything?" she asked Gravon.

"Oh, yeah, sure." He nodded to a series of human-like dummies at one edge of the room.

Silver trotted up to them, her tail scraping along the ground and the extra length cutting a small crevice. She whipped her tail at one of the wooden dummies, and was delighted when the end pierced its chest. She slowly drew her tail back to its normal state. That would be useful later.

"That was impressive," said Gravon honestly, a little nervous at what else she could do.

She smiled at him. "Don't worry. I won't be doing any of this to you anytime soon. Unless you annoy me too much."

Daquan walked over to them, anticipating Silver's next question. "Well, you could try something similar with your wings."

* * *

For the rest of the day Silver trained with her newfound abilities. She found she could create a large club-like edge on the tips of her wings, and figured out how to create spikes on different parts of her body, like her wings, and propel them without having to move. She trained in her full-metal form as well, discovering she could lengthen her claws into razor-sharp edges that could even match the sharpness of her wings and tail. It was all very exciting and by the end of the day she found she didn't want to stop, but she knew she had to.

As she left the cave she stopped as Gravon called her. She looked back to see the gravity dragon bounding over to her.

"Hey, you know you don't have to sleep in the hatchling cave tonight," he said.

"What?"

"Yeah, if you want you can come and spend the night down in my cave. It's just opposite this one, but a little lower," he grinned. "You should. It'll be fun."

Her suspicion of the gravity dragon rose again. "Thanks, Gravon, but I think I'll stay in the other cave for now. I have my own nest there."

"I have spare nests. You can sleep in one of those," he insisted.

"No, not a straw nest. Metal dragons don't like straw nests. I made one myself, and I can't exactly move it," she said, knowing perfectly well she could.

"Oh, okay." He drooped a little, nearly enough for Silver to reconsider. "See you tomorrow then? Same time?"

She nodded and jumped out of the cave before her conscience changed her mind. She really did feel bad for the dragon, but she didn't like him. She couldn't, knowing who his mother was. Sighing, she glided down to where the under-eights were heading back to the nest.

Raize saw her coming and frowned. He stopped and waited as she landed beside him.

"Where were you today? Gretta said you had something important to do but she didn't elaborate."

"I've started my 'speciality training' with the other rarer dragons," said Silver. "I found out some pretty cool stuff today."

For some reason, Raize seemed a little worried at that. "She's already taken you up there?"

She nodded.

"Be careful, Silver. Iraliene's a good leader, but she always goes to great trouble to get what she wants. I don't want you to become one of them," he said.

Silver snorted. "As if that will happen." She quietened down to a whisper: "I hate her."

"Yes, I know, you told me what happened. But all this seems like a ploy to get you to choose quickly," he said.

Silver sighed, knowing what he meant. "I don't care. I've already become quite a bit more powerful, and that was within one day. Imagine what two months will do to me. By that time, maybe I won't need to fear her anymore."

Raize hesitated. "I hope so."

"You two! Stop whispering! Get into your caves!" Gretta yelled at them.

Silver nodded a goodbye before following the fire dragon's orders. Maybe she should've joined Gravon in his cave after all, if only to get away from the insufferable dragoness she could probably destroy with a single swing of her tail. Snarling, she shook her head, not allowing herself to think like that.

"I need to see Zepos again," she murmured to herself as she slipped into her metal nest.

CHAPTER 26:
EIGHTH HATCHDAY

SILVER felt the two months left to her eighth hatchday slip through her paws. It passed like a fire, full of action and discovery. She got lost in the attraction of her new powers, growing more powerful and confident the more she trained. Gravon was always there, encouraging her, trying to get close to her. She ignored him most of the time, but occasionally they fell into conversation, and she hated herself for it. And she hardly saw Zepos, who was kept so busy that she suspected he was being kept from her on purpose. They saw each other only once or twice, and barely exchanged a word before they were whisked away from each other.

As the fateful day came close, Silver realised she still hadn't chosen a dragon, and she began worry. There were only two she could consider, and while she would rather Zepos than Gravon, it seemed Iraliene was pushing her strongly towards her son. But she still felt that this whole situation was despicable, until finally a third option came to her mind that seemed much more palatable, even if it was dangerous and a little stupid.

The night before, Silver had found herself falling into a frightful sleep. Nightmares plagued her. Worry gnawed at her. For she knew the following day she would have to make a decision that would affect the rest of her life.

***

Silver woke reluctantly the following morning. She was eight years old today, arguably the most important birthday of a dragon's life. The only upside she could think of was that she wouldn't have to stay in this damned cave any longer. With a groan, she got to her feet to Gretta's call and ambled towards the entrance of the cave.

As soon as she exited the cave she spotted the emerald green dragoness she dreaded so much, sitting where the earth dragon had perched himself before. She froze, but Iraliene saw her and smiled. Knowing she couldn't avoid her, she traipsed over to the leader of Sky Mountain, her head down.

"Silver. I hope you feel refreshed. Today is a big day for you, after all." The life dragon grinned.

"Elder Iraliene." Silver nodded her head politely.

"So, who have you chosen?" she asked.

Silver hesitated. "No-one yet. But I still have till the end of the day."

Iraliene nodded. "But only until then. Tomorrow morning I'm choosing for you. But being the kind dragon that I am, I will give you the day off from any classes or training. I suggest you use that time wisely."

Silver nodded glumly and winced as the life dragon took to the air with a thrash of her wings, whipping up dust. She rose with her customary grace and flew back to the cave that looked over the rest of The Nest. With resentment, the metallic dragon watched her go.

"Don't let her bum you out," Raize said, walking up behind her.

She jumped in surprise and snarled, "Don't do that."

He laughed. "Come on, sis, lighten up. It's our eighth hatchday. The greatest day of our entire lives. Let's rejoice."

"I wish I could, Raize, I really wish I could," sighed the dragoness.

Seeing that his attitude didn't lighten her up, he nudged her. "Hey. Everything will turn out alright. Trust me."

She smiled weakly at him. "I can only hope."

"Hey, how about—"

"Raize, I appreciate your help, but right now I just want to be alone. Get my thoughts in order, you know," she said.

He bobbed his head slowly. "Fine. I'll see you later then?"

"Yeah," she turned away from him and mumbled to herself, "maybe."

Before he could ask what she meant, the dragoness took to the air, flying towards The Centre. She flew over the heads of the dragons who had chosen to walk, towards the exit of Sky Mountain and into the sun. She sighed with relief as the cool Chinese wind brushed past her shell. She caught an updraft and let herself be taken upwards without even flapping her wings.

Once she was high enough she began to circle the top of Sky Mountain, looking over the place that had been her home for the past couple of months. It was truly beautiful. The evergreen trees of the surrounding forest all had the same jade lustre, and she knew they housed many creatures that had grown used to the dragons' presence.

The crater that supported Sky Mountain rose at its edges, creating a bowl-like landscape. The walls would make it extremely difficult to get anything bigger than a small army with minimal equipment through, on foot anyway. The mountain range provided protection from planes and other aircraft. It was hard to fly a machine through such dangerous terrain. One wrong move and they would end up on the side of a mountain in flames.

Some dragons undergoing flight training slowly exited the mountain. They were mostly either very young dragons, one or two years old, or older dragons who had chosen to become scouts. They practised techniques of speed, agility and stamina, qualities needed for quick getaways. Silver already knew most of what they were being taught.

One dragon, flying separate from the rest, caught her eye. It didn't take her long to recognise Gravon. He was the only gravity dragon in the air that day, and was flying straight towards her. Silver growled, annoyed. How did he even know where she was? For a moment she contemplated flying away from the dragon, but instead she stopped and hovered, letting him approach.

"Silver! What are you doing all the way up here?" he said, coming to a stop a few metres away.

"Getting some fresh air," she replied. "I'm rarely able to fly anymore. And I mean truly fly, not some stupid training exercise."

"So you like flying, huh? Same." He flapped his wings and began to move, flying around her. "It's … the best thing about being a dragon."

Silver agreed, but didn't say anything. "What do you want, Gravon?"

"Straight to the point, huh?" he smirked. "Well, I know what my mother has been telling you lately, and I thought we should get together. I think we would make a great couple."

"That's a matter of opinion." Silver was surprised he was being so open about it.

"And why shouldn't we? We're both strong, independent dragons. Powerful. The hatchlings of two great leaders. Rare. We disregard the rules and dislike authority. We're very similar, you and me. It only makes sense. Plus, I'm experienced in … many areas. I could make it wonderful."

Silver snorted. She guessed she wasn't surprised to hear that he had mated before. Iraliene had probably made him do something like what she had told Silver to, but he had been much more eager. Male dragons usually were.

"You're missing one thing from that list, Gravon. One very important thing. We don't love each other, or at least, I don't love you," Silver said.

"Does that matter?"

"To me? Yes. Yes, it does."

"Well … I'm sure we can learn to. As I said before, we have similar interests. Love would come soon after."

"Maybe."

"Come on Silver. It'll be fun, for the both of us."

He flew up to her and brushed his wing against hers. The metallic shell could be surprisingly sensitive, and she growled, backing away from the dragon. Gravon backed away to hover in front of her, waiting for her decision.

"I'll tell you tonight what I have decided," said Silver. "Wait until then."

A worried look went through Gravon's eyes, but he nodded and tucked in his wings, diving from the sky. Silver watched him go and breathed her relief. No, definitely not him. That only left two options, and the dangerous one was becoming more and more attractive.

* * *

She ended up down near the pond where she had first met the gravity dragon. It looked the same, except for the thin layer of clear ice that had accumulated on the surface. It broke easily when Silver pressed a claw against it, sending cracks running across the lake. The cracks running across the clear ice made it look as if the water had been broken. It made her smile.

With a grunt, she fell to her side, looking up at the sky. It was surprising how easy it would be to just leave, fly over the mountains and never return. No-one would know until later that night, and by then Silver could have made it halfway across the world. She could be anywhere, and she was sure there were other dragon havens out there besides Sky Mountain. Why they had to come this one she couldn't figure it out. But she doubted she would get far without either D. E.D. or A.O.D.H. finding her. Still, that option loomed in front of her, waiting for her to take it.

She stayed at the lake for hour after hour, letting her thoughts take her wherever they wanted. She thought about her time away from the nest, the year and a half that had passed since Dragon Valley. Her time on the farm, escaping from D.E.D., all of it. She had grown a lot, not only in size but also in confidence and power. She had led a group of dragons and done something that had never been done before. It reminded her a little of what her father had done.

Since he hatched, he had been trapped at A.O.D.H., where they drilled the mind-controlling device through his skull. For ten years he followed every order they gave him, killing, destroying—acts he wasn't proud of. But when they were going to force him to take a mate, he had refused. Even with the mind-controlling device, he had resisted, making him the first dragon to ever do so. And soon after that had he ripped the device off his head, only to have it placed back in, stronger than ever. Still, he hadn't given in, and soon after he had found a human who told him of the device's weakness, and he tore it off once again. After that, he gathered an army of freed dragons and laid waste to the A.O.D.H. base. That was eight years ago, and her father was now back in the same organisation that had enslaved him for years. And yet he still resisted. Silver knew he did. So why couldn't she?

"Silver?" the familiar voice of a certain electric dragon drifted over her.

She looked up at him, and couldn't help but smile. "Hey, Zepos. What are you doing out here?"

She got up to her feet and faced him.

"Raize broke me out of class. He said you needed help with something," he replied.

She nearly laughed. That sounded so like her brother. She wouldn't be surprised if he was now making sure no-one disturbed them, though it was a little pointless. No-one could find this place unless they were looking for it.

"How did you find me?" she asked.

"I asked around. A dragon said they had seen you fly in this direction, so I came here and saw you sitting by the pond," he said. "So, what do you need help with?"

"Oh, nothing much. Raize was overreacting," she said. "But now that you're here, why don't you stay? We haven't seen each other much."

"I know," huffed Zepos, walking over to her and sitting down. "It's been frustrating me."

"Yeah." Silver sat down next to him. "Sometimes I wish we hadn't come here."

"The only thing that keeps me here is I know A.O.D.H. and D. E.D. are worse," replied the drake. "At least in this place they aren't really forcing you to do anything."

"Well, not exactly." Silver looked at the floor.

"What do you mean?"

She looked at him and decided to tell him what had transpired in the past few months. She told him of her time in the under-eights' cave, of her training with Frezron, and then with Gravon. She told him of her longing to be free again, like she had been at the valley, and her wish to fly again. To truly fly. And she told him of Iraliene's rule, and what she was being forced to do.

Zepos was silent, thinking through what she had said. "So … what are you going to do?"

She sighed. "I'm still deciding. But I'm not ready, Zepos. I'm not ready to find a mate. To settle down. You know me. I'm wild. I hate being trapped. And here, here I feel like I'm trapped."

"But surely here is better than D.E.D. or A.O.D.H.?"

"I know. Don't think I'm that daft. I would rather be here than any of those places," sighed Silver. "At least here I have a chance to fight back."

"So, you're going to refuse?"

"No … well, maybe. I don't know. You've only met Iraliene once, so you don't know how truly small she makes you feel. She may as well be a mind dragon, because whenever she tells you something, you are obliged to do it. And my brother, he said that she would do whatever it takes to get what she wants. So if she wants a metallic hatchling to be hatched, she'll make that happen."

"That's … horrible."

"I know." Silver sighed and lay her head down on the ground, watching the water filter through the cracks she had created in the ice.

They sat in silence for a while, Silver in her thoughts and Zepos watching the dragon he had come to love. The thought of her being with another dragon was hard for him to bear, but he knew all too well he couldn't force her into anything.

"What's this Gravon like?" asked Zepos.

Silver looked at him, surprised at the question. "Why?"

He shrugged. "I'm just curious."

"Well, he's the son of Iraliene, so that tells you quite a bit about him. He's headstrong, and not in a good way. He thinks he's the centre of the world and seems to be able to draw dragons to him. Other than that, he's alright. I mean, he's good-looking, confident and powerful. Someone most dragonesses would fall head over heels for. But he's prideful; he thinks he can get away with what he wants, whenever he wants. Much like you were back in Dragon Valley."

"Hey! I wasn't that bad."

She tilted her head at him, a dragon's equivalent of raising an eyebrow.

He looked down at the floor. "Okay, maybe a little."

Silver smiled and bumped his shoulder with her muzzle. "Don't worry. You've changed quite a bit now. In a good sense. Maybe that year you spent in A.O.D.H. did you good."

He snorted. "I would rather have not gone there."

"I know, but I guess bad experiences help you realise just how fragile the world is. They help you grow and become wiser in your decisions," she said.

"Your father told you that, didn't he?" Zepos grinned.

"Yep," Silver laughed. "You really think I could have come up with something like that by myself?"

"You have your wise moments," he said.

"Humph. Rarely."

They laughed again, glad to be able to talk with each other once more. They continued to chat the rest of the day away, exchanging stories, boasting to each other, listening to each other's troubles, and staying well away from the problem at hand.

To Silver it was the best day since her flight from Dragon Valley. She forgot everything that had happened and focused on the dragon in front of her. Sometimes it was better to forget. But as the sun began to dip into the horizon the two dragons knew that soon they would have to leave each other again.

"It's been fun, Zepos," Silver said as the sun finally slid below the horizon.

"Yeah," he sighed.

They stayed with each other for a moment before Silver shuffled and got to her feet. She stumbled slightly, her legs having cramped a little from sitting in the same place for such a long time. With a grunt, she stretched, groaning as the sore muscles unwound.

Zepos stood as well and shook himself off. He watched her, the last evening lights dancing off her shell in luminous patterns and radiating orange and yellow through the clearing. She was beautiful at this time of day—well, more beautiful than usual.

"I'll see you tomorrow, Zepos," she said.

"Wait, Silver," he said, before she could take off.

She turned towards him and grunted in surprise as he stepped forwards and kissed her. A dragon's kiss is different from a human's, dragons usually rubbing their muzzles against each other's as well as pressing their lips together.

Silver kissed back. Her first kiss, and one she would remember for as long as she lived. She purred, a deep rumble coming from her throat as she moved closer to Zepos. And when Zepos pulled back she found she wanted more, much more. But she couldn't go on.

"Silver, I love you," Zepos finally said, "and I couldn't bear to see you with another dragon. So, please, before you go back to Sky Mountain, know that no dragon will ever love you as much as I do. I know you aren't ready, but consider choosing me as your mate. You're the only dragon I could ever be with."

Silver gulped, surprised at his sudden confession. It only made it harder to choose. Oh, how she wished she weren't being forced to take a mate. If only they'd flown in the other direction.

"Zepos … I can't deny that I have strong feelings for you," she spoke slowly. "I just don't know if it's love. I just don't know. But I do know that I will not be choosing a mate anytime soon, no matter what Iraliene says."

The electric dragon nodded, looking at the ground. He took a deep breath, seeming to gather himself. "So … what are you going to do?"

Silver looked to the sky, her resolve hardening. "Let's just say, don't expect me to be here tomorrow morning."

CHAPTER 27:
THE SEARCH

RAIZE sighed as he looked out of the opening of his new cave. It was only a little higher than his previous one, but it was smaller, with fewer dragons: five males and five females. It was comfortable, and the dragons he had met seemed nice. There were a few other fire dragons, and one of the females seemed to have already taken an interest in him. While he had shared a cave with his sister for most of his life, it was strange to be living with females again, though he supposed he could get used to it.

What truly worried him was Silver. He couldn't help but think that something horrible had happened to her yesterday. And if Gravon had gotten to her before Zepos … He shivered at the thought. So instead of waiting to be called out of his cave for his now more advanced classes, he left the cave at dawn, hurrying to the outside of Sky Mountain. The sun had barely touched the horizon, but one of the many skills of a fire dragon was to be able to detect nearby heat sources, allowing him to find living beings in the dark.

He flew to where he knew Zepos had been pointed the day before, and soon found a clearing that seemed like a place Silver would like. It was a small cave near a pond with deep water and long reeds around the bank.

He first checked the cave, hoping to find Silver and Zepos wrapped in each other's wings, but when he saw nothing he began to worry.

He leapt down from the cave and checked the forest around the small clearing, wondering if the two had slept in there. Still not finding anyone, he began to think that maybe he was at the wrong place, when he saw a messily scrawled message in the rock.

'Hey bruther. I know you wood come hear evenchally. But if this is some other dragon, bugger of. Me and Zepos have left sky moutain to search for anuther dragon haven. Sorry for not bringing you, but it is to dangerus. Once we find anuther haven, we will come back for u.'

A small growl left his throat. She had left him! Again! He read the message over and over before stepping back and creating a fireball in his throat. He blasted the wall, destroying the message so no other dragon could find it. Oh, this was so like Silver, doing things without thinking them through. Didn't she know that A.O.D.H. had recently been on the move, approaching this very mountain range? He turned, debating whether to warn Iraliene or not. No, he wouldn't, not yet. First he would gather some friends and see if he could find Silver.

With an angry snort, he threw himself into the air with a beat of his wings, flying as fast as he could back to Sky Mountain. He needed to find her before it was too late.

* * *

Gravon paced in his cave, one of the highest in The Nest. He had slept badly that night, wondering when Silver would come, but she hadn't. It had left him angry, frustrated and confused. Why hadn't she come to him? Everyone else had, eagerly even. But this damned dragoness was just so … He snarled at himself before stalking to the edge of the cave and looking down over the mostly empty nest, as it usually was this early in the morning. A few dragons slowly rose and flew around, mostly teachers preparing for their classes. But one dragon caught his eyes: a young fire dragon who couldn't be more than eight years old.

He frowned with suspicion and leapt from the cave, spreading his larger-than-normal wings and descending towards the dragon. He knew that Silver had two brothers, both fire dragons, and one of them resided at Sky Mountain. This dragon was young enough to be her brother, and they had some physical similarities as well.

Seeing that the fire dragon was in a hurry, Gravon manipulated the gravity around him with a thought, drawing himself towards the ground with greater force and making himself fall far faster than normal. Before he hit the fire dragon he opened his wings, lessening the gravity and coming to an almost perfect midair standstill. The fire dragon yelped in surprised, reflexively speeding up to escape the threat from above. When he realised that there was no threat, he turned around with a growl, looking at the dragon who had disturbed him. Gravon laughed in contempt.

"Why such a hurry, hatchling?" asked the gravity dragon, knowing very well that this dragon was far from a hatchling.

The flame drake narrowed his eyes dangerously, but didn't retaliate with an insult of his own, much to Gravon's surprise. "None of your business. Why did you try to attack me?"

"I didn't," Gravon replied. "Though it was amusing to see your reaction."

The fire dragon huffed, before turning as if to fly off again.

"Hey!" growled Gravon. "Don't you turn your back on me! I haven't finished with you yet!"

The fire dragon turned back to look at him. "What?"

"Are you Silver's brother?"

"I am. My name is Raize, if you ever wanted to find that out."

"Do you know where she is?"

"Who?"

"Silver! Do you know where she is?"

"No, I don't." Raize replied abruptly, as if he had anticipated the question.

Gravon frowned, suspecting that he wasn't telling the whole truth, but there was no way he could prove it.

"When did you see her last?" he asked.

"With Zepos."

"Zepos?" Gravon frowned. "Who's he?"

"An electric dragon, one of Silver's … very close friends," the fire dragon replied.

Gravon narrowed his eyes. He remembered that dragon now; they were in some of the same classes, when he bothered to show up, that was. And his mother had mentioned some competition for Silver's affections, but he thought he could easily trump any other male in Silver's life. It seemed he was mistaken.

"And where is he now?"

"With Silver, so I don't know."

"You know, Raize, I don't believe you."

The fire dragon shrugged. "Good for you."

He turned to leave again. Gravon snarled and manipulated the gravity around the dragon, forcing him to the floor. Raize yowled in surprise and tried to get up, only to find that he was far too heavy to lift himself. Still, he struggled, not allowing himself to be defeated so easily. Gravon landed in front of the downed dragon, a grin on his face. Fire dragons were so easy.

"Now, tell me the truth or I will crush you into the ground," he threatened.

Raize snorted and opened his maw, sending a torrent of flame towards the unsuspecting dragon. Fire was not affected by gravity because of its lack of weight, so Raize hit his target. Gravon screeched in pain as the flames scorched his scales. He lost his hold on Raize, turning away and shielding himself from the flames with his wings.

The fire dragon took advantage of Gravon's lack of sight and pounced at him, colliding with his side and knocking him over, pinning him to the ground. The gravity dragon snarled and tried to throw Raize off, but he had underestimated the strength of the younger dragon, and yowled when Raize pressed his claws into his flanks, drawing blood.

"You stay away from my sister, worm. She's too good for the likes of you," Raize snarled.

Gravon roared in pain and looked at the fire dragon above him. He manipulated gravity again, but this time in the opposite direction. Raize growled in surprise and nearly let go of Gravon as he began to fall upwards. But he kept a hold of him, and they began to fall together. Raize bathed Gravon in flame. He screeched, losing his control of gravity and sending the pair back towards the ground.

With a thump, Raize slammed Gravon into the rocks below, breaking a few bones in the rarer dragon's wings and back. He roared in pain before falling limp against the rock. Suddenly worried, Raize checked to see if he was still breathing, and sighed with relief when he was.

He took a step back from the broken dragon and snorted his contempt. Spreading his wings for flight, another voice stopped him.

"Hey, you there!" cried an older earth dragon who had seen the whole thing.

Raize growled in annoyance and turned towards the dragon. "You may want to get him to a life dragon. He's badly injured."

"Oh, I'm taking him to a life dragon alright, and you as well," the earth dragon snarled.

He landed next to them and scooped up Gravon's broken form. The drake groaned, but stayed unconscious. The earth dragon looked at Raize angrily, as if it was his fault. The fire dragon snorted. He could just fly away, but he knew that the alarm would be raised and every dragon in Sky Mountain would be looking for him. Best to go along quietly and hope they believe his side of the story.

The earth dragon took off, and Raize followed.

* * *

Iraliene looked at the large screen in front of her, worry hard on her chest. The screen showed a map of the mountain range stretching through western China. On the screen were hundreds of tiny dots, all moving in a jittery fashion towards their location. Every one of those dots represented a machine or dragon from A.O.D.H. But from all her resources she knew that they didn't know where Sky Mountain was, unless they had just found the general location and were now searching the mountains for them.

She turned from the screen and began to pace. While Sky Mountain was well defended, losing even a couple of dragons to them was something she couldn't risk. Their numbers were already minimal, and A.O.D.H. had nearly twenty thousand dragons under their command.

"Laang," she said, speaking in Mandarin to a human working at a desk in the cave, "call the Chinese government. We need as much help as they can give us."

"Yes, Elder," he said, reaching to a phone on his desk.

With a sigh, Iraliene looked back at the screen. If this was going to be a fight, then they were going to have to fight with their utmost power. It was time to test the true capabilities of Sky Mountain. She turned and began to walk out of the cave, ready to give the order to lock down the mountain.

But she was stopped when an earth dragon landed at the entrance of the cave, accompanied by a fire dragon. He seemed surprised to see her, and bowed before laying something at her feet. Her eyes widened in surprise. It was her son, Gravon, badly injured.

Gathering her power in her maw she quickly breathed green energy over the gravity drake, healing his wounds with an ease granted by centuries of practice. She stepped back, worried as Gravon slowly regained consciousness. He jumped up suddenly, snarling. The fire dragon growled back.

"Who did this?" snarled Iraliene.

"He did!" Gravon accused, looking at Raize with red anger in his eyes.

The life dragoness turned towards the red dragon and narrowed her eyes. Raize took a small step back, intimidated by the giant dragon in front of him.

"I'm sorry, Elder Iraliene," he said, bowing his head, "but he attacked me first. I merely defended myself."

"Lies!" snarled Gravon, taking a step forwards.

The elder dragon snorted, not believing her son. It wasn't the first time he had done such a thing and it probably wouldn't be the last. The question was why he would do it. There was usually a reason.

She voiced her thoughts: "Why would my son attack you?"

"He wanted to know where Silver was. I didn't know, and he didn't believe me, so he attacked me, and I retaliated."

At the mention of the silver dragon, Iraliene frowned. "Do you know where she is?"

"No."

Iraliene took a step forwards to the dragon, boring into his eyes with her intense gaze, asking for the truth.

"I'm serious. I have no idea where she is," Raize stuttered, taking a step back.

"Well, we'll soon know, won't we?" Iraliene said with a grin and yelled into the cave: "Fahre, would you come here a moment please!"

A moment or two passed and a mind dragon revealed himself from the cave. He was maybe a hundred years old, and was experienced with extracting information from other dragons' minds, or humans'.

"What do you need, my queen?" he asked with a bow.

"Would you please read this young dragon's mind and tell us what we want to know?" Iraliene said.

Raize took a step back, wondering whether it would be a good time to run. He stepped right into the earth dragon, though, who shoved him forwards and sent him sprawling onto the ground.

"With pleasure," Fahre said, turning towards Raize.

* * *

Silver woke up to a beam of light being shone into the cave. She groaned and forced herself upright, looking around at her new surroundings. It was a small cave, one that she and Zepos had found the previous night. She didn't know how far they had flown but she doubted it was very far. They had flown for less than an hour before deciding to stay here for the rest of the night.

Zepos was still sleeping, curled up around himself and snoring gently. Silver smiled slightly at him before yawning and getting up. While sleeping on rocks was better than sleeping on straw or sticks, it was nowhere near as great as sleeping in a metal nest. She would need to get used to the rough life again.

With a groan, she stretched herself out, cracking a few joints as she began to warm up. She checked her wings and tail for any sign of the rust that occasionally formed on the surface, and, finding none, she grunted contentedly and turned towards the sleeping dragon. It was almost a shame to wake him up. Almost.

She walked over to him and prodded him with her tail. He murmured, refusing to wake, so she jabbed him again, a little harder this time. He opened his eyes and growled at her.

"Come on, Zepos, we need to get moving."

At first, she thought it was a bad idea to bring him along. She didn't want to endanger another dragon through her actions, but Zepos had come up with a winning argument. If they met any dragons from A. O.D.H., they could free them easily and even create their own small dragon haven. So Silver agreed to let him come, not that she would have been able to convince him otherwise.

"Aargh, do I have to?" he groaned, closing his eyes again.

"Yes, unless you want me to leave you here," she smirked.

Zepos quickly found his feet and stood up. "I'm up, I'm up."

He yawned and stretched like a cat. They had grown accustomed to sleeping in comfortable nests over the past few months, and now they were back to roughing it. Silver laughed at him and shook her head.

"You're getting lazy," she said.

"No, I'm not. I'm a growing dragon. I need my rest," he snorted back. "I'm surprised you managed to wake …"

He froze as the light shining into the cave was blocked. Silver frowned and turned, expecting to see a dragon from Sky Mountain, come to take them back. But as she saw who it really was, she froze, staring in a mixture of shock, fear and joy.

Standing at the entrance of the cave was the dragon she had spent her whole life with, the only other dragon of her species. He was smaller than she remembered, his metal shell reflecting the light away from the cave. His eyes were full of sadness and remorse, and the mind-controlling device stuck in his head was bleeping a red light.

"Hey, Silver," Elron smiled sadly.

"D … Dad?"

CHAPTER 28: FATHER AND DAUGHTER, PART ONE

Elron looked at his daughter with painful pride. She had grown so much since he had last seen her, from the size of a small horse to that of a large car. Her eyes spoke of fearlessness and confidence. Her posture was stronger, more self-aware, and he could see the slight wariness in her eyes that told him that she didn't allow her emotions to control her.

"It's been a while," he nearly choked.

When A.O.D.H. had detected the bio-signatures of two dragons in this cave, he had hoped against hope that it wasn't his daughter, but as soon as he landed at the edge of the cave, that wish had been dashed. He just prayed her skills in battle had improved enough to defeat him, because there was no other way this was going to end.

"Dad," Silver said, taking a step back, not knowing whether to run to her father or away from him. The device on his head seemed to blink more rapidly than before, trying to force him forwards.

Elron bowed his head. "I'm … I'm sorry, Silver, but I've been ordered to take you in."

Her heart nearly broke at those words but she strengthened her resolve and let out a shaky breath. "You know I won't come easily."

"I hope you don't. I hope you manage to defeat me and fly away. I hope you find a place where you can live safe from A.O.D.H. for the rest of your life," her father said. "But ..."

He growled, shaking his head, fighting the compulsion to pounce straight into the fight and destroy the two dragons in front of him with a single swipe of his talons. The thought of laying a talon on his daughter repulsed him, but even as he resisted the device's power he began to walk forwards, slowly, making the two younger dragons back away.

Silver looked towards Zepos, and a silent agreement passed between them. They prepared themselves: if this didn't work, then, trapped in this small cave, they wouldn't stand a chance against an elder metal dragon.

Zepos opened his maw and shot a bolt of electricity at Elron, but the metal dragon was fast, far faster than they had anticipated. Before the bolt even left Zepos's mouth, Elron flicked his tail, volleying metal spikes at the electric dragon, sending his aim astray so the bolt hit the roof. He grunted as the spikes slammed into him, sending him into the cave wall.

Silver let out a cry of horror, for a moment thinking he was dead, but when she saw that the metallic spikes had been blunted and Zepos was merely unconscious, she exhaled in relief, turning her attention back to Elron. She cursed. Without Zepos, she had no chance of freeing her father.

"I'm sorry, Silver," he said, the remorse plain in his voice.

"I know," replied his daughter.

She looked behind him to the cave's exit. She could only win this if she managed to get outside. The only strength she had over her father was agility, and for agility she needed space to move.

Silver nearly yelped when her tail touched the back of the cave. She needed to think of something fast or there would be no hope for either of them. Deciding to act rather than think, she thickened the edges of her wings and leapt at her father, aiming to uppercut him in the underpart of his jaw. Elron growled and stepped back, bringing up his paw and catching the wing. Silver stepped forwards, swinging her other wing sideways at her father's head. This one he didn't see, and she was rewarded by a clang as it collided with the upper part of his head, jarring her wing as metal struck metal.

The strike didn't injure Elron, but his head whipped to the side and the ringing dazzled him. He let go of Silver's wing and growled in pain, closing his eyes against the dull throbbing. Silver took advantage of her father's momentary lapse and pounced over his back with a flap of her wings, leaving a clear path to the exit of the cave. She took it, running as fast as her legs could carry her. Tail spikes flew past her, a few ricocheting off her back and stabbing the walls and roof. She stumbled slightly but didn't falter, and with a roar of victory leapt into the open with her wings spread.

Elron wasn't far behind, the machine having taken complete control of him. He was no longer himself, completely enraptured by its mental snares. Elron roared as he flapped his wings, heading straight for the silver dragoness now flying up to the mountains' peaks.

Silver's heart thudded hard against her chest as she looked down at her father. They had sparred many times and she had never beat him, and she had a feeling he had been going easy on her. She guessed another advantage she had in this fight was her will. She would do everything—well, almost everything—she could to win, while Elron was being forced to something he didn't want to do.

She turned in midair, coming to a hovering stop, before folding her wings and plummeting down again, straight towards her father. She opened her maw and rapidly fired small metallic spikes, like bullets, at Elron. He snarled as they pinged off his shell, some cutting the underside of his unprotected maw.

As the dragons passed each other, Silver flapped her wings, trying to dodge Elron, but her father anticipated the move and spun, catching her in the side with the upper face of his wing. She snarled in pain as she was shoved into the mountainside.

She crashed headfirst, putting her wings out in front of her to brace herself. A lone tree managed to slow her down slightly, but she crashed right through it, rolling down the mountainside with a cascade of rocks following her. The speed of her crash didn't help. She rolled herself as much as she could into a ball, but when a sharp pain seared through her left hind leg she couldn't help but scream.

The silver dragon finally came a stop on the valley floor, moaning. A sheared-off tree branch jutted from her injured leg and scratches marked the unprotected portion of her body. Scales had been ripped out and blood trickled from the wounds. Her body throbbed, and she breathed in ragged gasps. She was lucky she came out of the fall so well, her shell having protected her from the worst of the damage.

With a shaky groan she hauled herself to her feet, dislodging a rock that had fallen on her back. She stumbled slightly, limping. Turning around to the worst injury, she gripped the tree branch in her jaws and, with a deep hiss, ripped it out. Blood poured from the wound, but it threatened neither life nor limb.

So focused she was on patching herself up, she nearly didn't see the dragon plummeting from above. She leapt out of the way just in time to dodge Elron as he slammed into the ground where she had been. The rocks below his feet cracked, and the metal dragon grunted in pain, not having expected to hit the ground so hard.

Silver snarled and lengthened her tail into a whip, swinging it forwards with the expertise of months of training and landing a solid strike between her father's eyes. To their surprise, the sharp whip cut a small groove in Elron's armour. The slash quickly filled with metal, but they both realised their shells could be cut by another metal dragon.

Silver lashed again, this time aiming for his unprotected legs. Elron had already pounced forwards, crashing into his daughter and driving her into the ground, back first. She hissed and clawed at his legs, cutting long bloody gashes in them, but Elron hardly noticed. He reared up and pounded her into the ground again. Silver gasped as the air was knocked out of her and a few of her ribs cracked.

As Elron reared up a second time, Silver opened her maw and shot a thick stream of metal at his neck. The force of it staggered him backwards on two legs. She formed her tail-whip into a mace and swung as hard as she could at his legs. Elron roared in pain as he was toppled over by the surprising strike. Silver wasn't sure, but she thought she felt a bone break.

Both dragons struggled to their feet. Sharp pains shot up Silver's spine with every breath, and Elron favoured his right hind leg as he limped backwards from her, trying to gather himself.

Suddenly Elron's eyes seemed to clear, as he gained some control over the device on his head. "You've grown better, my daughter."

"Yeah?" Silver hissed. "It still hurts."

"A cracked rib?"

"More than one."

She coughed and shook her head, her heart lightening; this was the first serious fight between the two, and despite its solemnity, they found a strange satisfaction in the battle. Elron was the first dragon Silver had fought that she could go all out on without fear of seriously injuring him. Still, she hoped to hold him off until Zepos regained consciousness or—though this was a longshot—knock him unconscious herself.

"That was a hard fall you took," he said, gesturing to the trail of destruction she had wrought down the mountain.

"It wasn't too bad. A few scratches, that's all," she said. "How's your leg?"

"Bruised, not broken," he replied.

"Damn."

"Nice try, though," he said, before snarling as the machine once again started to take over his consciousness.

Silver saw the strike before it happened. Elron formed spikes on his tail before launching them at Silver. She leapt into the air with a flap of her wings. Pain ran through her at the movement, but she ignored it, forcing herself higher and higher into the air.

Elron took a little longer to follow, but when he did she couldn't help but growl in annoyance. He had transformed into his full-metal state, his armour shining in the sun as he rose out of the dust the two of them had thrown into the air in their scuffle.

Silver flung a storm of tail spikes in her father's direction, landing a direct hit. Most of the spikes ricocheted harmlessly off his impenetrable shell, but a few lodged in his armour. Elron roared his anger and Silver shivered. She needed to get that device off his head.

Turning in the air, she flew away from him, not willing to attempt another dive attack. The last one had ended badly enough. She twisted her body, hearing the unmistakable sound of spikes whizzing through the air. The bullet-like projectiles flew past her, a few imbedding themselves into the shell on her back. Snarling, she dove, forcing her far heavier father to pursue her again. He was slower than her in his unarmoured state, and armoured as he was, he was nearly at a standstill. She could fly circles around him. The problem was making sure she didn't get hit.

Flying upwards again, moving unpredictably, she passed over her father, narrowly dodging his grab at her wings. She came to a stop above him again and flung another volley of spikes in his direction. Another hit. But still no damage.

Her eyes narrowed in frustration. She could do nothing to pierce the armour, unless she spent hours flying around him and filling it with spikes. She would eventually break it, but Elron would have figured out a way to best her long before then. She wondered if this was how other dragons thought when they tried to fight her and the invincible armour she wore.

And then there was A.O.D.H. If Elron was here, she knew they wouldn't be far behind. They wouldn't let their most prized possession fly around without protection, despite his invincibility.

Taking a deep breath, she decided on a tactic. Her shell expanded, covering her form once again, and she flew at her father. If this was going to be a fight of strength, power and will, then so be it. Elron

snarled and met her challenge, and they clashed in midair. A booming clang rang through the mountain range as the only two metallic
dragons in the world came together with all the ferocity and power
they could muster.

Silver roared as her ribs took the clash badly, but she held herself
together, latching onto her father's neck with sharp teeth and clawing
grooves into his belly. Elron thudded her chin with his own claws,
shocking her into letting go of his neck. He then gripped her throat
with his claws and flew straight towards a mountain.

While Silver had grown in their time away from each other, Elron
had also, and was bigger than his daughter. While Silver was the size
of a large car, he was easily bigger than a small bus, and his extra size
gave him far greater momentum.

Silver was sly, though. She shaped her tail into a razor-sharp blade
and plunged it into Elron's armpit. It was just sharp enough to pierce
his armour and wound the pressure point she had aimed for. He
growled in surprise, loosening his grip on her neck just enough for
Silver to twist free and grip her father's shoulders, pushing upwards
with all her strength. She lengthened her tail again, whipped it around
Elron's neck and flew upwards with a powerful sweep of her wings.

Now with an advantage over her father, she flapped her wings again,
flying as hard as she could in the opposite direction. She wasn't quite
strong enough, though, and grunted in surprise as her tail was nearly
ripped from its socket as Elron continued his flight towards the mountain. Snarling, she whipped her tail again, unwinding it from him.

The two dragons turned to face one another once more. Silver was
gasping for breath, the throbbing in her chest becoming more and
more painful. It was making it hard to think and red stars danced
across her vision. With a growl, she shook her head and focused again
on the fight at hand.

Elron roared and launched a row of tails spikes in Silver's direction.
She ducked, but wasn't fast enough and they hammered into her chest,
knocking her off balance in the air. Her father shot forwards as fast

as he could, taking advantage of her incoordination and slammed into her again. This time there was no way she could escape from his grasp.

He drove her into another mountain, this time succeeding. Silver growled as she was slammed into the mountainside with enough force to crack granite. Her armour protected her, and she avoided injury, but that was before Elron hammered her chest with his mace-like tail. This time she screamed, her vision flicking off and on.

Elron landed above his daughter and struck her again and again, hammering her with claws and tail. Silver tried to move, tried to defend herself, but to no use. Everything was beginning to fade. Pain pulsed like water. Colours merged into a mass.

Inside, Elron was crying, screaming at himself to stop. He tried to get away from his daughter, tried to freeze himself, but the device was hundreds of times stronger than his will, and it was following the order given to it: 'Capture Silver. You are free to do whatever you can to do so, short of killing her.' They didn't mention that it would kill him if he did.

And so it continued, with a ragged scream every time Silver was hit, burying her deeper and deeper into the mountain, and a mental cry of rage and sorrow from Elron with every hit that landed.

But just as Silver was about to give into the pain and the anguish … a fireball exploded into Elron's side.

CHAPTER 29:
FATHER AND DAUGHTER, PART TWO

ELRON roared as he was thrown off his daughter's body. He quickly flapped his wings, steadying himself in midair, but another fireball blasted into him, knocking him backwards. Before he could recover, he crashed into the mountainside, and, much like Silver had, he rolled downward, crashing through trees and dislodging boulders.

Raize watched as his father fell from the sky, guilt deep in his chest. But suppressing his shame, he flew to his sister, stuck in the side of the mountain. Her head lolled to one side, her wings spread outwards. Her eyes were half closed, but she began to regain consciousness as the incessant pounding subsided.

"Raize?" she said, beginning to recognise the dull red blob in front of her.

"It's me," he said. "You look like you took a beating."

She groaned in response.

"Come on, let's get you out of here. Dad's not going to be down for long."

He gently pried her wings loose from the rubble, careful not to cut himself on the sharp edges. Silver fell from the hole, and Raize caught her on his back. He grunted at her weight, her metal shell making her far heavier than usual.

"Geez, Silver," he joked, "you need to eat less."

She snorted, but didn't object as Raize took to the air with her on his back. They were stopped when a clamorous roar clanged across the countryside. The fire dragon froze as their father rose from where he had fallen and flew towards them.

Silver snarled and tried to get off her brother's back, only to find she could hardly move. Her pain seemed too much for her to handle. But she needed to move. If she didn't, they would be captured. Raize, Zepos, her, every dragon in Sky Mountain. She needed to move.

"Raize?" Elron spoke, disbelief lacing his voice. "What are you doing here?"

"I came to find Silver, only to see you driving her into the mountain," Raize snarled back, the famous anger of fire dragons brimming just under his scales.

"It's not his fault," murmured Silver. "He's being controlled."
"I know that," snapped her brother, turning again to Elron, "but you resisted before. Why can't you resist now?"

Elron hung his head. "I … I can't. I keep trying … but no matter how much I do … I just can't." He looked back up at his two hatchlings. "I'm sorry, Raize, my son, but I've been ordered to bring Silver in. They won't allow me to let you go."

"So be it," snorted his son.

"Raize … don't. Get away while you still can." Silver grunted, trying to move again. "You won't stand a chance against him."

"Have a little faith in me, Silver. Please." He gave a half-hearted nod of assurance, knowing all too well that she was right.

"Raize, this is no time for jokes," his sister half-growled.

Raize snorted, looking at his father once more. "Will you at least let me put her down?"

Elron nodded his head once.

The fire dragon turned in the air and slowly flew to the ground. None of the dragons spoke. Raize and Elron had an idea of how it was going to end. The average fire dragon could never defeat a metallic dragon. The only hope Raize had was to stall his father long enough for more dragons to arrive.

They landed, and Raize gently slipped Silver off his back and onto the ground. She tried to stand, only to collapse again. He looked at her worriedly before taking a deep breath and facing his father. He took a ready stance on the ground, feet apart, wings open, and fire flickering through his throat. He only needed to stall him.

"I'm sorry, Raize," Elron said, before flicking his tail forwards.

The son anticipated the move, and before his father acted he pushed himself into the air with a sweep of his wings, dodging the spikes and quickly ascending. Elron snorted and leapt into the air after him, leaving Silver alone on the ground.

Raize began to go through his advantages. Speed, agility ... and that was it. It wasn't much, but it would have to do. He turned and saw that his father had transformed back to his normal state, making his underside vulnerable once more. He wasn't sure how fast Elron was in this state, so he would have to be careful.

He dodged a small metal ball shot at him and dived towards the ground, beating his wings frantically. Maybe if he led Elron away from Silver, she would have enough time to recover and help him. He growled in surprise as a spike scraped along his back, narrowly missing him.

* * *

Silver groaned as the pain in her ribs throbbed aggressively. She was still in her full-metal form, and was sprawled out on the ground. She watched the fight from afar, her brother far outmatched by their father. She needed to get to him, but she hurt so much.

Why can't I move? she thought. *The collars of D.E.D. hurt worse than this. And I broke them. I can defeat this. I'm stronger than this.*

Taking a deep breath, and ignoring the sharp spike of pain that lanced through her as she did, she forced her will into her legs and slowly hauled herself to her feet. She stopped every now and then, taking deep breaths of the numbing pain that assaulted her.

Once she was on her feet she took a shaky step forwards. Another deep breath. Another step. A scream pulled her attention skywards as Elron caught Raize as he attempted a risky turn to get around him. Fire lit up the sky, and somehow he managed to slip free, but not before suffering a grievous wound to his side.

A growl escaped the silver dragon and she opened her wings and flapped, using the anger and fear that plagued her to fight off the pain and rise into the air. The emotions drowned it out, giving her strength, and she flapped her wings again, shooting forwards into the air with as much speed as she could muster.

She collided with her unexpecting father, her full-metal form giving her the momentum she needed to completely knock him out of the air. They crashed into a mountainside and Silver formed the end of her tail into a mace. She jumped back and swung at her father's unprotected jaw, earning a hit. It was the first serious strike she had landed on him.

Elron groaned as his jaw broke under the attack, and for a few seconds he lost consciousness. He quickly formed his full-metal self once again, trying to ignore the throbbing pain in his jaw, and launched an attack on his daughter, smashing her in the side with his tail.

Silver growled, being flung to the side. She quickly caught herself before she crashed into the mountain again. Raize flew up beside her and nodded thankfully. They watched as Elron slowly hauled himself out of the hole he had created in the mountainside.

"Go to Zepos," said Silver, talking to her brother. "I'll hold Dad off long enough for you to wake him. He's in a cave near where we landed before. When you do, tell him to zap either Dad or me with as many volts as he can. Got it?"

Raize nodded and turned, flying back to the cave. Silver took another deep breath, hoping her father's pain matched hers, evening the odds and maybe even giving her an advantage. With a broken jaw, her father's attacks with his maw were accompanied by a great deal of pain.

The two dragons charged at each other again, a metallic ring echoing out like two swords clashing. They clawed at each other, striking with as much force as they could. Silver's strikes were weaker because of her injury, but she made up for it in speed. The adrenaline helped keep the pain away, but the injury still throbbed, especially when she took a hit to the chest.

Metal screeched and groaned as the two dragons fought, their armour protecting them from harm. They struggled to stay in the air as they fought, and slowly descended to the ground. Silver noticed this and snarled. The metal on her wings rippled and grew, creating a hook-like blade at the elbow of each wing.

She caught her father's horn with one of the hooks and wrenched his head forwards. She brought up her claw and struck him as hard as she could in the jawline. He roared in pain, flapping backwards with all his might. Silver followed the attack by forming her tail into a mace and swinging it around, colliding it with her father's jaw again. Elron's head was wrenched sideways as he struggled to stay in the air under the pain.

Silver spotted movement at the corner of her eye and turned to see her brother flying back towards her, with Zepos right behind. She sighed, glad that he was okay, and relieved now that they had a far greater chance of freeing her father.

"Now, Zepos!" Raize yelled.

The electric dragon gathered lighting through him, his body emitting yellow bolts of static electricity. He opened his maw and a streak of lightning shot towards Silver. She opened her wings and closed her eyes as the electricity surged through her like a tidal wave.

She looked down at her father, who had stopped and stared at her in surprise, wondering why Zepos had just struck her with electricity. With a snarl, Silver flapped her wings again, launching herself at her father. A long-range attack wouldn't do much good seeing as he could probably conduct the lightning as well, but she couldn't hold the electricity for too long.

With a roar, she clashed with her father once more. The electricity surged from her body and into his, finding a far greater source of metal for it to conduct through. It spread out evenly over the two dragons, growing in power and becoming more dangerous by the second.

Elron growled in surprise, unable to roar through his broken jaw. The surge of power had taken him by surprise. A tingling sensation ran through him, and it only took a moment to realise he could control the energy. But Silver wielded it as well, and much more efficiently than her father.

The electricity surged upward into her father's head and towards the device. This time Elron roared, shaking himself to shed the massive power, but Silver still had control, and with a snarl she forced the electricity into the device. It sputtered, and a hole blew open in one side before the red light switched off and the device died.

Elron's eyes glazed over from the shock. His body went limp and he fell from the sky, unconscious, as Silver gathered all the electricity from his form and unleashed it into the sky in an enormous crackling lightning bolt that shot through the clouds and lit up the mountain for miles around.

Silver gasped as the last of the energy left her. She felt lightheaded, never having held that much lightning. Looking down at her father, who was now lying on his back, she noticed that the device had been torn off by the fall. She smiled. They had done it. Her father was free.

With a grin she began to descend towards him, only to be stopped by an angry cry that rang through the mountain range.

"*Silver!*" The unmistakable voice of Iraliene rang through the mountainside as the queen of Sky Mountain flew towards her, a small army of dragons at her back.

CHAPTER 30:
THE BATTLE PLAN

SILVER snarled, debating whether to flee. When she looked down at her father, though, she knew it was time to face Iraliene. She didn't care what the life dragon said, she was leaving Sky Mountain. With a snort, she descended to where her father lay, wings splayed like a target. She landed beside him and stared up in defiance as the life dragon followed her.

Raize and Zepos landed beside her. The electric dragon nuzzled her, glad she was okay. He hadn't seen the fight but by the state of surrounding mountains, he knew it had been intense. Silver nuzzled him back, but kept her gaze on Iraliene.

"Are you okay?" asked the lightning dragon.

"Yeah. A few cracked ribs, and that's about it." Silver smiled weakly.

"Raize said you took quite the beating."

Silver nodded. "Just a little. I'll be fine, though."

Even as she said it she felt herself leaning against Zepos for support. Now that the fight was over, and her adrenaline rush had dissipated, she felt the full extent of the pain shoot back through her. Her breathing was laboured, and the salty tang of dragon blood filled her mouth. A small groan escaped her, and her metal shell retracted to its original state.

Zepos felt guilty, looking over her bloodied legs and sides. If he hadn't been knocked out so easily they could have defeated Elron without her suffering these injuries, and be gone by the time Iraliene arrived. If only he had reacted faster at the start of the fight.

The large green dragoness landed with a thud in front of them, glaring with anger in her eyes. She opened her mouth, ready to yell at the young dragons for daring to defy her, but when she saw Elron lying belly up and unconscious, she closed her mouth, staring in surprise.

"What? Is that who I think it is?"

"Yes." Raize stepped forwards. "That is Elron. The first metallic dragon and the first dragon to escape A.O.D.H., the leader of Dragon Valley and our father."

Iraliene blinked, speechless. She hadn't expected them to defeat the metallic dragon, nor remove the device between his horns, which lay a couple of metres away with a hole blown in its side.

Iraliene's dragon army—about a hundred strong—landed around them, every species in their midst, though most were common dragons. Gravon was among them, and he padded up to Elron, glancing at the unconscious dragon warily. He hadn't realised Elron was so big. Wasn't he only eighteen years of age?

"How did you free him?" Iraliene demanded.

Raize snorted. "We don't have to tell you anything."

Her eyes narrowed. "Do you remember what happened last time you refused to give us information, young one?"

The fire drake stepped back, a little nervous. When the mind dragon had invaded his psyche, he had nearly screamed. It had hurt, a lot, bringing up memories that weren't his to take. When he had found the information he wanted, he had stayed in his head a little longer, before withdrawing and leaving Raize weak and lightheaded.

"If you electrocute the device with enough power, it overloads and short-circuits," Silver said. "After that it's a simple matter to take it off." With this, Silver coughed up a glob of blood.

Iraliene frowned, a little worried for the silver dragon. She took a step forwards, studying her wounds. They didn't look too bad, though the blood meant there was an internal injury, which could be far worse than her surface wounds. The life dragon gathered a little of her power and breathed it over Silver, healing all her scrapes and broken bones, and restoring the energy she had lost. Silver breathed a sigh of relief and stood up straighter, no longer needing Zepos to hold her. She nodded her thanks to the life dragoness.

Iraliene then turned towards Elron and did the same, healing him through his armour. His jaw set, and his gashes and wounds sealed, though none could see the healing energy at work. A few moments later, Elron groaned and opened his red eyes. Seeing the dragons, he rolled to his feet and growled, before realising that his movements were no longer being controlled.

"What … how?" He raised his tail and touched the place between his horns where the device had been.

"Dad!" Silver smiled as she padded up to him, nuzzling him. "You're free again."

He nuzzled her back, still surprised. He laughed his freedom, remembering the fight they had just been through. He recalled the electricity that had surged through him, and had an idea of how they had broken the device off his head. Raize leapt towards them, embracing his dad, and Elron chuckled, holding his children close with his wings.

"You two are amazing," he said, letting the armour around him retract.

"I know," Raize replied with a smirk.

Silver swatted him over the head lightly with her tail and stepped back. Raize let out a playful growl. He seemed far happier than usual, nearly giddy. If he was as glad as Silver was to have their father back, then she wasn't surprised. They had both had missed him dearly.

"I'm sorry to spoil this for you," said Iraliene, sounding anything but sorry, "but we have a far greater threat to deal with. Namely the A. O.D.H. army converging on *this very location!*" She took a big breath, seeming to control her rage. "I would like to be back in the safety of my mountain before then."

"That's a bad idea," said Elron.

"What?"

"If we go back to Sky Mountain they will surely find it. We … they … haven't found the mountain yet. If we head back there now, yes, we will be safe within the confines of the mountain, but this army is just a scouting team. Once they find your base they will send all their forces to capture it. So, we have to make our stand here, and make sure they don't get to the mountain."

"But what about all of us?" Iraliene growled. "I'm not going to risk some of the rarest and most powerful dragons from Sky Mountain."

"You risk them anyway. In fact, you risk them far more if we go back to the mountain," Elron said. "If we fight them off now we may have a chance of stopping them before they reach the mountain, which will buy us more time in the future."

Iraliene hesitated, angered by her inability to counter his argument. "Well, what do you propose?"

As Elron and Iraliene argued, Silver noticed Raize deep in thought. Her brother looked to the sky, then at Gravon, then at her and Zepos, and his eyes brightened. He nudged his father in the side, but Elron was too focused on coming up with a defensive strategy.

Silver ducked under her father to Raize. "What's up?"

"I have an idea, and it just might work as well," he said. "I just need to know some things for it to work."

She nodded and turned to the two leaders. She opened her maw and let out a metallic roar like two gongs clashing. Elron and Iraliene nearly jumped in surprise and looked down at Silver quizzically.

"Raize has an idea," Silver said.

"Thanks." He grinned at her before stepping forwards.

Iraliene snorted. "Let's hear it, youngling."

Raize took a deep breath. "Okay, what type of machines are they using, Dad?"

Elron seemed a little surprised, but replied, "They are humanoid machines, giant suits of robotic armour controlled by humans inside them. They're made from elronium, so they are extremely hard to break. They have planes and dragons as well, of course."

"Elronium?"

"The name they gave a metallic dragon's metal."

"Oh. And their numbers?"

"Around three hundred."

"Okay, that's all I needed to know," Raize said, turning to Iraliene. "We will need a gravity dragon and as many electric dragons as you have. And bait; two metallic dragons would be irresistible, I would think."

"What are you getting at?" frowned Iraliene.

The mischievous grin that Silver knew so well formed on her brother's face. "Here's what we need to do."

* * *

Silver flew swiftly through the mountain range, searching for any sign of the enemy. At her flanks were two other dragons, a mind dragon named Buri and Celestia, who had chosen to come with Iraliene, though she still had her eggs to nurture. It was the first time in a while Silver and the light dragon had been able to spend some time together, even if it was for a risky purpose.

There's a group just up ahead, the mind dragon spoke to the two of them telepathically. *Land at this mountain just ahead.*

The three dragons landed on a small ledge and crept forwards. Silver made no effort to dull her shell—the idea was to be seen. Clouds blocked the sun from shining off Silver's shell, but that was where Celestia came in.

The dragonesses looked around the mountainside and Celestia growled in surprise. Flying slowly through the valley was a squadron of five of the humanoid machines Elron had described, each bigger than the average ten-year-old dragon. They looked bulky and slow, but her judgement of their capabilities was tempered by the familiar glint of what Silver now knew as elronium. They may have looked slow, but their armour was light and the strongest on earth.

"You ready?" Silver asked her two companions.

They each nodded their heads. Taking a deep breath, Silver stepped slightly into the open. The light dragon opened her maw and emitted a small beam of light. It struck Silver's shell, reflecting brilliantly over the mountainside. Celestia then ducked back behind the mountain and looked at the mind dragon expectantly.

Buri frowned, and then smiled. "They saw it, and they're coming. They have contacted the rest of the group, and have been ordered to follow you and capture you. More are coming, though, faster ones as well, so we better get going."

The three dragons leapt from the cliff ledge and began to wing their way back to where their trap lay. Elron—also acting as a decoy on another mountain—had no doubt been spotted as well, and would also now be flying back to that small set of mountains. The whole plan rested on these four dragons' safe arrival.

Silver didn't fly fast, knowing they would easily lose them if they did. Buri kept a close mental watch on the humans, though, making sure they always knew exactly where the dragons were. More machines of war were joining the humanoids, though, and when the mind dragon told them to fly a bit faster, they complied.

Turn now! he suddenly yelled. *They're coming down in front of us!*

Silver and Celestia instantly turned to the right, maintaining their speed, and flew between two mountains before righting their course. They would have to take a detour, but it wouldn't add much to their flight time.

As they reached the familiar range of mountains, Silver felt her heart beat faster. If Raize's plan were to work, every part of it needed to happen at the right time. As Silver passed between two of the mountains, Buri and Celestia broke off, flying into two caves on opposite sides of a ring of mountains, leaving Silver in the centre.

On the other side, Elron swooped in, snorting when he saw his daughter. They had made a bet before they left that each one would reach the valley before the other. It seemed Silver had won the race, but only just. They met in the middle and grinned at each other.

"Ready?" asked Elron.

"As I'll ever be," Silver said, nervousness peeking through in her voice.

Besides A.O.D.H.'s attack a year and a half ago, this would be Silver's first major battle, and if everything went to plan it could be over within the hour, and even if it didn't work quite so well, it would create at least a dent in A.O.D.H.'s forces. She glanced over to her father. He was scanning the mountain range intensely, seemingly undaunted by the impending combat.

As soon as the first plane flew into the valley, Elron and Silver armoured themselves, leaving two fully shielded metal dragons to face the army. Following that first plane another came, and then another, and another. They circled the dragons, as if waiting for something. The father and daughter made no effort to move, though, waiting until every A.O.D.H. machine was in the valley.

The humanoid machines came next, and instead of circling with the planes they launched their attack, flying towards the two dragons. Silver and Elron moved this time, dodging the first assault by splitting up momentarily. Silver sent a volley of tail spikes into one of the robots and Elron launched a metallic ball from his maw with enough velocity to dent another.

Make sure to stay together, said an unknown mind dragon. *There are still more coming.*

How many more? growled Silver, ripping her claws through another machine.

Not too many, was the annoyingly vague reply.

Sighing, she did as she was told, and father and daughter fought together, staying as close to each other as possible and making sure to stay in the centre of the battle. More machines began to pile in, and a few dragons, though the rarest among them was an acid dragon.

And the plan is being enacted ... now, said the mind dragon.

Silver felt a strong force act upon her, and the two metallic dragons suddenly magnetised to each other. They both grunted in surprise, even though they were expecting it. The machines, planes, and even the dragons began to fall towards them. The human pilots cried in surprise and the dragons roared as they struggled in vain to fly away from the two metallic dragons.

"This is gonna hurt," Elron grimaced slightly.

"Great," murmured Silver, and braced herself.

The first robot hit them with surprising velocity, knocking the metal dragons apart, only for them to be magnetically pulled back together. Another robot crashed into them, and then another, and then another until they were surrounded by a ball of flailing machines. A wind dragon came next, ramming into one of the robots. Soon after that even the planes were drawn towards the gravitational force that was combining them in one massive metallic ball.

Planes crushed a few of the unluckier dragons. Explosions fired around the edge and a few of the robots in the centre were flattening under the pressure. In the very centre the two metallic dragons were beginning to struggle under the weight, but their armour was holding.

Outside the ball, on top of one of the mountains, stood Gravon. His wings were raised, and he shook slightly as he focused on the sphere of machinery. His teeth were bared as he used his power to create the small planet. It was exhausting him, and he wouldn't be able to hold out for much longer.

"Raize! Do it now! I can't continue!" he roared.

Responding to a mental message, several electricity dragons rose out from their hiding places. Zepos was amazed to see the pure power of a gravity dragon. How the drake was managing to hold them together he had no idea. Rather than worry about it, he opened his maw and blasted lightning into the metallic mass. The other dragons quickly followed his lead and soon the ball was crackling with streaks of lightning, until the machines, planes and even the devices controlling the dragons began to short-circuit.

In the centre, Silver felt the charge strike her back, and she growled, before forcing the electricity outward, creating a surging current that pulsed throughout the hovering behemoth of wrecked machinery. Elron did the same, finding it surprisingly easy to control.

Gravon held on for as long as he could, but eventually it became too much for the young dragon. He let his power go and collapsed to the ground, falling unconscious from the effort. The mini-planet broke apart as he did, but his job was done. None of the machines that had entered the mass were still functioning, and many of the humans inside had been killed by the electricity. Sadly, a few of the dragons had as well, but that couldn't be avoided.

Silver and Elron felt the pressure holding them together release, and instantly flapped their wings, flying up through the mass as it fell apart. The machines rained from the sky and into the valley below. Explosions rang out from the planes, and a few of the robots simply fell to pieces.

Silver let out a roar of victory—their plan had worked! A few roars accompanied her own but were quickly cut short by the distant sound of jet engines. Over the horizon appeared another A.O.D.H. army. This one was a little smaller than the one they had just defeated, but it was still large enough to pose a threat.

Elron growled, "We missed some."

CHAPTER 31: SILVER'S SORROW

SILVER felt her heart thud in her chest with each pulsing beat of a jet engines. There were more of them? Despite her wounds being healed, she was exhausted from fighting. She had spent most of the day in the air, and the sun was high. The pounding she had taken just a moment ago didn't help. Her body throbbed and she was wobbly in the air.

But, as before, she forced herself upwards towards the coming threat. Elron rose next to her, glancing at his daughter worriedly. He hadn't expected this. A.O.D.H. hadn't told him that they had a spare hundred or so machines ready to fight off any dragons that defeated them.

The other dragons in the valley slowly rose up as well, some looking terrified. A muttering rose among them, speaking of surrender or retreat. Few of the dragons there had seen battle, and now they faced one of the most dangerous armies in the known world.

"Don't fall now!" Elron yelled. "Stand and fight! We have no chance if you retreat! All of you will be captured, killed or worse if you fall now. Would you do that to yourself? To your mates and hatchlings? Don't let yourself be frightened by them. Use all the power you have. Don't think you can't win! You can!"

A few of them looked at him in surprise, and their fear lessened. Others remained afraid until they saw Iraliene rise from a mountainside. If their own leader was going to fight with them, then the fight was worth it. She nodded at Elron, a mutual understanding passing between them. As wicked as the dragoness was, she understood what it was like to fight for something she believed in. She had been doing so all her life.

Raize flew up beside his sister and the two exchanged a nod of solidarity.

"Think that the same idea would work?" asked Silver.

"No, Gravon fainted," replied her brother.

She snorted, "Of course."

They laughed slightly, both shaking out their nervousness. The army was approaching quickly, and one of the robots was different from the rest, sleeker and more humanoid, with a glass pane at the head, revealing the human inside.

It took a moment for Silver to recognise him, but when she did her heart nearly burst from her chest. It was the scarred man she had fought all that time ago. He had the same looks and crazed grin. His eyes sparkled with inhuman insanity. The throbbing scar on his throat didn't look any better, and stood out from the rest of his body like an unnatural growth.

A growl escaped the silver dragon, and Raize looked at her in confusion, wondering where this sudden anger had come from. He hadn't seen the scarred man before, having escaped before Silver's encounter with him.

"It's the hunter that captured father before," Silver explained, "and nearly defeated me, without even breaking a sweat."
"What?" Raize frowned, having not heard this story before.

"You two ready?" Zepos said, flying to meet with Silver and Raize before the dragoness could say anything else.

Silver nodded her head at him, this time not smiling. Her hate for the scarred man made her blood boil and her nervousness completely dissipate. She was going to destroy him, along with his fancy-looking machine, making sure there would be nothing left.

Zepos frowned at her, wondering what had got her so worked up. He glanced at Raize, who shrugged back, also unsure. The three dragons joined the others, flying towards the approaching army in readiness to protect their mountain.

Suddenly another noise rose up—more planes. A few of the dragons turned to source of the din, and murmurs of fear rose up again as more planes appeared behind them. There weren't any robotic machines in this army, but it was far bigger than anything else A.O.D. H. had thrown at them so far.

"Don't fear, my friends!" yelled Iraliene over the crowd. "It is the Chinese. They've come to help!"

Silver blinked in surprise. She knew that Sky Mountain had an alliance with China, but she didn't know it was strong enough for the country to actually aid the dragons. A smile spread across her face; now they far outnumbered the A.O.D.H. army. There was no way the enemy could win now. With a roar she charged forwards, flying as fast as she could towards the approaching dragon hunters. The rest of the dragons followed, hope renewed now that they had the upper hand.

Silver was in the frontline, and as they clashed the dragoness took the brunt of the attack. She twisted through two robots, striking with her tail to break their armour. The strike didn't do much, though, the robots being made of the same substance as her shell.

Persevering, she formed a hook with the edge of one of her wings and gouged it into the back of a robot. The hook sunk deep into the machine's back, and Silver found herself stuck to it. Snarling, she wrenched the claw out, leaving a long, deep gash that sprouted severed wires. She couldn't but grin as it began to malfunction.

She turned to face a scene of chaos, though the dragons were easily winning. The Chinese planes swooped above the army, loosing rockets at the robots and lighting up the sky with explosions. A few machines were knocked from the air.

Silver rose higher, above the army, and began to look for a particular machine. She spotted it, right in the middle of the battle, fighting Elron with destructive ferocity. Elron's razor-edge wings carved through the air and his mace-like tail whooshed behind him. The machine that the hunter controlled was fast, though, far faster than any of the other robots, and Elron struggled against the punches and kicks thrown at him.

Silver dove towards them, lengthening her tail. While the robot was fast, dragons were faster. She dove past it, whipping her tail around its foot. The man inside grunted as he was suddenly pulled from the air, leaving him open to Elron's next attack, a strong strike from his mace-like tail. The glass cracked, but didn't shatter.

Silver pulled up before she hit the ground, still dragging the robot with her, and felt a satisfying thud at the end of her tail as the machine crashed into the ground. It was a stupid idea to have glass in the machine. That substance was so much weaker than metal, and if the man in the machine hadn't been visible, he wouldn't have attracted the fury of two of the world's most powerful dragons.

The machine's pilot hurriedly pressed a few buttons and flicked a switch, raising the robot to its feet once more. Silver, her tail wrapped around its leg, simply pulled, yanking the two-legged machine over again. She snorted in satisfaction. A hail of bullets zipped her way, and she growled as a robot landed on her from above, driving her into the ground.

With a grunt, she unwrapped her tail from the machine's leg and retracted it to its normal length, before striking at the robot that had attacked her. She was still in full-metal form and was well protected. Her armour was stronger than theirs because it was alive, whereas the metal she breathed wasn't, or at least, that was what she had been told.

The robot grabbed her around the neck and picked her up, slamming her into the ground again. She snarled, clawing at its hand. She was so used to fighting flesh and blood creatures that she expected the hand to pull away, but robots don't feel pain. With a grunt she was rammed into the ground once again.

Giving up on trying to tear the arm apart, Silver bladed the end of her tail and stabbed the robot's chest, piercing the armour easily and spearing the human inside. At first the robot didn't do anything, but then its grip on her weakened, and before it fell on top of her she rolled out of the way.

The battle overhead was turning in their favour. A.O.D.H. seemed to be retreating, the machines flying away from the dragons as fast as possible. It hadn't even taken the dragons and Chinese an hour. The dragon hunters seemed unused to fighting aircraft, and had no defence against them. Raize and Zepos fought together in the air, working together to destroy machine after machine. Iraliene was like a giant green demon, big enough to grab to machines in her paws and crush them together.

Life dragons were named so because their breath could heal and restore life, but it could also do the opposite. Powerful life dragons could drain another creature, stealing their life force. They could also heal themselves, so whenever Iraliene's scales were pierced, the wound instantly closed, like she was immortal.

Gravon had finally joined the fight as well. While he was still weak from using his power on the first wave of enemies, he still had enough to create havoc. He crashed two machines into each other with such force that they were flattened. Others he guided into zero-gravity wells where they couldn't control themselves, flying into them and knocking them to the ground.

It was the first real use of power Silver had seen from Iraliene and Gravon, and she was almost impressed by it. Almost. Turning back to her father, she saw that he had crushed the scarred man's machine into a mountainside, shattering the glass. Raising his tail, he brought it down on the man inside, before he stepped back and turned with a snort.

Silver smiled and leapt into the air with a flap of her wings. The rest of the robot pilots were retreating to the horizon, trying to preserve their own lives. A victory. A.O.D.H. wouldn't trouble them for a while, fearing all-out war with China.

Sighing, she turned back to her father. He was still on the ground. They smiled at each other. Suddenly a movement from behind him caused her to roar a warning, but it was too late. The scarred man's robot leapt at the grounded dragon, grabbing his neck and swatting him across the maw. Elron grunted as he was thrown sideways, landing on his side.

Taking his advantage, the scarred man made his robot grip Elron's neck again, shoving him into the ground. One of its hands slid back into the robot's arm, creating a cannon. The man, seeing that the dragon's body was covered in impenetrable armour, shoved the cannon down the dragon's throat.

Elron and the scarred man made eye contact. Somehow the hunter had survived Elron's crushing blow, and his body was still intact. His eyes narrowed and his grin widened, knowing he had the dragon. There was no escape from him this time. It had happened too fast for anyone to save him. The hunter fired the cannon.

"*Dad!*" Silver screamed.

Elron's body convulsed, the inside not being nearly as protected as the outside. The hunter slowly drew the now bloody barrel of the cannon from the dragon's mouth. With a metallic clang, Elron's body fell onto the ground, limp and still. And just like that, half of the world's metallic dragons were gone.

A scream of rage erupted from Silver and she pulled in her wings, diving headfirst at the creature that had killed her father. He laughed, opening his robotic arms for her, leaving himself wide open. She didn't think, aiming directly at the man, claws outstretched, maw open, ready to rip him to pieces. The man simply swatted her out of the air and she tumbled through the trees, before springing to her feet again.

But the man was already gone, retreating with the rest of A.O.D. H. into the sky. Silver cried out after him, opening her wings, ready to take off and destroy every last one of the creatures. She lifted herself into the air, but something tackled her to the ground again.

"No, don't, Silver. Don't. You'll just be captured," Zepos said, pinning her to the ground.

The dragoness struggled viciously against her friend, trying throw him off, "I'll kill them all! I'll destroy them! Let me go! *Let me go!*"

"Silver, please!" Zepos cried out.

This time she heard him, and fell limp on the ground. The electric dragon hesitated, before letting her go. She rolled to her feet slowly and got up. She walked over to her father and collapsed by his side. He was still in his full-metal form, and no-one would know that he was dead except for his stillness and the blood trickling out of his mouth.

"Dad?" Silver whimpered, not allowing herself to believe that he was gone. "Please … please."

She buried her head in the dragon's side and let the tears fall from her eyes. "Y … you can't be dead. You just … you just …"

The silver dragon keened, a haunting and mournful cry echoing through the mountain range. It sounded over and over, tears trickling down her jaw and neck. The dragons around her lowered their heads in respect. And Silver cried. For the first time in her life she opened the emotions she had held and let them out into the world, her wail like a death knell.

Raize landed a few feet away and nearly collapsed. "No … no." He walked up to his sister, staring in disbelief at his father's limp body. To the hatchlings he had been invincible, impossible to defeat. The ultimate hero. To them, he was immortal. He did the impossible, and instead of becoming enraptured in his fame and power, he continued to work towards the betterment of himself and others, loving his family the whole way.

Iraliene landed nearby and bowed her head. Her heart was heavy, and she couldn't help but feel guilty for the death of this mighty dragon. She looked at the silver dragon and her brother: she was mourning, and he was standing, staring with hate-filled eyes.

Silver looked back to the queen of Sky Mountain, and suddenly hope blossomed, "You can bring him back, right? You're a life dragon. You can … bring him back!"

Iraliene lowered her head. "No … I'm not powerful enough."

She had tried once before, in a similar circumstance, and it had nearly killed her. The dragon she had tried to heal hadn't been revived either and she had mourned, just like the silver dragon was now. But Silver refused to give up.

"Try, at least … try," she sobbed.

Iraliene hesitated, before nodding her head. She took a step forwards and gathered her power in her chest. She opened her maw and let out a streaming blast of green energy. It entered Elron's body, illuminating it. Every dragon there looked on, hope filling them at the sight. Iraliene continued to pump the body full of life energy, hoping, praying that it would work. She couldn't let another dragon die like this. As she depleted her energy she began to feel weak and faint, but she continued, refusing to give up. It went on for minutes, until the queen could not give anything else. She collapsed to the ground, huffing in exhaustion, but her eyes fixed on the metal dragon. Every eye was fixed on Elron. And … nothing happened.

"No … no!" Silver cried again, fresh tears coming to her eyes. "You have to do more! You have to!"

Iraliene only sighed. "I … I don't have anything left."

"Please! He's my father." She collapsed by his side again. "He's … he's my father."

Raize said nothing.

Zepos moved over to her and lay by her side, wrapping his wing around her. He couldn't believe it either. He had spent the first few months of his life in A.O.D.H., and didn't remember it that well, but he did remember what it was like being freed. And Elron was the dragon who did that. It was part of the reason he had fallen for Silver in the first place, because her father was his hero.

Silver buried her muzzle into his side, weeping. Great shudders ran through her body and her shell dulled to nearly black. Zepos held her, not knowing what else to do. He glanced at Raize. The fire dragon still stared at his father, shuddering with rage. A single tear trickled from his eye before he turned and, without a word, took to the air, flying back towards the mountain.

Zepos looked back at the dragon he loved, now broken. He nuzzled her neck gently. "We … we should go."

She looked up at him and nodded her head. She slowly got to her feet, standing next to him. The rest of the dragons gradually took to the air, flying away from the dead dragon. Zepos opened his wings and flew, Silver close behind. A few dragons picked up Elron's body and together they flew back to Sky Mountain.

EPILOGUE

"*You idiot!*" A resounding whack stung the scarred man's face. His head whipped to the side, but he was otherwise motionless. The pain was numbing, almost wonderfully so. The man who hit him turned his back and marched to a wooden desk.

They were in a large room, empty but for the single desk with one seat and papers scattered across it. Each paper listed names, each marked with 'active' or 'inactive', or a red line scrawled across it. Most of the names had a green 'active' next to the name, but at the top of one sheet, the first name had a thick red line, like blood, running through it: 'Elron, metal dragon'.

"I should kill you," continued the man, sitting down at his desk. "In fact, if it wasn't for your record of success you would be laying on the floor with a bullet deep in your head."

The scarred man continued to stare straight ahead, still silent. He couldn't speak: the scar on his neck was left by a dragon talon that had ripped out his voice box. It was the very dragon he had killed earlier that day, and he didn't feel the least bit sorry for the loss. He didn't care what type of dragon Elron was.

"You don't have *any* idea what you have done, do you?" the man at the desk said.

Silence.

"I can't just leave you unpunished, Jurien," the man continued, "so I'm stripping you of all ranks and privileges. You will forever be a private, serving under people higher than you."

This time a croaking cough of protest escaped Jurien. He stared at his superior in horror, not believing what he had just heard.

"Now. Leave me. Before *he* kills you," said the man.

Jurien hesitated, before saluting and turning regally, marching out of the room with as much modesty as he could muster. The man watched him go, a deep frown on his face. How could this have happened? It set them back significantly, not to mention the importance of the metal dragon.

Maybe it's time for a change in tactics, a strange voice resonated through the man's mind.

"Maybe," he replied out loud.

We must get the silver dragon. We have no other choice, said the voice.

"Yes, and this time she won't escape us." The man stood up. "We will make sure of it